Maureen Murphy
— 2019

# Graciella

# HANDLING THE RANCHER

## SARA OHLIN

Handling the Rancher
ISBN # 978-1-83943-803-5
©Copyright Sara Ohlin 2019
Cover Art by Erin Dameron-Hill ©Copyright October 2019
Interior text design by Claire Siemaszkiewicz
Totally Bound Publishing

# HANDLING THE RANCHER

# Dedication

To my mom, Mary,
for giving me a love of words and for always
telling me I could be whatever I wanted.
And to Greg, who is my home, no matter where we
are. I love you.

# Chapter One

Cruz stood at the edge of the bluff above the Pacific. The ocean brooded, inky-dark and dangerous, while the wind whipped it onto the shore. He let the cadence of wild, crashing waves and gusting wind wash over him. He loved the water in its fierce and powerful nature as much as he loved it when it was calm and patient. Wide and open, the beach stretched on, completely untouched by footprints, secluded and vulnerable all at the same time.

He took one lasting breath of the misty sea air and headed towards his farm. *His farm.* He still had moments when he couldn't believe it.

Wispy slips of fog teased and lifted around Cruz, revealing the morning dew on the grass as he made his way up towards the main house of Brockman Farms. Mornings on the farm were his favorite, the way the new light barely stroked the land, how the hues of everything were rich in those few moments of soft sun and leftover darkness. The salty air mixed with the scent of damp earth as it rose up. Home — Cruz was finally home — a place most people took for granted.

He'd been back in Graciella for five weeks after more than a decade away. His relief on hearing that his father, T.D. Brockman, was finally dead had been such that he'd nearly wept like a baby when his brother Adam had called with the news.

Thank goodness no one had seen his near breakdown. And that it hadn't lasted long. He could finally breathe clear and easy here on this land he loved, knowing the monsters were gone. He aimed to do more than breathe easy, however. It was his time to take care of the farm and all the people who depended on it — and to put his stamp on something valuable.

As much as he liked helping out at the barns, this morning dictated that he make a dent on the estate paperwork and duties. That didn't mean he had to do it without a fresh cup of coffee. Cruz entered the main house through the back to grab a mug of their housekeeper Elena's rich espresso brew in the kitchen before he got to work.

Fueled by caffeine, he sat at T.D. Brockman's old desk, going through bank statements and employee schedules. Since he'd returned, the phone hadn't quit ringing with condolences for his father's death and calls from the press. He wasn't sure which group won the award for insincerity.

Who could blame them? T.D. Brockman had taken pleasure in his ruthless way of doing business. But he'd been a wealthy bastard, owning most of the commercial properties in downtown Graciella. And the farm was spread out over two hundred and fifty thousand acres, nestled between Oregon wine country and the prized breathtaking Pacific coast. Money was involved, and where money was involved, people were curious. What would happen now that he was dead? Everyone wanted to know.

The phone rang again. "Brockman Farms," Cruz answered, the words clipped at one more interruption.

"Mr. Brockman? This is Ms. Selby from the *Oregonian*."

*Another reporter.* "The family has no comment at this time."

"Please, Mr. Brockman—"

"No comment!" Cruz said through clenched teeth and slammed the receiver down. The only reason he'd left the damn thing plugged in was because there were legitimate calls from banks and people regarding T.D.'s investments that Cruz had to deal with as executor.

"You must be Cruz Brockman."

Cruz looked up at the musical voice. Normally he wouldn't have to force a smile for anyone, let alone for an elegant woman. "Hello," he said and tried to punch down his irritation. "Can I help you?"

"Do you ever wait to see who's on the other end or are you that rude to everyone on the phone?" she asked as she walked into the room. Her body language might have said *cool* and *put-together*, but the haughty tone in her voice gave away one serious, pissed-off attitude.

"Excuse me?" He pushed his chair back and stood. "This is my office and if I remember correctly, I smiled and said hello. Perhaps you'd like to start over—"

"Mr. Brockman," she snapped.

He locked his gaze with hers and came around from behind the desk. "I said, perhaps you'd like to start over." His tone was sharp, no longer concealing his frustration.

"I'm Miranda Jenks, the audit accountant. I've been trying to contact you for days to let you know when I'd be arriving, but your phone etiquette made that impossible. The times you actually picked up the phone, you hung up on me before I could say more than three words. I finally got hold of your lawyer. He should have mentioned I'd be here today."

*Gorgeous and haughty, what a combination, like a goddess rising from the morning's crashing waves.* The image, unbidden, teased through his temper. Cruz half-listened as he studied her. In her charcoal-gray suit and black high heels, with that tone of reprimand in her voice, she reminded him of his finance professor in college, who'd believed Cruz's choice of photojournalism a waste of time. That was where the similarities came to a screeching halt. His professor had been in her sixties, very short and very thick.

The woman in front of him certainly wasn't sixty, short or thick. In fact, she looked more like she could stand to eat a good meal or two. Contradictions surrounded her. Deep, confident and extremely sexy, her voice was like a rich port. It also vibrated with indignation. But the rest of her seemed guarded. Her long dark hair was pulled back and held in a simple ribbon at her neck. Tall and stiff, she did a good job of trying to pretend calm. Gaunt cheekbones shaped her face and dark circles rested under her eyes. Very green, very frustrated eyes. That expressive gaze and sultry voice were at odds with the rest of her controlled, veiled demeanor.

"Mr. Brockman?" Impatience sliced the woman's words.

"Accountant? Jake never mentioned you were coming today."

"Yes, I did, Cruz." Jake walked in. "Sorry I'm late, Ms. Jenks, I'm Jake Burns. We spoke on the phone."

"Nice to meet you, Mr. Burns."

Cruz watched her almost-smile at Jake and enjoyed the way her face warmed and softened a hint. *Wonder what she looks like when she really lets herself smile?*

"Cruz, good to see you." Jake smacked him on the shoulder. "Ms. Jenks, thanks for your patience. Cruz, Miranda Jenks—the accountant I told you would be auditing the books if we plan on settling this estate."

Cruz had a vague memory of the conversation. One of about five hundred he'd had about the estate since the funeral. "I apologize, Ms. Jenks," he said. "The phones have been on fire since T.D. died and I lost my patience with them days ago." He flashed her a grin in apology.

He held out his hand, and when she took it, his nerves sizzled. Every pulse point in his body awakened. He nearly tugged her closer so her entire body could touch his. She closed her eyes and quickly removed her hand, one that had trembled slightly in his and had such soft skin that he wanted to hold it again. She opened her briefcase to search through her paperwork.

"Excuse me, it seems my phone's busy today," Jake said. He took out his cell and walked into the hall.

"Ms. Jenks, thanks for coming all the way from…?" Cruz began.

"Houston."

"How was the trip?"

"The trip was fine. Shall we get to work? I'm certain none of us has any time to waste."

*All business.* Cruz sighed. From experience, he found accountants shallow and driven by money. But he needed one to handle the books. Cruz had lived most of his adult life traveling from one assignment to another, documenting the beauty and tragedy of the world, photographing and writing other people's stories. He had not been running a large company or settling estates, meaning he needed help to get things reconciled. Only then could he begin making lasting improvements and changes to Brockman Farms, fulfilling his dream of making this place something to be proud of.

"I'll need all the records your father kept. Bills paid, bills due, revenue, assets, expenses, wages, tax forms from the past few years, receipts, investments." She drew him out of his thoughts with her long list of demands.

Cruz looked around at the piles of paperwork covering the desk. "Most of it is here somewhere, but it's a mess at the moment, a mess I've been trying to sort through. Jake and I have some things to take care of. I know you've come a long way. How about if we begin in the morning? That will give me some time to get things more organized for you."

"Certainly."

*Damn!* The force of that word breathed at him like a dragon's fire. He could almost see the inner turmoil as she fought the need to roll her eyes at his incompetence. "But time isn't something you have a lot of, Mr. Brockman. I'm sure you're aware of that."

"I realize the importance of this, Ms. Jenks, but it's not exactly life or death now, is it?" He grinned at her again, trying to prod some emotion out of her. At the least he wished she'd relax. At the most he wanted to see her smile again. He liked the way it softened her face, gave her a bit of mystery, as though she was holding a special secret or two. He'd even take the fierce side of her—it showed her strength.

"That depends on how you feel about the IRS shutting you down for good."

"What the hell's that supposed to mean?" he demanded.

# Chapter Two

How quickly all humor and warmth had left his voice, Miranda noticed. He was completely ignorant. Ignorant and pissed off and taking it out on her. Her patience was shot. Combine that with serious jet lag and three nights without much sleep and her calm façade cracked.

*No surprise.* He epitomized the relaxed playboy who'd just swooped in from his latest vacation, come home to receive his inheritance, trying out Daddy's chair for size. A wrinkled white linen shirt with the sleeves rolled up accentuated his dark skin, and his black hair was tousled as though he'd never even entertained the idea of combing it. At the moment, however, his body simmered with anything but relaxation.

Why was she so unsettled by him? She was used to clients yelling at her, trying to manipulate her or simply ignoring her. Right then she wasn't sure which she preferred, but being ignored seemed like the safest choice, with that storm in his eyes. She could practically hear the thunder.

"Your attorney didn't mention how serious all this is?" she asked. *Is he really that unaware?* He was angry, there was no doubt about that. "Brockman Farms has been under investigation by the IRS for the past few months. I—"

*"Investigation by the IRS?"*

Now the storm thundered in his harsh, incredulous words and he stalked closer to her. She braced for the impact. "Explain," he ordered.

"There have been hints of large-scale tax evasion, Mr. Brockman. You, or I'm guessing Jake, hired me to conduct an outside audit. We need to see how much this farm owes the government. Often in cases like this, it's substantial, especially if it's seen that taxes haven't been paid properly in years. If you're lucky, you'll owe a lot of money. Just how much will be determined."

"Lucky?" he said, unable to conceal the shock. "And if luck decides not to show up?"

She hesitated, caught for a moment at how different his face looked from only a few moments ago. His grin was gone and the stark lines of his forehead spoke of serious concern. "The government could seize all of your father's or, rather, your assets and revenues until they've gotten what they're owed. If that's the case, everything could be shut down temporarily. It could also be permanent."

"Jesus." Cruz let out his breath. But he looked more like a bull getting ready to charge than someone breathing in relief. "How much time do we have?" His tension filled the room, reminding her of the moment before someone seriously loses their temper, the way her mother had done when Miranda had been a child and her father had lost all their money to another scheme.

"Less than two months. You can take longer than that to fully settle the estate, but the IRS and the Department of Justice want this matter solved first. Jake hired me to help you. An outside audit may benefit your case as we try to prove that, even if there was fraud committed, it was done with T.D.'s knowledge only, and that you're willing to pay back the fines. The IRS will perform their own audit as well. Right now, they've only mailed you documents, which you're responsible for filling out. If that goes smoothly, they won't have to send anyone out here. I can help you with their paperwork. The audit's due the third week in May. Sometimes they grant extensions, but it's unusual."

His eyes never wavered from hers as she explained, and his body calmed, although the heavy air still surrounded them like a too-long, extremely hot, humid summer, full of unwanted family secrets.

"I had no idea." He walked even closer. Okay, maybe he hadn't calmed at all. Maybe he'd channeled his energy in a different direction. All she knew was that she was in its path.

Miranda gathered her bag and purse in an attempt to put something between them, or protect herself—she wasn't quite sure which. If he was truly unaware, it would be a huge shock to him, and she suspected he might like some time alone. "I'll be back in the morning. Is eight a.m. too early for you to begin?"

"Where do you think you're going, Ms. Jenks?"

*So much for defusing his temper.* "Siesta Hotel, off the highway. I have a reservation and since you said you weren't ready for me, it doesn't make sense for me to hang around today. I have preparation work I can get done."

"You should stay here," he said, looking at his watch, all business now. "We've plenty of room. There's a guest house you could have to yourself. I'll have Javier show you. He's on his way here now. We'll need to get started as soon as we can, and I'll need to cancel some appointments for later in the week."

"That's all right. I already have a reservation — "

"By your calculations, we have about six weeks." He cut her off again. "That means we don't have time to waste. You'll save yourself over an hour a day driving back and forth. That much should appeal to your sense of efficiency. Besides, I'll bet you a beer that our guest house is much more comfortable than the Siesta Hotel. I'm surprised that shack is still standing. It was built in the early sixties and not that well to begin with. Anyplace would be more comfortable than that hole."

*Depends on what you mean by comfortable,* she thought, staring at him. *Because being in close proximity to you is anything but comfortable.* What was he doing joking about a hotel and making beer bets? She'd told him his farm, his lifeline, was in jeopardy. He was vulnerable. She found herself searching for his smile, the way it made her feel. She wanted that feeling, that warmth again. But work and emotions did not go together, ever. *So ignore the feelings he's stirring.*

Her body had other ideas. Every time Cruz spoke, something fine and delicate vibrated inside her, a violin being played with light fingers, the bow barely touching the strings, bringing the music to life. And it only got stronger the closer he'd gotten to her. Normally she had nerves of steel — nothing affected her. But Cruz Brockman was... God, even if she'd been able to find her breath, she wasn't certain she'd know what word to use to describe him. *Intense? Gorgeous? Fierce?*

At over six feet tall, even in rumpled clothes his presence commanded attention. Although tall herself, Miranda felt completely overwhelmed by his height. His dark skin looked more like it had come from a hidden pirate bloodline rather than irresponsible days spent in the sun as she'd assumed. And the sharp look on his face paired with his piercing blue eyes hinted at danger.

The sooner she got the job finished, the sooner she could move on and the sooner she could add one more paycheck to her savings, which, for the first time in her life, she could do what she wanted with.

She stared at him as he threw out the offer to stay. *Ha!* It was more like an order, and her intelligent brain knew she should refuse, but a hotel sounded unbearably awful right about then, with the fatigue from the last month dragging her down. It was the beginning of the week, yet she felt like she'd been running for miles — days — until her limbs wouldn't hold her up anymore.

"All right."

Once more he extended his hand. She looked down at it then back up at him. No way was she touching him again. She was already unsteady enough in his presence.

"Normally in a bet you shake hands," he said.

*Right, I can do this.* She reached for his hand and pleasure washed over his face. A minute earlier he'd been openly shocked and angry at learning his farm could be shut down. He didn't hide his emotions, she thought, and she couldn't predict his reactions to anything.

Lord, how she wished he'd go back to being angry. At least then she could keep him at a distance. An angry Cruz Brockman she could manage.

"Ah, Javier." Cruz let go of her hand. "I've got Jake waiting for me. Would you do me a favor and show Ms. Jenks to the guest house?"

A handsome older man had walked into the room. He carried his cowboy hat and his silver-gray ponytail trailed down past his neck. Next to him was a woman, her arms overflowing with a flat of yellow pansies.

"Mom, what are you doing here?" Cruz kissed her cheek. "Here, let me take those for you."

"No you don't. I don't trust either of you with my babies." She smiled at Javier and Cruz. "Last week I set a flat down, and when I returned, I found half of them trampled by a boot print about your size." She stepped back and noticed Miranda. "Hello, I'm Katie."

She reminded Miranda of a sparkly, small, but not insignificant shooting star. Auburn hair with a hint of gray curled around her rosy cheeks and sky-blue eyes lit her face with joy.

"This is Miranda Jenks. She's here to audit the farm's books," Cruz said, staring at her with that intense gaze again.

"It's nice to meet you," Miranda said.

"I offered her the guest house as she has an extremely tight deadline."

"Oh, it's quite lovely, Ms. Jenks. We recently updated a few things. I'm sure you'll be comfortable there. You must be exhausted from your travels. Why doesn't Javier walk you over, and I'll set my flowers down in the garden and grab a few things from the kitchen to bring to you?" Katie was already walking away as she spoke. Light and warmth trailed behind her. Even Jake kissed her on the cheek as they passed each other in the doorway.

Silent, but no less intriguing, Javier nodded a greeting and gestured for Miranda to follow him. She didn't like being dismissed, and she felt out of place and anxious when she wasn't balancing books and calculating figures, yet was swept up in the current. With one glance back at Cruz, she turned and followed Javier down the long hallway and out of the back door. They walked through a garden quietly awaiting its plants, and down a wandering path till they arrived at a small red cottage.

She was grateful for the silence as Javier led the way and she used the walk to get a handle on her emotions.

She'd been doing this job long enough that she'd learned to build a hard shell around herself to face her clients, to protect herself. Why now, all of a sudden, did she feel like she was losing it?

"The cottage is a special place. It has Katie's touch." Javier's deep, gravelly voice had a strong Spanish accent curling around his words. "And this time of year, you should be able to smell the sea through the windows. It's good for the soul."

As if sensing her unease, he steadied her with his hand on her shoulder then handed her the key. With that he put his hat back on and left.

Well, as uncomfortable as she felt, there was no place else to go. Miranda took a deep breath and opened the door into the small entryway. She was hit by sunlight flooding in from the gorgeous windows. It was as if the whole place was designed to welcome the light, from the wall of windows in the back where the kitchen faced west to the blond hardwood floors and the soft white slip-covered sofa in the living room. It wasn't large, but open and airy and absolutely wonderful.

Miranda soaked it in. She'd had no idea she'd been craving light, or how much her body had wrapped itself inward in her mother's stuffy bedroom during these few last weeks.

Miranda set her purse on the coffee table and noticed the large photograph over the fireplace. It was a black and white photo of three girls kneeling at a river, washing clothes. Their baskets sat beside them, with one lone acacia tree in the distance and the cracked desert stretched out before them. She could practically taste the dusty landscape on her tongue. *C. Cooper*. Miranda would have recognized his work anywhere.

She remembered that day last year when she'd accidentally caught his showing of photographs from

Africa. She'd never seen so much emotion expressed through only black and white before. The man was a genius with a camera. He told a whole story with one picture. The one that had caught her eye was the one she'd bought for herself that very afternoon. She'd gotten a raise and a promotion and had no one to share the news with. And there in the window had sat the photograph of the mother elephant and her baby. Her perfectly organized budget left almost no room for personal indulgence, but she'd tossed responsibility out of the window that day.

"It's lovely, isn't it?" Katie said.

Miranda had been so lost in the photograph that she hadn't noticed Katie's arrival. "Yes," she replied. "I love his work. There's so much open emotion in each shot. To be able to do that in black and white is humbling, isn't it?"

"Indeed."

"I bought *Mother and Daughter* last year. I couldn't seem to resist it."

"Oh yes, I know that one very well, the elephants. Such love in that shot." Katie turned toward the kitchen. "I brought over some homemade bread, a dozen eggs, wine, cheese and crackers, apples and a bit of leftover pasta salad. There's a gem of a market at the southern edge of the farm where the town starts, and a small grocery store in downtown, but I thought you might like a few things to have on hand right away. Oh, and coffee. I made certain there was coffee."

Katie began putting the groceries away. "I don't know about you, Ms. Jenks, but the world would be an unhappy place for me without coffee in the morning. Now I'm off to plant flowers and lay down some compost. Let us know if you need anything else. There's always someone around."

"Please, call me Miranda. And thank you for this." Miranda looked around the room. "It is quite lovely, Katie."

"Enjoy yourself while you can, Miranda. I'm sure you'll have plenty to keep you busy once tomorrow starts."

And with that Katie was off again, out of the cottage and up the path back towards the main house.

A charming guesthouse on a coastal farm. Exhaustion, longing, confusion and something unknown all flowed open inside Miranda. And she couldn't stop thinking about those fierce blue eyes.

*What kind of an assignment have I stepped into?*

\* \* \* \*

"Tax evasion? What the hell is going on?" Cruz asked Jake.

"I know it's a shock, Cruz. I just found out last week when I notified the IRS about T.D.'s death. We need an accountant to help with the estate anyway, and I did some research. Her record for handling large business audits is impeccable. The IRS and the DOJ suspect T.D. of withholding taxes for the past few years. They're not sure how he's done it."

"Unbelievable." Cruz didn't know whether to let out a breath or take a deep gulp of air for the battle that was to come. This was a disaster Cruz had never anticipated. "It never even occurred to me that T.D. was cheating the government. But hell, why not? The man cheated everyone else." Cruz almost laughed. Once T.D. had died and Cruz had come home, he'd thought everything would be different. Here in Graciella was where he belonged, where he'd only ever belonged. Even though T.D. had never made him feel that way, the people had. Cruz felt a connection to the earth and to this community.

Now everything he had, everything the workers and people of Graciella had, was in danger. He'd been wrong about the ghosts of his past. They still lingered.

"What do we do?" he asked, running his hands over his face, feeling weary now at the thought of losing what he'd waited so long to claim.

"We let her do her job, help her in any way we can and hope for the best."

He looked at Jake, one of the few good friends he'd had since college. "Bet you never expected this kind of a mess when I asked you to help me settle the estate, did you? Knowing T.D., it's probably bad. Hoping for the best could be a pipe dream."

"True," Jake said. "Maybe T.D. simply made some mistakes."

"Not T.D." Cruz rubbed the lines on his forehead one last time, as if he could massage away this unexpected disaster. "If T.D. hid money, he did it on purpose. And it looks like he left a nightmare behind for us."

# Chapter Three

Hours later, jacked up on frustration and adrenaline from trying to organize some of T.D.'s papers, Cruz headed toward the back yard, where he found his mother in the garden. He knew her presence would calm him. She walked through the raised beds, inspecting the small sprouts she'd transplanted as though they were her babies.

"Hello, darling," she said when she saw him come down the steps.

"Mom." He kissed her cheek. "How's your day going?"

"Fine. Better than fine. I still can't believe you're back in Graciella. After all these years." She searched his face and Cruz wondered what she might be looking for. Did she already know the trouble the farm could be in? She'd known and done so much more over the years than he'd been aware of as a kid.

It wasn't until he and his brother Turner had left Graciella as teenagers that he'd begun to learn why she'd stayed, and why she'd stayed with a man like T.D. It wasn't until then that he'd had the guts to ask her.

In the beginning she'd stayed out of fear, but also because she loved the land that had been in her family for generations. And behind T.D.'s back, she'd done what she could to help the workers, many of them migrant, many illegal. She'd brought them food and medicine when she could, shoes and clothing for their children and cared for them when they were sick.

It was from her dedication and spirit that Cruz had gotten his desire to travel the world as a photojournalist. He wanted to help others and bring their stories to light. But his mother had something he didn't— bravery. She'd stayed here in the face of T.D.'s wrath to help the people closest to her.

"Cruz, Javier got called back down to the barns before he could get Ms. Jenks' luggage in the foyer. Why don't you take it over to her and see if she needs anything else?" Katie suggested before kneeling back down to work with the plants.

*A successful, beautiful woman with lots of money would have luggage.* Cruz was surprised when he saw only two small suitcases sitting inside the front door. He picked them up and walked the short distance to the guest house.

As if from someplace else entirely, the cottage welcomed and warmed. It was just as Cruz remembered, painted deep red with white trim. On the porch sat two ancient rockers and an old porch swing and yellow pansies spilled out of the window boxes.

For a moment it struck Cruz as sad that this cottage had the look of loving care, the way a home should look, where the main house didn't. Perhaps it was the charm, and the way it felt hugged by the landscape, or maybe it was simply because it didn't hold all the bitter ghosts of the big house.

He set the bags down and knocked. It took a moment for Miranda to open the door, and when she did, her appearance caught him off guard. She was still in her fancy blouse and skirt, but she'd shed her suit jacket and shoes. Her deep green eyes were a bit red and damp, and when she saw him she quickly crumpled a tissue into her fist.

"Yes?" she said. Her voice was clipped. It held a fine line between control and falling off the edge.

"Everything all right?" The question was out of his mouth before he knew what he was saying. He felt the need to comfort, to wrap his arms around her and make whatever it was that had made her cry disappear.

"I thought we agreed to get started in the morning." Her voice sounded harsh, but her eyes revealed sadness and a long-hidden pain. Without thinking, he reached his hand up to her cheek and wiped away a tear.

She seemed frozen as a look of confusion washed over her face.

But her recovery was rapid. She stepped back brusquely. "Was there something you needed, Mr. Brockman? I could start billing my hours now if you've changed your mind and are ready to get to work."

*Billable hours?* She was either the ice queen or seriously closed up. *And can she please quit calling me Mr. Brockman?* That name splintered at the headache he already had.

"Do all accountants have to perfect that coldhearted tone or does it come naturally?"

He watched her face change from that cold mask to pissed off in one smooth move. *So she's not immune to me.* "I thought you might like your luggage," he said, matching her clipped tone.

"Oh, I…" Miranda looked down at her suitcases. Before she could say anything else, he strode away.

Miranda carried her bags inside, shut the door then leaned against it to catch her breath. *Damn him!* What right did he have to judge her? He didn't know anything about her life. But she was mad at herself as well. As soon as Katie had left her alone at the cottage, she'd climbed the stairs and discovered the sunlit bedroom. Complete exhaustion had taken over and she'd fallen asleep. She'd been dreaming of herself as a child, searching for her mother, and she'd woken in tears to his knock at the door. Rarely did she cry, and simply because he'd caught her in a moment of exhaustion and embarrassment, she'd been a complete witch when he'd asked if she was okay.

*Coldhearted.* He'd hit a nerve, a sensitive one that was raw and stretched, a brittle old wire waiting to snap.

It was true that she had gone into accounting in business school so that she could make a lot of money, but it wasn't for purely selfish reasons. After her father had died and left them penniless, she and her mother had done everything they could to scrape by. She'd vowed never to be financially dependent on a man again. Then her mother had gotten sick and Miranda had had to provide for both of them.

Hired right out of college by one of the top five accounting firms in the country, she'd never looked back. Along with the paychecks came a workload that left her little time for anything else. Maybe that did make her coldhearted.

Yet coldhearted was the label that scared her the most when she looked deep into herself. Was she? She had gotten through a lot of her career and life with a hardened attitude, especially after...well, *that* certainly wasn't an experience she wanted to remember. Ultimately, she had discovered very few people over the years she could trust.

Miranda brushed her hair out of her face. Following her dreams had never been an option, at least not while her mother depended on her. In fact, as accounting had become her life, Miranda had hidden her real longings.

But now her mother was dead. It all felt like some strange time warp. One minute Adelaide Jenks had been awake, complaining about too much sunlight in the small cramped room of their old house in Houston, and the next minute her heart had given out.

After the funeral, Miranda had packed and left as she'd always done, except this time her mother wouldn't be there when she returned. The entire foundation upon which she had built her life, the one thing that allowed her to stay buried in work, no longer existed. Now Miranda was responsible for no one but herself.

*Freedom.* Something she'd secretly longed for, but now that she had it, did she even know what to do with it, how to step out of the careful shell she'd built around herself?

Thinking of Cruz Brockman, the oldest son, heir and executor of the Brockman estate, she walked to the window and drew back the curtain. He was rude and callous, and he'd insulted her.

But he'd done something else too. He had touched her, and his touch had seared into her with a shock that had caused her to pull away when what she'd really wanted was to feel his strong hands warming her entire body. A body that had been asleep for a long time. The sky darkened slowly as the sun began to set. Miranda watched the light fade. She wasn't sure what she was more afraid of, being coldhearted and closed off, or the feelings Cruz had opened inside her with the caress of his finger and his almost predatory gaze.

\* \* \* \*

Cruz stormed through the main house, annoyed at himself for having met her rudeness with his own. He got into his truck and headed back to the dairy barns on the other side of the farm.

Miranda Jenks was a puzzle—soft and exposed one moment, sharp as a knife and closed up the next. Cruz liked puzzles, but this lady was a serious distraction he didn't need right now.

He had plenty to do to keep the business running while settling the estate, and he wanted this chance to make Brockman Farms something to be proud of.

Cruz had been waiting to return without thoughts of revenge, hate or nausea at the memories of his father. When he could breathe a sigh of relief and walk through the orchards, when he could stand above the barns, smell the crisp sea air and watch the sun dip into the ocean without fear. He'd known this day would come. What he hadn't known was that T.D. would name Cruz as executor.

Cruz suspected his father had done it on purpose, knowing that Cruz would do his duty—T.D. knew what drove his sons, all three of them. *Manipulative bastard! Even from the grave you try to mess with us.*

In naming Cruz executor, T.D. had dragged Cruz back. T.D. thought he'd beaten him one last time. But this time, Cruz was the winner. He was determined to be nothing like his father, the reason he had bristled when Miranda had called him Mr. Brockman with disgust in her voice.

His mind lingered on her as he drove. When he'd brushed his fingers across her cheek to steal the tear from her face, the featherlight touch of her skin on his had felt like a welcome. He'd wanted to leave his hand there to feel her softness and the fire that was building inside him. For a minute, as the blush bloomed across her cheek, he'd felt she wanted the same. But she'd composed herself again, become so cold, so reserved.

What he needed was some good physical labor to clear his head for a while. The threat of tax fraud wasn't in his plans. Neither was a stunner of an accountant with a voice like steel that shot right to his gut.

# Chapter Four

Miranda was up before the dawn, which was normal for her. What was unusual was not knowing what she was supposed to be doing. Or, rather, when she was supposed to start. She assumed people who had a farm and animals must be up early, but it was quiet here by the cottage. Looking across the landscape, she couldn't tell if there were lights on in the main house yet, and the land around her was beginning to wake up.

Uncertainty made her restless, and she did not like that feeling. The thought crossed her mind that she could call Cruz, but she quickly tossed that idea out, remembering how hard she'd tried to get hold of him this week. Just because he owned a cell phone didn't mean the man answered the damn thing.

By the time she'd showered, gotten ready and made some coffee, she could see a light on across the large garden in the back of the main house.

"Well, nervous or not, it's time to get started," she told herself. Grabbing her laptop case and her soft cardigan, she headed outside.

It might have been spring, but the chill hit her as soon as she stepped out, soaking right to her bones and nipping at her throat as she breathed in. Shivering, she wrapped her arms around herself. She'd completely forgotten her coat for this trip. Not that she ever really needed one in Houston, but she was used to traveling and always came prepared. Her mind had definitely been exhausted last week. She looked up at the clear morning sky, which was a beautiful lavender starting to lighten into blue.

"You do realize it's not even fifty degrees, and we're on the coast here, don't you, Ms. Jenks?"

"What?" Miranda turned and put her hand to her chest.

"Sorry, didn't mean to startle you," Cruz said, reaching out to steady her. "You're shivering."

His voice sounded like a reprimand and his face had that angry look. She shifted enough to remove her elbow. "Sneaking up on people a habit of yours, Mr. Brockman?"

"Barns. Path. House." He pointed. "Just walking along my path from my barns to my house to help you get set up this morning. Not sneaking up on anyone."

"Right."

"Shall we?" He gestured towards the house and they turned to walk together.

"I wasn't sure what time you wanted to begin. I neglected to pack a jacket. It's in the eighties in Houston." *Stop babbling,* she silently told herself. She walked alongside him. His hand had been warm on her arm — even through her sweater she'd felt the heat. *Neglected to pack a jacket. God! Could you sound prissier?* Quiet might be her best course of action until she untied her tongue.

Apparently, he was fine with the silence too, as he said nothing while they walked. She almost preferred his clipped tone—at least then she wasn't so tuned in to her nerves rattling around inside. When they reached the back porch, he held the door open for her and followed her into the warm steamy kitchen that smelled of cinnamon and sugar and fresh coffee.

"Good morning, Ms. Jenks." Jake sat at a worn wooden stool at the kitchen island, drinking coffee.

"Hello," she said.

"Elena," Cruz said. "This is Ms. Jenks, the accountant who's going to be helping us settle the estate accounts. Ms. Jenks, this is Elena. She's been the housekeeper here since before I was born. And she makes the best cinnamon rolls you've ever tasted." He winked at Elena, grabbed a roll out of the baking dish and nearly fumbled it. "Hot!" he said.

"Come here, young man." Elena drew him down to her in a hug. "And you, Miss, it's very nice to meet you." She took Miranda's hands in both of hers. "Goodness, you're freezing, and you're too thin. Sit down right now. Tea or coffee?" She gestured to a stool next to Jake's.

"Ah, coffee sounds wonderful," Miranda said.

"Cruz, get this lady some coffee." Elena swatted him with her towel. "Where are your manners? You let her walk over here in that thin sweater so she'll catch a cold. Your mother and I didn't teach you better than that? What is wrong with you?" she asked, while she fixed a plate of eggs, sausage and a steaming cinnamon roll for Miranda. "Now, honey, you eat and get some energy for your brain and meat on those bones. You're too thin. I'm here five days a week till four. You need anything at all while you're working, ask me. I know everything that goes on around here."

Miranda was too startled not to smile. "Thank you, and please, my name's Miranda." She snuck a look at Cruz and had to swallow slowly. She couldn't tell if he was annoyed at her or himself, but he wasn't calm and settled, that was for sure. He got Miranda some coffee then poured himself a cup.

"Cruz," Jake said. "You look rough."

*Rough and dangerous,* Miranda thought as she ate her breakfast, trying hard not to stare at him. Not at all like the clean-cut rich playboy she'd seen yesterday in his office. In fact, 'clean-cut' was the last thing that came to mind.

"I'm not sure I can handle all these compliments this morning." His voice was frosty, but she also caught the quick grin he tried to hide behind his steaming coffee mug.

Jake laughed. "Sorry. Late night, or early morning?"

"Both." Cruz pinned Miranda with a look before he dodged around Elena for another roll.

"The breakfast is delicious," Miranda said trying to ignore those vibrations that spread through her when his gaze locked on her.

"Elena is the only reason I put up with Cruz." Jake winked at Miranda.

"Stop." Elena blushed.

Cruz snorted. "Elena's the only reason you ever see a home-cooked meal."

"Please," Jake said, "I haven't found the perfect woman yet to marry me and cook for me. What do you say, Ms. Jenks, you and me, wanna get hitched?"

Miranda nearly choked on her coffee. *Are they always this open and informal with each other?* She smiled at Jake. "While I'm certain I've never received a more charming offer, I think I'd better focus on the audit I'm here to do." She got up to take her plate to the sink, but Elena took it from her.

"You boys leave this lady alone with your teasing now. Go on, all of you, out of my kitchen."

"Whenever you're ready, Ms. Jenks." Cruz picked up her laptop bag for her and led the way out.

"You should be comfortable in here," Cruz said as they followed him into the library. "It's much bigger than the office." *And we can stay out of each other's way.* It was barely eight o'clock in the morning and he felt like a stumbling drunken idiot around her.

"It's huge," Miranda said, looking around at the room.

Cruz studied it. The ceilings were twelve feet high and books lined every wall except the floor-to-ceiling windows along the front of the house. Despite those windows, the room looked dark and cold.

"T.D. didn't believe in doing anything half-as — I mean small. Bigger was better, according to him, even in a room he never used with books he never read."

She gazed around the room at all the books, awestruck, but something more as well, almost as if she was trying to solve a problem in her head. She studied things intently. He'd watched her do the same thing yesterday when she met his mother, as if she was taking notes or drawing pictures in her head. And this morning before he'd caused her to jump out of her skin, she'd been staring up at the sky, swallowing in the clear morning light.

He had manners. He'd thought to offer her a jacket. There were several hanging in the cottage she was staying in. Heck, he'd meant to offer her his own, dirty as it was. But that had been before she'd turned to him with that startled look on her face, the soft sunlight surrounding her, before he'd held her arm, and before any reasonable thought had been sucked right out of his brain.

"Unfortunately for you, Ms. Jenks," Jake said, "it's also a huge amount of files and accounts and paperwork."

"I've built my career on big businesses and the work they provide me. I never complain about that. I'm sure I'll be fine."

*She works hard to be snotty.* Cruz hadn't slept well at all for thinking of her. For some reason Miranda's pale face, with a hint of flush and her startled eyes, had played havoc with his mind all night. He'd gotten up early and been down at the barns since before five a.m.

"I'm sure you will," Jake said. "Your reputation is excellent. I know it can be stressful in the beginning trying to reorganize someone else's system, and T.D's system was a mess. We'll help in any way we can."

"Well, I've certainly handled messes before. I'd like to get started. If it's all right with you, I'll take some time by myself and see what's here." She turned on the desktop computer and set her laptop next to it.

"Sounds great," Jake said. "Cruz and I have several meetings today. Then I'll be back in Portland for most of the week. Cruz should be easy to find as he practically eats, sleeps, breathes and, come to think of it, rolls around in the farm, from the looks of him this morning." Jake smacked Cruz on the back. "You might want to think about cleaning up before we head to the bank."

Cruz looked at himself. Hosing down barns and milking cows wasn't exactly clean work.

"Right. I need to get cleaned up. Ms. Jenks," Cruz said and nodded at her. "I'll meet you at my place, Jake." And he turned and strode from the room.

She let a breath out, at ease now that he'd taken his broody presence out of the room. The fact that she'd been able to feel his gaze on her even when she wasn't watching him unnerved her. *How odd,* she thought, as she surveyed the shelves, the large mantel over the fireplace, the wide leather chairs, *to have a room built specifically for books you never read. And the tone Cruz used when he spoke of his father wasn't one of kindness and love, that was for sure.*

What Miranda knew about Brockman Farms didn't seem to match what she'd encountered. A wealthy family running a business that had been handed down through generations. On paper it was polished and perfect, something to be envied. On paper it was simple, an audit she had to perform and a report to hand in.

Here among them it felt anything but simple.

Jake picked up his briefcase, stirring her out of her thoughts. "You have both our cell phone numbers in case you need anything. And good luck. I know accounts like this are a common, everyday thing for you, Ms. Jenks, but these people mean a lot to me, so please let me know if I can help."

She was touched by his words, simple, honest, sincere. She'd seen the bond between the men, witnessed their good-natured teasing, their easy talk. Here was true friendship. She'd had two good friends in college. They'd all drifted apart soon after graduation. What must that be like, to have those bonds still in her life, to have someone like Jake looking out for her?

"Certainly," she said. "And please, call me Miranda. From the looks of things, we'll be working together for a while."

"At least we'll have Elena's cooking to keep us well fed," he said. And his easy smile was back.

# Chapter Five

After several days of working on the Brockman Farms account and attempting to weed through piles of paperwork without much real auditing going on, Miranda was grateful for the end of the day on Friday. Her brain needed a break. She couldn't decide if she'd been working all that hard or if she was exhausted from the unorganized hell the accounts were in. How did these people expect her to audit? How could she do her job when such a shoddy one had been done before her? In all the years she'd been an accountant, she'd never seen accounts so messed up.

So little of the information was in the computer, too much was a disarray of old-school paper files, and the accounting that had happened before her... *What accounting?* She wanted to scream as she entered the cottage and sank down into the oversized couch. Often where there was such disorder in a suspicious account it meant the client was hiding something. Or many things. In this case, she already knew that was a possibility. The IRS Criminal Investigation Division and the Department of Justice had been looking into Brockman Farms right before T.D. died.

So far, she hadn't discovered any suspicious information, but she knew she'd barely even scratched the surface. Her instincts told her she was working with honest people here at Brockman Farms, but the numbers would ultimately reveal any fraud.

She'd spent the week working alone. After Jake had left her in the library with all the paperwork and computer accounts, she'd gotten to work. That was that. She'd seen glimpses of Cruz in passing, rushing from his office at the main house back down to the barns. She'd spotted Katie working in the garden early Wednesday morning, and aside from that the longest conversation she'd had with anyone had been Elena, who made the best coffee Miranda had ever tasted and brought her some each morning along with a selection of pastries, every one better than the last. For lunch she delivered crisp fresh salads and sandwiches.

The audit was going to be hell, but a girl could get used to the delicious offerings of food.

Her eyes drifted closed, and for the first time in her life, she actually contemplated taking a nap on purpose. But then she thought of all those buttery pastries she'd been eating. She faced the photo of the girls washing and looking off into the vast flat distance beyond them, and she wondered what they were thinking, what wisdom they knew that they could share with her. Or were they as lost as she was?

"Exercise is what you need," she said aloud, "if you think a photo's going to answer you back. And sketchy audit or no, this place is breathtaking. You might as well enjoy the beauty while you're here. Let's go exploring, Miranda."

She left the cottage and found a staggered path that led through the orchards. The ground was soft and a slight breeze flowed through the branches and new pink blossoms. It felt good to walk outside, especially in this clean crisp air. She was so used to working out in a gym or running that she never really took walks, but she felt both her body and her mind relaxing. And she lost track of time, which she'd never done before in her life.

It was the middle of April and all she could see around her were acres of farmland, grassy hills and rows and rows of trees on the gently sloping hill to the west. In certain places she caught a glimpse of the coast. The trees' limbs were bursting with pale pink and white blossoms that gave the rows of dark trunks a fluffy, ethereal look against the bright spring green grass. All things she hadn't ever seen or paid attention to in her life—a farm, apple trees, new sprouts barely pushing up through the dirt.

There was so much space here. She was in awe of it for the rugged feeling it delivered, a landscape she'd never seen. She followed a rocky path down a hill and let out a breath at the staggeringly wide beach and ocean in front of her. "Wow." Such extremes here, the cliff and tall fir trees behind her and now this gorgeous expanse of beach and dark blue water stretching out to forever. She betted on a stormy or windy day the water crashing over the rocks and onto shore could be wild with fury, but today the clear blue sky and still air left everything around her feeling calm. She walked the length of beach, breathing in the scent of seaweed and salt, and let it take away her responsibilities for a while.

Climbing back up the path, she turned and took one last look from the top of the bluff. She wasn't here on a calming vacation. She was here to perform an audit on books that most likely would turn up something illegal. It could take a toll on a person, being face to face with greed and deceit as a daily part of her job. But she'd done it. She was good at what she did, and she depended on her paycheck—two things she had always been certain of.

Standing on the rise looking out toward the water and listening to the rolling waves, she wasn't certain of anything anymore. Nature had a way of making a person and all their to-dos seem so insignificant.

She headed toward a row of trees. Reaching the end, she looked down a small, rough, grassy hill to a few small farm buildings and several large barns. Alongside one russet-colored barn was a fenced-in area full of calves and men. The late afternoon sunlight drifted down behind them, making the horizon a sea of blue melting into lavender and pink.

*What a great picture that would make.*

A truck arrived, kicking up dust, and Javier stepped out of it. He would make a great shot too, especially in black and white with the wisdom he carried in his weathered skin contrasted by the childlike glint in the laughter lines on his face.

Javier walked towards the men. One of them turned and met him as he climbed over the fence. Narrowing her gaze, Miranda saw that the other man was Cruz Brockman. He had changed out of his nicer clothes and wore dusty jeans, a dark brown work shirt, old boots and work gloves.

The two men shook hands and spoke closely, gesturing towards the calves. They paused for a moment as two young skinny children, maybe eight or nine years old, ran from the other side of the orchards down the hill towards them.

The girl kept running, climbed up on the fence and leaned over it to watch the calves, but the boy ran right into Cruz's arms. Cruz tossed him up in the air, caught him and held him upside down for a moment. The boy's laughter echoed through the orchard. Finally, Cruz set him down and pointed the boy towards the barn. Miranda noticed Cruz's smile as he watched the boy run.

She had never been one to stare or eavesdrop, but she seemed to get lost watching. Cruz was their boss, son of the infamous tyrant T.D. Brockman, and yet he was working alongside the men, laughing with them, teasing their children, getting dirty and being extremely gentle with very small calves. The man was definitely full of surprises.

Cruz patted Javier on his shoulder as they finished talking. It was then that he looked up and stared at her, his face hard and silent. He put up a quick hand in acknowledgment, then turned and walked away into the barn.

*Intense.* It was that gaze again and his rugged stance that caused those curious feelings to race across and under her skin. The sun was setting and reluctantly she turned to head back before she found herself in the middle of an orchard in the dark. She wondered what she'd done to make him see her at all. She was a good fifty feet away standing up against the trees. Initially the walk had felt refreshing, but arriving back at the cottage with her mind on Cruz Brockman, she was rattled.

The scene she'd witnessed wouldn't leave her mind as she shut herself away in the cottage. She wanted to do this audit carefully and as fast as she could and get away from these unsettling emotions running through her.

She took a shower and the heat helped soak away the tension. But the sensations that she couldn't wash away were the ones Cruz's searing touch and penetrating gaze sent through her body. He'd awoken senses in her that she couldn't turn off.

# Chapter Six

The next morning Miranda was completely engrossed in examining financial records. She meticulously organized everything. Her job took patience and to do it in a hurry would go against her work ethic. Rushing was a good way to make mistakes, and Miranda didn't do that, at least where numbers were concerned. But for the last half hour, she'd had trouble concentrating. She'd decided to approach the unorganized mess as a puzzle. It was a challenge, and she liked challenges — at least numerical ones. But at the moment she needed a break.

She hadn't seen Cruz all morning. Still, she couldn't get him out of her mind. Taking off her glasses, she sat back and looked around. This house was very different from the guest house. The guest cottage, with its bright colors and abundance of light billowing in through the windows, exuded a general feeling of cozy welcome.

The main house, where she sat now preparing to work, was anything but cozy. The library, although grand and beautiful, held absolutely no warmth. In fact, aside from the kitchen, she didn't feel much warmth in the house at all. *What a waste.* All these rooms, all this space, all this wealth and the people who lived here didn't seem to notice it or enjoy it.

She let herself imagine for a moment. Instead of an enormous dreary house with unused rooms, it would make a great bookstore with different genres in different rooms and plenty of oversized cushy places to sit.

Or, she could picture a café or wine-tasting room in one section with a shop full of local things like specialized foods, art from local artisans, photography, native plants and garden gifts spilling over into the other rooms. A gourmet market showcasing the Oregon Coast and Brockman Farms, with something for everyone.

They could make and sell artisanal cheeses, homemade jams and apple cider. It would be a place to welcome and draw people, not an empty shell of unwanted space.

Miranda sighed. Who was she to be fantasizing about this place? Not only did it not belong to her and she would never see it again once she was gone in a few weeks, but it wasn't up to her to decide what other people did with their homes. *And since when do you fantasize about anything?* Years. She'd been a girl with dreams, even after her father had died and left them broke. In a way, all her scrapbooks of pictures cut from magazines, pictures of exotic homes, families on vacations, travel photos—her secret longings for beautiful places, for connection and belonging—had kept her going. But after years of struggling to make ends meet and take care of her mother, of being lonely, she'd learned they had been ridiculous dreams. And dreams could hurt.

*You're an accountant who has a job to do and that's it,* she told herself firmly. This was certainly not the time or the place to wonder how her life could be different.

Miranda had moved the two large arm chairs to spread her papers on the floor. The desk was not nearly big enough for the way Miranda preferred to work, with room to spread everything out around her.

"Well, aside from all those files, I'd say you look quite comfortable there." Katie Brockman startled Miranda out of her thoughts.

"Oh, I'm sorry I've made such a mess in here," Miranda apologized.

"Please don't worry about it at all." Katie motioned for Miranda to sit back down. "It's nice to have someone in here using this room. It's been a long time. When I'm back here, I spend so much of my time in the kitchen or in the garden and the sitting room out back where there's more light and less stuffiness. I like to be where it feels a little less ghost-like, if you know what I mean."

Miranda followed Katie's gaze over the bookshelves and furniture. "I do." She studied the woman for another moment and wondered what she'd been doing with a man like T.D. Brockman. Katie's warmth and kindness were so completely opposite from that man, whose horrible reputation had preceded him.

"Elena made a pitcher of ice tea. I thought you might like some." Katie handed Miranda a glass full of tea and mint leaves.

"I'd love some." She reached up to take it.

"It looks like there's enough here for a whole team of accountants, not just one," Katie said.

Miranda laughed. "There is a lot, but I seem to work best by making a huge mess, reorganizing it under my own system and assessing the records. That way I know I have everything in my head, that I haven't missed anything, especially if another accountant has been working on the account previously." Miranda glanced at Katie. "Sorry, I'm babbling."

Katie sat back into one of the chairs. "It sounds like me when I'm laying out my garden each spring. Clear the space, sort all my plants and seedlings out in front of me to see exactly what to do with it all. Then put each one in its perfect place. You must love what you do, Miranda." Katie looked at the younger woman with a question in her eyes.

The truth was, Miranda didn't love her job. Not anymore, maybe not ever. She'd been driven and successful because there was no other option in her mind, but the thrill of audit accounting for big businesses wasn't something she loved. And lately she'd found her patience about unethical accounting practices wearing very thin.

Miranda envied the joy that came through Katie's voice. "I…" Miranda looked around at the boxes. "I'm good at it and it pays well," she finally said, not sure she wanted to pour her heart out to this woman she hardly knew.

"It must be lonely, though, traveling all over by yourself."

"I have someone who depends…depended on me," Miranda began. Although she and her mother had never been close, it was still hard for Miranda to get used to the idea that she was gone. "So…"

Katie nodded. "Sometimes we do things because we have to, not because we want to."

As his mother rose to leave, Cruz walked into the room. He intended to come in sooner, but when he'd stepped up to the doorway and seen Miranda sitting on the floor, her hair pulled back from her face and the light from the open window illuminating her profile, something inside him had tightened and he'd stood there, unable to move.

It was unsettling, the effect she had on him. He couldn't explain the way his nerves revved when he was in her presence—heck, even when he wasn't, she stayed in his mind. And yesterday, when he'd been talking to Javier outside the dairy barn, he'd felt her presence. When he'd looked up, she'd stood there, staring back at him from the edge of the trees.

Now, as those roles were reversed, he saw another side of her. She and his mother were speaking as if they were old friends and when Miranda laughed, he wanted to drink in the sound, that deep throaty, playful laugh that made others want to join in. But then he had heard Miranda's words, "I'm good at it, and it pays well." Miranda Jenks' audit could destroy the livelihood of all the people he held dear.

"Mom." He kissed her on the cheek and looked down at Miranda. "Ms. Jenks."

The smile disappeared from her face and the warmth in her greenish-hazel eyes faded to a spark when he turned to her. She stood and smoothed her hands down her black pants. Her long-sleeved blouse was ivory silk and sheer and he could make out the lace from her camisole underneath it. Desire shot through him.

"Mr. Brockman."

"Cruz, good morning," Katie said. "Miranda, have a good day and if you want a break, come visit me in the garden and I'll bore you with details of all the plants."

"I'm sure you wouldn't bore me, Katie. Thank you for the tea." Miranda smiled openly at Katie.

Cruz watched the light return to Miranda's face when she spoke to his mother. When Katie was gone, Miranda looked at Cruz and caught him staring at her. The flustered look came over her and she turned away.

Cruz glanced around at the files again. "I brought you some recent paperwork on the banking Jake and I have been taking care of. You'll probably need it. How's everything going?"

"Slowly. I'm still organizing everything. These files look like they've been mismanaged for a long time." There she was again, all tightened-up and guarded. "Once I'm done sorting and organizing, then I'll be able to begin the audit. I don't want to keep you from your work either, Mr. Brockman."

Cruz enjoyed watching her try to be calm and put-together, but he could see that he was picking at that reserve. He let his mind drift to the way her skin had felt when he'd wiped the tear away and he wondered what the rest of her skin would feel like as he uncovered every part of her.

Miranda gestured towards the mess on the floor, "I'd better get back to work. We coldhearted ones aren't very good at chatting."

"Oh, yes, work." Cruz tried to dispel the image of her naked body. What was he thinking? His intention wasn't to take this woman to bed. *Get a hold of yourself, Cruz.* "I should apologize for my rudeness," he began as he forced his thoughts off seducing her.

"That's generous of you, Mr. Brockman." She was calm, but her voice was as chilly as the crisp morning air.

"I'm trying to apologize, Ms. Jenks," he said through gritted teeth. He brushed one hand through his hair in frustration and walked towards the window. "I'm not very good at it." That was the truth. He wasn't good at it because he never did it. He wasn't used to being wrong. He looked back at her. She looked puzzled at his admission. There was a knot in his gut as she stared at him. For an instant he could have sworn she felt it too as she stood caught in his gaze.

She rubbed her hands up and down her arms as if she were cold. It was that change again, from fiery to vulnerable, that intrigued him.

"I overreacted," she said. "I need to get back to work. We have a deadline, Mr. Brockman."

"Always this cool and matter-of-fact with your clients, Ms. Jenks, or doesn't the thought of them losing everything they own touch you at all? No feminine compassion?"

"Of course it concerns me, Mr. Brockman," she fired back. "But my first responsibility is to complete the audit. That's my job. The sooner I can complete your audit, the sooner you can settle your estate and you won't have to deal with a woman any longer." Miranda met Cruz's demeanor with steel.

"You think it's the fact that you're a woman that bothers me?" Cruz said, and some of his frustration eased away. "It isn't. It's the fact that you're an accountant. I don't like accountants."

"Lots of people don't," she said, backing down a bit.

"So why become one?" he asked.

"I don't care about most people, Mr. Brockman," she said, giving an answer without really answering.

# Chapter Seven

"If you don't mind, Ms. Jenks..." Cruz softened the tone of his voice as he walked towards her. "I prefer to be called Cruz. Mr. Brockman reminds me of my father and I don't like to be compared to him in any way."

She snapped her head up, a look of confusion meeting his gaze again. "Certainly. I assumed... I didn't mean to insult you."

"It looks like neither of us is very good at apologies, are we?" He stepped closer and watched her eyes widen, her breath hitch. He liked having that effect on her. She certainly did something to his nerves. He'd lied when he said the fact that she was a woman didn't bother him — everything about her being a woman, her slight curves, the gorgeous green gaze, her scent, like wild roses in a field, was driving him mad.

"I really should get back to work...Cruz."

"You're intense when it comes to your job, aren't you?" His smile spread as he studied her, captivated by the shimmer of gold that sparked through her eyes. He was close enough to see annoyance flash across her face as any trace of calm vanished. "Do you ever relax, Miranda?" He smiled as he drew her name out. He was baiting her, couldn't seem to help himself.

The sparks turned to fire. "Not all of us have the leisure" — Miranda waved a file folder in front of his face — "of playing with our father's money all day."

In a flash Cruz grabbed her arm and pulled her close. Miranda sucked in her breath. The folder and its contents spilled onto the floor, papers scattering everywhere.

"Let go of me," she said, enunciating each word with an edge.

As quickly as his temper came, he reined it in and dropped her arm, but he didn't step away, couldn't pull himself away from her, that spicy floral scent that hovered around him. He could feel her breath, sense her pulse racing, "Certainly, but let's get one thing straight, Ms. Jenks."

"I was trying to make polite conversation." Anger, frustration, lust all laced his slowly spoken words as an ache spread through him. "I work hard and I do not, nor have I ever, 'played with my father's money'. Got it?" And with that he brought his head down and crushed his lips to hers. Strong and insistent, he drank her softness in like some forbidden potion.

He was on fire at the touch of her. There was no thought, only movement. He tasted her, breathed in her scent. More, he wanted more. Her body responded with a shiver as she opened to him. Only when he felt her shudder and heard her moan from somewhere deep inside did it register what he had done. Abruptly pulling away, Cruz drank in one last look of her, then turned and stormed out of the library. His last glimpse was of her standing frozen and stunned.

"Got it," Miranda whispered to no one as she slumped into the chair. She touched her fingers to her lips to feel the throbbing sensation left from him. *What in the hell just happened?* As shocked as she'd been when he grabbed her arm, she was overwhelmed with the intense heat that had poured into her from his closeness, the way her body tingled throughout, and that didn't begin to explain what she'd felt when he'd kissed her, the way he plundered. How she'd wanted him to plunder. With one kiss he'd completely shattered all the walls she'd built up over the years.

How long had it been since she'd felt that way? Had she ever?

*Focus, Miranda,* she told herself, although not too convincingly, as she came down from the high Cruz had taken her to. Focusing was harder than she thought as her heart pounded.

Miranda gathered the spilled papers and willed her hands to stop shaking. She hadn't meant to insult him like that. In fact, she didn't know where that stupid comment about playing with his father's money had come from. Since she'd walked into his office on day one and he'd hit her with those wolf eyes, his presence had set her nerves on edge, and biting, cold retorts seemed to be her default in dealing with him.

She didn't know much about what Cruz Brockman did here at Brockman Farms or who he was. She'd let her own assumptions and temper get the better of her and acted stupidly. She may have built walls up to remain indifferent to people around her, but it was unlike her to be downright nasty.

"Dammit!" She put her head down on the table. "Now I'll have to apologize." He might be rude and arrogant, but she could and would apologize for her own insulting comments.

# Chapter Eight

"Dammit!" Cruz had never let his desire or his temper guide his behavior. He'd acted like a complete asshole. "It's her eyes, I couldn't think straight while looking at her, and those legs of hers that go on and on...then she throws that haughty voice at me and insults me, insults me about money."

"Hey!" Adam smacked Cruz on the back.

Cruz whirled around. "Jesus, Adam, you scared the hell out of me! What're you trying to do, give me a heart attack?"

"I've been standing here calling your name, Cruz. What in the hell's wrong with you? You're talking to yourself, or talking to the hay—not sure which is crazier. And, man, you look like you're involved in some heated battle up there." Adam pointed to Cruz's forehead. "Ah ha! It's the accountant. She's got you all tied up in knots. Javier said she was the prettiest accountant he'd ever seen." Adam leaned back against the wall and grinned.

Cruz scowled at his brother and kept raking out the stall he was cleaning.

"You know, we have employees who get paid to do that. In fact, I think you're cleaning a clean stall, Cruz."

"It's not like I intended to kiss her, not exactly." Cruz waved the rake around. "And it's not only the way she looks, I mean stunning is a word, but there's something else. I can't..."

"You're still talking to yourself, aren't you?" Adam put his hand on the rake. "Cruz."

"What?" Cruz came back to the present moment.

"Stunning, huh?"

"Shut up." Cruz grabbed the rake and stalked away.

"Legs that go on and on?"

Cruz stormed back around to face Adam.

"Whoa." Adam laughed. "Calm down. I'm trying to get your attention. Want to talk about it?"

"No."

Adam smiled again. "Okay."

"I'm not making any sense, am I?" Cruz stopped and looked at his brother.

"Enough." Adam put his arm around Cruz's shoulders. "Come on. Let's go check on the new filly. Ana and José should be here any minute."

Miranda was too restless to make any dinner when she got back to the cottage. She couldn't get Cruz Brockman off her mind, not his behavior, not her behavior, and especially not the way his scorching kiss had ripped her open. And the look he pierced her with. She'd bet he could slay dragons with it

She still tingled where he'd touched her. *Who can think of food at a time like this?* And it was too early for bed. It was only five o'clock. Too early for anything. A walk — she needed a walk. Down to the beach. After throwing on some jeans and a sweater, she grabbed a pair of rain boots from the back porch and headed off in the direction of the water. Perhaps the rough sound of the waves, the heavy wind and the empty stretch of beach would settle her. She was barely a few yards from the cottage when a young girl came streaking by and nearly ran into her.

"Oh, *lo siento, lo siento*, I'm sorry. My brother's chasing me." The girl screamed as her brother raced down the path towards her. She hid behind Miranda as the boy skidded to a halt. He was all smiles and racing breath and one big gap where both his upper teeth were missing.

"Who are you? I'm José, and this is my sister, Ana."

"Nice to meet you. I'm Miranda."

"We're racing to the barns—a new foal was born last night and whoever gets there first gets to name it," he said.

"Come with us, you have to come with us." As if they'd never met a stranger, they raced off, pulling her with them.

Before Miranda knew it, she was running to keep up with the two kids down the slight hill. They all but dragged her into one of the barns. "Uncle Cruz, Uncle Adam," they yelled. "We're here!"

Cruz popped his head around the last stall in the barn where he was leaning over the rail next to another man. When he noticed the kids, he smiled that wide, brilliant grin. Even as dirty as he was, he still radiated that cocky energy. She shouldn't find that combination so attractive—the scruffy mess, the welcoming grin, mixed with his surely temper from before. But there was that quick tremble in her belly. *So much for pretending that kiss never happened. Uh oh.*

"Over here," he said, his smile vanishing as he saw her with the kids.

The storm brewing on his face replaced the easy pleasure. It wasn't as though she could turn around and escape without him seeing her. With a child hanging on each arm, she said, "Hi."

"Ms. Jenks." The angry tone in Cruz's voice from earlier had faded, but she certainly wouldn't call him relaxed. He looked as edgy as she felt.

"We found the beautiful lady, Miranda, and brought her along. She wants to see the new baby horse too." Ana nearly fell out of her skin with excitement. "Can we see it? Is it a boy or a girl? How big is it? Can it stand yet? Oh, Miss Miranda, can you believe it?" They drew her over towards the stall and peeked in.

"Beautiful indeed," Adam said under his breath and elbowed Cruz as they looked at Miranda.

"I'm Adam, by the way, I'm the youngest and the handsomest and the cleverest of the Brockmans." He reached over and offered his hand.

"You forgot most humble," Cruz snorted.

"It's nice to meet you. I'm Miranda, the —"

"The stunning accountant, I know. Word spreads fast around here." Adam smiled.

Her cheeks flushed at the open compliment. *Talk about smiles.* His was wide and generous and playful without a thing to hide. He was taller and bigger than Cruz and he had the fair Irish skin of his mother, with dark brown hair curling out from under his cowboy hat, and bright sky-blue eyes. *Good looks sure run in the family.*

"It's a girl, a filly," said Cruz as he put his hand on Ana's head and pointed to the foal.

"Oh!" was all Miranda could say at the scene in the stall before her. The newborn foal was wet and shiny. She was standing but still a bit wobbly and her mouth was latched on to her mother's teat as she sucked down milk. She nursed quickly, trying to stay steady on her new legs that looked gangly and too long for her. Her glossy mahogany coat was still matted in a few spots, but she was gorgeous.

"Quite a sight, isn't it?" Cruz said.

"I've never seen...how could you...what an amazing, it's amazing. Wow," she said and put her hand to her mouth. "She's beautiful." Miranda looked at the three men, ripe and dirty from a hard day's work on the farm. "Did it take all three of you to help her?" The astonishment carried through her voice. She could only imagine what it must have taken for the mother to push that baby out.

"Luna, the mother," Cruz indicated with his head, "did it all by herself. Most horses do, unless there's a problem."

"By herself? But the baby must weigh seventy or eighty pounds." Miranda couldn't believe it.

"Eighty-two pounds, fifteen ounces." Adam smiled proudly. "Stood up a few minutes after she was born and is already into her fourth meal."

"Who gets to name her? Who gets to name her?" José interrupted, tugging on Adam's arm. "We got here all at the same time." José climbed up Adam's back and onto his shoulders.

"What was the deal?" Adam asked. "Whoever got here first? If that's the case, it was Cruz. He was here at five a.m. this morning right after she was born. He even beat me, can you believe it?"

"Oh noooooo, noooooo, nooooo." José nearly fell off Adam's shoulders with a dramatic full-body slouch. Cruz stepped over, caught him and started tickling him.

"Stop!" the boy screamed through his laughter, "Uncle! Uncle!"

Cruz peeled him off Adam and let him go. "I think we should let our guest name her," he said as he straightened and looked right at Miranda.

"No. I couldn't," she said, trying to ignore the directness of his gaze.

"I'm practicing being polite." He flashed her a wry grin.

Was he teasing her? Or maybe he was making fun of himself? She was so bad at reading these kinds of social cues, these innuendos, especially with him and all that energy swirling around him. Well, at least he didn't stay mad long. Although, if he always kissed the way he'd kissed her senseless in the library maybe it wasn't bad at all. *Get a hold of yourself, Miranda.*

"And besides, she's never seen a newborn foal." Cruz crossed his arms and looked at the kids, all seriousness now.

Both kids stared at her, as if she had a foot growing out of her head, "You've never seen a baby horse before?" Ana asked, taking her hand again and looking up at Miranda.

"Never, only photographs." She leaned down towards the girl as they both carefully watched the foal try to lie down.

"Oh, you must name her. Naming's important," Ana said with reverence.

"Well," said Miranda, as seriously as she could, "I suppose if I'm going to be the one to name her, I'll need some help. Why don't you tell me what you're thinking of naming her now that you know it's a girl?"

She could feel Cruz watching her and glanced at him briefly.

"Oh my." Ana took both of Miranda's hands as if this were the most important decision in the world. "We could name her Starlight because her mother's called

Luna, like the moon. Or, I love Cassiopeia because it sounds so beautiful. I love the names of all the stars. I know all about the stars. Then there are flowers. I love flowers too. Do you love flowers? Sunflowers are my favorite, what are yours? Oh!" And as quickly as she'd begun chattering, Ana stopped for a second then said, "Sunflower, because her mama eats all the sunflowers in the garden when they grow, that's what I think." Ana looked up at Miranda.

*Puppy-dog eyes,* was what Miranda thought of when she looked at the big brown circles glittering with hope and excitement before her. And smart as a whip, it seemed. "Sunflower it is then," she said squeezing Ana's hands. Ana kept a hold of her as they both turned back towards the foal.

"It's a good name, Ana," Adam said, patting the girl on the back. "I've got to get the afternoon milking started. Ms. Jenks, hopefully I'll see you around soon. Cruz." Adam grinned. "Ana, José, want to help me with the cows?"

"Yes! Yes, please!" They followed Adam out into the afternoon light towards another barn.

The sudden empty quiet around them struck her. Miranda stood with Cruz as the silence stretched out between them.

"She really is beautiful." Miranda watched the mama horse and her baby. "Both of them."

Cruz leaned up against the stall door, next to her. "It's been a long time since I've seen a newborn. I remember the first time. I was six or seven, and I thought right then and there I wanted to be a cowboy or cowhand, or whatever I had to do to be near horses. I wanted to get my sleeping bag and sleep here at night. I thought the foal was my new pet, like a puppy."

Even without looking, she could feel the smile in his words. It was nice, hearing his voice, rich and full of love for his horses, talking about himself as a child. *Nice when we're not jumping down each other's throats.* His arm was close enough to touch hers and she could feel the warmth. "Miranda, I was a jerk inside, earlier," he said. "I lost my temper and I shouldn't have. I shouldn't have treated you that way."

"I upset you. Not that that's any excuse for your behavior." She flashed him a quick look then turned back towards the horses. It was much safer to look at the horses. "But I had no right to assume anything about what you do. I'm not usually so rude, and it's none of my business what you do or don't do with your money." She let out a breath. "I mean, I guess it is, since I'm auditing your books, but not in that way. I'll shut up now since I sound like a complete idiot."

"For the record, I don't normally treat people like that."

*Shouldn't things seem easier between us?* He'd apologized. They'd cleared the air on that whatever-it-was that had happened in the library. 'Kiss' was too mild a word. He'd practically blown all the fuses in her brain. He'd devoured her. Nothing felt easier. Instead the space seemed to shrink and she felt as though someone had sucked all the oxygen out of the barn. She started walking backwards toward the barn door.

"I should go."

"I need to get —"

They spoke at the same time. He laughed and let a breath out as he faced her. "Miranda."

"Yes," she said, caught in his gaze.

"I'm not sorry for that kiss," Cruz said, his face serious again as he pinned her with that look of desire. He took a step toward her. "I'm sorry for being rude, for putting you in an awkward position." He continued walking closer. "But I'm not sorry for that kiss, for feeling what I felt. You confuse me."

"Bossy accountant not your type?" She tried to joke, but the words came out jagged.

His strides were long. In an instant he'd caught up to her so their bodies were almost touching. "I don't know what my type is." His voice deepened. "I haven't been in one place long enough or spent enough time trying to figure out if I have a type. The only thing I've ever been sure of is my work and this land, the farm, the people."

He tucked a stray hair behind her ear. The intimacy startled her more than his gaze. She felt raw inside with need. She only had to stretch up a little to meet him. Her lips could be on his again. That delicious fire could consume her, which was exactly why she took a large step back and kept going.

He let her go. "That was nice, the way you handled Ana. She's taken with you, and she loves horses. Clever, letting her name the horse in that roundabout way. I don't think she'll ever forget."

She grinned at him then. "I didn't want to mess it up, and anyway, who could resist her pure delight, and those eyes of hers? I didn't have a chance. She has a way of making you feel as if you're a long-lost friend. I think I'm smitten with her." She paused a minute before she turned to leave. "Your filly's beautiful. Thanks for letting me see her. I'll see you," she said and was gone.

It was all he could do not to follow her, but he'd recognized her deliberate retreat. Speaking of eyes, he found himself wanting to dive into Miranda's every time he got close enough to see them light up. "Anytime," he said more to himself as he walked to the doorway and watched her disappear. She turned once, quickly, to glance back. Her hair flew around her face in the breeze, a rosy flush tinted her porcelain skin, then she was out of sight.

Desire for her raced through him, like a fierce need to be near her, to touch her, to be back in the library kissing her all over again. And more.

Maybe he'd find a way to get close enough soon. Which was possibly the stupidest thought he'd had in his life. Her presence and the job she had to do could potentially ruin his dream and the lives of people he loved. Not to mention a real relationship was the last thing in the world he was capable of. Getting closer to her was a mess of complications, some of which were so shameful he wouldn't even know how to explain them to her.

Complication or not, he couldn't quit thinking about her. Cruz wanted her, but he'd seen the fear in her look. Fear and uncertainty. He wasn't sure of what, but it was there. He didn't want her to be afraid. Nervous he didn't mind, but fear was a different thing entirely. Cruz walked back toward Luna and Sunflower and watched the mother and baby together while he remembered what her lips had felt like under his. No, the last thing he wanted at this moment was for her to be afraid of him — because he fully intended to kiss her again.

# Chapter Nine

If Cruz thought he'd get a chance to see Miranda again soon, the farm and his responsibilities had other plans for him. A new electronic milking system needed to be researched and ordered. He'd spent all day yesterday helping replace glass panes on the two long greenhouses. Pea seeds and onions were going into the ground and more seeds had been started. They were interviewing more employees. And all that was only the top of a very long list of things to be accomplished.

The farm's ongoing demands never stopped. That was one of the things Cruz loved. It felt constantly humming with movement. It was definitely a challenge for him to manage all the farm work while trying to settle the estate at the same time, but toss the gauntlet down in front of him and he'd always thrived, testing himself to see what he could accomplish.

Risk, fear, the possibility of failure, hopefully success — these had all attracted him to the life of a photojournalist. He'd had talent in photography, from the very beginning of his freshman year of college, and he'd always had a knack for storytelling, but it was the thrill of going into often dangerous, tricky situations to get the story that had driven him. For a time, it had fed him, but he'd grown weary of the danger, the pace, the transient lifestyle.

He hadn't tired of challenges, though, and he felt revived coming home to Graciella. As happy as he was to be here dealing with all this, right then, poring over agriculture and scientific journals to research the safest and best ways to protect his apple trees from pests was putting him to sleep.

What he needed was food and fresh air. What he wanted was Miranda. He'd only seen her once the last few days. She'd been on the phone and he'd been racing to meet the civil engineer who'd come out to consult on the irrigation problems in the orchards. And his thoughts still battled with whether or not he should stay away from her.

She hadn't been in the library when he'd returned from the barns a few hours ago—he'd checked. Maybe he'd see if she was there now, engrossed in her work with papers surrounding her. Maybe he'd be able to watch her for a few minutes before she noticed he was there. Maybe he'd convince her to kiss him again.

*Empty.* The library was empty. He made his way to the kitchen. Elena was gone for the evening too. He hadn't eaten and his truck was down at the barns. Who knew what was in his fridge at home? If he knew Elena, the fridge here would be well-stocked, and she always kept a few of his favorite foods here.

Cruz smiled when he opened the freezer. Homemade strawberry ice cream. It had been his favorite as a boy. Some things never changed. He made himself an overflowing sugar cone and set off across the land down to the barns. *My land,* he thought, looking around at the landscape surrounding him in the twilight, with that special light infusing everything around him with deep color. The grass was fairytale green like the hills of Ireland. The orchards, although suffering, sat full of pink blossoms shimmering against the deep blue sky. Off in the distance the silver silo towered over the barns and behind them, the subtle rolling hills with rows of sprouts and vegetables as far as he could see. And even though he couldn't see the coast from where he stood, he could hear the waves, smell the air. He felt like a kid with a whole set of new toys.

Then Cruz saw Miranda, the evening surrounding her in softness as she gathered groceries from her car.

"Let me help you with those." Cruz's voice startled her, her arms full of bags. She hadn't seen him at all the last few days, but he hadn't left her mind — another novelty for her. No man had ever hummed through her every thought like this.

"I think I've got them," she said, trying to balance the two, but he took one from her arms with his free hand before she could gather her thoughts. He looked handsome and happy, and dressed to kill in his tailored gray slacks with the sleeves of his blue dress shirt rolled up. The contrast of that professionalism with the enormous silly ice cream cone made her smile.

"I'm fine, Cruz. I'm perfectly capable of carrying two grocery bags."

"I know. Taste?" He offered her his cone. "I guarantee you it's the best ice cream you've ever had. Elena's secret recipe," he said when she hesitated.

He was so informal, so easy. She took the cone from him and he maneuvered the other grocery bag into his arm.

"Dessert? Oh, delicious." She practically moaned as she took a taste.

"More like lunch," he said. "Long day. I didn't get a chance to eat. Maybe you could get the door."

"Right." She opened the cottage door and stepped in. She'd been caught up in his presence, the way his eyes took in every inch of her every time he saw her. "You can set them on the kitchen counter," she said as he followed her back.

He set the bags down and sat down on one of the stools. "Nice glasses," he said. "I didn't know you wore glasses. They make you look even smarter, and prettier. Gorgeous Miranda with the glasses." He grinned at her.

Embarrassed, she handed him back his cone. He seemed perfectly comfortable sitting there across the counter from her and she was anything but. She couldn't remember the last time someone had called her gorgeous while she wore her glasses.

"Sometimes looking at the computer all day, I need a break from my contacts." She took her glasses off, set them on the counter and began to put her groceries away.

"Maybe you'd like a break from looking at the computer all day."

"Pardon?"

"Tomorrow morning, I could give you a tour. I'd give you one now, but it's getting dark, better to see it all in the daytime." He finished his cone and leaned his arms on the counter, watching her. "It might be helpful to see how things work around here too, don't you think, to understand the whole business? To see how all the smaller parts work together as our livelihood, a picture in my mind always works better for me than numbers in a column."

She kept her hands busy putting groceries away and avoided his gaze. It *would* be helpful to understand how things worked, which she could mostly do on paper through written reports about the farm and corporation, or by talking to him and his employees, but it seemed everyone was so busy that if she was going to actually have a conversation about the estate, a tour might be a better way to get the job done. "All right," she said. "I'm up early."

"Me too." He grinned and asked, "So, what are we making for dinner?"

"What?" She turned around to face him again.

"Dinner. I'm assuming you haven't eaten yet, looking at all your groceries. And I'm still hungry." His grin was no less powerful when he was sitting there relaxed and content in her kitchen.

She stepped out of her heels and rubbed one ankle with the other foot. "I haven't...I was going to panfry a steak and mushrooms and roast some asparagus."

"Sounds perfect. Want some company?"

"I..."

"I can help," he said, standing up and putting on the apron hanging by the back door.

That shameless charm and the silly flowered apron he put on brought out her own grin. She could handle this, eating a simple meal with him. "Fine," she said, smiling. She handed him the bag of mushrooms. "You slice. I'll change quickly." She grabbed her heels and went upstairs.

In her bedroom, Miranda plopped onto the bed, her body a mess of emotions. She tried to talk herself down from the crazy feelings. She wished she had a close girlfriend she could talk to. He wanted to stay for dinner. What did that mean? Was this a date? It couldn't be a date. He was in her kitchen with an apron on, slicing mushrooms. She had to get changed.

He'd opened a bottle of wine and was peppering the steak when she walked into the kitchen. He'd already made himself at home and finished the mushrooms. She was glad he'd invited himself in—more than anything, she wanted to sit with him and enjoy a meal together. Hopefully she could focus on more than his lips, or the sound of his voice and the way it felt like a caress on her skin.

"Wine?" he asked, handing her a glass.

"Thank you," she said. She moved carefully around him and got a cast iron skillet out for the steak.

"Anything else you need me to do?" He sat back down at the island with his wine and watched her get the asparagus ready to put in the oven. *So much for fixing an easy dinner.* With him so close, she could barely concentrate. She'd left her hair down and put on jeans and a black blouse, with her feet bare. Was she too casual, too exposed? She could feel his gaze following her and wanted to linger by his side. Her senses felt acutely tuned to him. Her hand shook as she salted the asparagus. At this rate, they'd never eat.

"Miranda, it's just dinner. We sit, we eat, you tell me about your day. I tell you about mine. You look like I'm ready to eat you alive."

She stopped, looked at him and took a deep breath. "I don't know what to do with this, this feeling in the room when you're close to me," she said quietly. She twisted the dish towel in her hands, betraying her unease.

He smiled long and slow and she felt it like a caress. Holy cow, she was completely turned on from it.

"Stop that," she said.

"We could go back to insulting each other," he teased.

She let her breath out and grinned. "I'm not very experienced at this sort of thing, and I work for you, and I don't know what you want. Annnnd there I go babbling again."

"I want you."

Hell, he'd blurted it out. Obviously he was having trouble maintaining his composure around her too, which made her relax a bit. "But aside from what you might believe, I can behave like a gentleman. As for working for me, technically you work for your bosses. For the moment, let's enjoy a meal together. We can even talk about work if that will make you feel better. We could call it a business meal."

"Okay," she said and heated the skillet for the steak. "How was your day, Cruz?" she asked giving him the briefest of smiles.

They sat at the island and he couldn't remember the last time he'd had a more enjoyable meal.

"Dare I ask how it's going with the audit?"

"Ugh, like a stopped freight train, but I think I finally finished organizing everything this morning. Now I can move on to all the tax returns that were filed for the past few years. You've been busy this week too," she said. "I see you being pulled in many directions."

"Keeping tabs on me, huh?" He grinned at her and watched the embarrassment flush her face. "It is busy around here, but it's a kind of busy I love. Tell me something you enjoy doing, Miranda. And by the way, this steak is excellent." He wanted to keep the attention on her. He loved peeling away her layers bit by bit. She was full of contrasts, like the ocean and like the most beautiful black and white photos, so many hidden nuances inside her.

She stared at him and put her glass down. "Enjoy?"

"You know, hobbies, things that people do for enjoyment. Some people enjoy cooking, others travel — maybe you're a blacksmith and I don't know it."

"A what?" She laughed.

Good, he'd gotten her to relax and smile again. "Seriously, though, what do you like to do when you're not working? Come on, name one thing. I know there has to be more than work in your life."

She studied him for a moment. Jesus, she had killer eyes.

"I like music. I like to read murder mysteries when I'm not too tired. I sew."

"You sew?" He was intrigued and raised his eyebrow at her. "Like clothes?" It was like pulling teeth to get her to talk about herself.

"Yes, like clothes, Cruz. Don't make fun."

It hit him in the gut how much he liked this almost relaxed side of her, and it worried him, because he liked it more than he should. "Sorry, I'm not making fun. I find it interesting. My mother had a sewing machine when I was growing up and I could never figure out how the damned thing worked. It used to drive me crazy. I took it apart once and couldn't get it back together the right way. I don't think I've ever seen my mother that mad at me."

"You didn't," she said, and giggled.

"Honest. I think it took me a week to fix it, and even then I had to get help from my friend Miguel's dad."

"What do you enjoy?" Miranda asked.

"Well, right now I'm enjoying looking at you." *So much for keeping things casual.* But, man, he liked catching her off guard. Her eyes got bigger and unshuttered, and he could almost see past her confusion to what lay inside her. He wanted to see deeper, her to open up to him. He'd been thinking about these things all week. He must be losing his mind. "I also like to read. See, we have something in common. But I'm more of a science fiction nerd. I love baseball, and I love old movies." He was about to pour more wine into her glass when she yawned.

"I'm so sorry," she said while he smiled at her.

"I'm that interesting, huh?

"No," she said, trying to disguise her laugh. "I enjoy listening to you. I've been up late working the past few nights and haven't slept that well, and I'm relaxed at the moment. It's nice, Cruz. I don't relax very often."

With her bare feet and her hair soft around her shoulders, she looked young and free, and innocent. And if he was really going to behave, he'd better leave now. The way she was looking at him, tired and vulnerable, made him want to ravish her.

"You're tired and I'm going to let you get some sleep," he said, clearing his throat of the ache inside him. "I'll come by around six tomorrow morning. The sun'll be coming over the hills. Should be a beauty of a sky at that time. Perfect way to see the farm."

He got up and took their plates to add to the dishwasher. He loaded their glasses, then she was standing there next to him. He stared at her a moment, searching her eyes again. So much was written in their depths. *Openness, curiosity, want.*

All he wanted was to kiss her. Instead he reached around her to the counter and picked up her glasses. Putting them back on her face, he tilted her head up to his. He took one long look into those green pools of hers and something in his gut tightened again. "See you in the morning, gorgeous Miranda," he said and walked out.

"Mmm-hmm," she answered when the door shut behind him. She slid down onto the floor and sat there leaning against the cabinets, as her legs were unsteady all of a sudden. The feel of his fingertips grazing her ears and neck lingered and had flutters skimming down her back. She'd thought he was going to kiss her. She'd actually leaned towards him instead of away, not wanting him to leave, or their dinner to end.

She *had* felt relaxed, relaxed and happy. Except when he looked at her—then she felt edgy, and something she couldn't name. She'd been that way ever since that moment in the barn when he'd stood so close, apologizing but not apologizing. Staring into her face as though he was searching for secrets, he'd invaded her thoughts.

It was all silly. She was like a schoolgirl with her first crush, elated with each glimpse, melancholy when she didn't see him, counting the minutes till their paths might cross again. By this afternoon, picking up some groceries, she'd convinced herself that the simmering fire she thought was between them was simply all part of her imagination.

Then he'd shown up with that ridiculous ice cream cone, that teasing smile and a look in his eyes that said he wanted to sample her every bit as much as he sampled his ice cream. She rested her head on her arms and sighed. She'd certainly acted like an ignorant schoolgirl, stuttering and nervous and confused. She'd yawned while he was talking about himself. *Silly isn't the word. Idiot is more like it.* She'd acted like a complete idiot, one who couldn't talk or think straight.

# Chapter Ten

The morning was clear and chilly. Miranda pulled a knitted hat down over her head when Cruz pulled up. He was around the truck and opening the door for her before she reached it. "See, I have plenty of manners," he teased, helping her up into the cabin. "I thought we'd start out driving. The entire estate is pretty big. We'll go over by the actual farmland to start and end up back here by the orchards."

Gently rolling hills, with perfect rows of green, stretched as far away as Miranda could see. It was a sight to look at, and still somewhat indistinct this early in the morning. They drove up a hill and Cruz pulled over, stopped the car and pointed toward the horizon.

The sunlight was reaching up over the mountains to the east in the distance. It created a brilliant pinkish-red glow in the sky, making the trees close to them look lit up and on fire from behind.

"You were right about the sky, Cruz, it's beautiful." Gradually it faded to orange and pale blue as the daylight brightened everything up around them.

"Not a bad way to start the day, is it?" he said.

She caught him watching her and he brought his gaze away, started the truck and continued on alongside their crops.

"What do you grow?" she asked.

"For now, lots of lettuces, onions and garlic, sugar snap peas, some strawberries and raspberries. Now that it's up to Adam and me, and hopefully eventually Turner, we'd like to scale back the size a bit and grow a bigger variety, rotate the crops and let some of the land recover for a year or two. Unlike T.D., Adam and I would like to concentrate on growing delicious fruits and vegetables in healthy soil. I'd bet my life T.D. never once cared about the taste of what was grown here, just the revenue that came with it."

Little by little Miranda got a better picture of T.D. Brockman and was increasingly glad she'd never met the man. "And what's that?" Miranda asked pointing to a stretch of land that was dark brown dirt, a barren, empty canvas. It looked so out of place among all the spring growth—where everything else seemed to be clambering to keep up, this part of the farm appeared dead or neglected.

"That particular area gets battered by the coastal wind and hasn't ever produced as much. Right now, nothing's growing there. We've talked over the idea of putting some vines in, to grow wine grapes, but there's been too much else to think of at the moment."

"I did see lots of vines when I drove through the valley to get here. Do they do well here?" Miranda said.

"Yes, they handle the wind and the weather, but it's a huge investment, and takes a lot of knowledge. Neither Adam nor I know as much about growing grapes."

They drove in silence for a bit with crops on either side of them, the long white fencing rolling along with the land. They turned right towards the coast and passed more of the orchards.

"Is this all yours?" Miranda gazed over the apple trees to her right and lettuce crops to the left. Both seemed to go on forever.

"Yes, over two hundred and fifty thousand acres total."

"That's a lot of land, Cruz." She knew the number on paper, but seeing it all, driving through it made it more real to her.

"It is, but it doesn't matter how big it is—it's how efficient we make it. With the orchards and the crops, the grazing land, the dairy cows and horses, it's pretty well diversified, but damn expensive to run. One of my goals is to get our costs down but bring our quality up, and I'm not sure how that's going to happen yet."

"What are those?" Miranda pointed behind the orchards. Seven or eight cottages were nestled back into the trees.

"Ah, the workers' cottages." Cruz stopped the car. "They've been here for a long time, since the early 1860s. After the government forced the Native Americans off the land, white men were given acreage to begin mining and farming. The lumber mills started back then too. The O'Reilly family, my mother's family, settled here first and built your cottage. Then as their farm and orchards grew, they built more cottages for their workers."

"What will happen to the cottages now?"

"I'm not sure. Legally they belong to my brother, Turner. They're vacant now, have been for as long as T.D. was in charge. T.D. didn't believe in providing any comforts to his employees, especially the migrant workers. He saw them as dirty and beneath his stature."

"Why did they work for him? It sounds more like slavery." Miranda asked.

"In a way it was, but many of the workers were poor enough or were illegal immigrants, so they often took whatever work and wages they could find, scraping together here and there to make ends meet."

Miranda understood that. After her father died, she and her mother had done whatever they had to do to scrimp and save. Then Miranda had done the scrimping and saving after her mother's first stroke. She was a genius at making ends meet, but even though she'd often stressed over paying all their bills, she knew her struggle must have been very different from that of migrant workers and illegal immigrants. At least she had a degree and a home and didn't have to worry about not being a citizen. She'd been in her own bubble of unhappiness and struggle for so long it was good to learn that she was, in fact, extremely lucky.

"Taking much better care of the employees than T.D. ever did has been at the front of my mind since I returned after T.D.'s death."

"You haven't always been here?" She looked at him, surprised.

"I left when I was eighteen. Haven't been back here at the farm in over ten years."

It hadn't occurred to her that he had a life aside from this one. She'd assumed he'd always been here, the big estate farm, lots of money and power, surrounded by admirers, friends who hugged him. "I didn't realize you didn't live here. Another assumption. I'm rather good at those. Sorry."

Cruz waved away her apology. "It's not like we've had many, what you might call, calm, normal conversations about our lives with each other, have we?"

"No, calm and normal are not words I'd use to describe our conversations," she agreed and looked out again towards the cottages.

They drove back to the barns and Cruz parked his truck by several others. "Well, you've been in here to see Sunflower. We have twelve horses at the moment and over there is where we milk the cows." He pointed to another barn beyond as they walked. "We keep hay there, and feed over there." They passed a few workers, who waved hello to Cruz as they went to work.

"Adam's most likely milking with a few of the men. Right now we have over two hundred cows and that's way too many. Again, T.D. was concerned with bigger not better. We'd like to sell some eventually. And we're looking at investing in a new automatic milking system to replace the old one that seems archaic. We could use a new field cultivator. All the tractors seem to be older than me. Lots of changes need to be made. Not to put any pressure on you, Ms. Jenks, but as soon as the audit's done, and we can settle the estate, we can start making changes for the better around here." He nudged her shoulder with his.

She felt ridiculous suddenly for taking time away from the audit and enjoying the morning. "I know you're right, Cruz. I should get back to the main house to get to work."

"Miranda, I'm teasing you." He put his hand on her shoulder and turned her towards him. "I see how long you work every day. I know the accounts are a mess. I do want the audit to be done, but I know you're having to work long and hard at it because of the way T.D. left things when he died. Come on, I'll walk you back." He took her hand in his.

She looked down at their connected hands. His warmth soothed her. "It's all right. I know you're busy. I can walk myself back."

"I'm certain you can," he said. "But my day starts at the house too with phone calls and paperwork, trying to find out about some properties listed as part of the estate. In a way, you could consider it helping you because you'll need the information I dig up. Besides, I'd like to walk you back."

"You make me nervous," she whispered, looking at him, her hand in his large one, the warmth spreading throughout her.

"I know." He flashed his smile.

While she was practically falling into a puddle of lust, he helped her up the rocks to the path back to the house. He didn't let go of her hand as they walked. And she didn't try to pull away.

# Chapter Eleven

Miranda looked up at the night sky as she crossed to the small market outside the farm's main entrance. She'd forgotten how amazing the stars looked out in the open like this. Over the big city, it was as if they disappeared. Tall buildings all but obscured the sky and stars. But out here, ah, it was beautiful. The world felt huge and peaceful. Somehow the night wrapped around her and comforted her, which made her less aware of the loneliness inside her.

Even with the few spring rain showers of the past couple of days, the temperature this evening was warm and pleasant. There was a gentle, balmy breeze, and the scent of wet dirt and new flowers from the flower garden traveled through the air towards her.

She felt almost...relaxed. Cruz had rattled her when he had gazed into her, calling her coldhearted, then again in the library when he'd pricked at her inability to relax. Even now, with what she might call a friendship building between them, when he looked at her, he looked right through her guard and made her acutely aware of her feelings—feelings about life, about pleasure, about him. Last night he'd completely stumped her when he'd asked her what she enjoyed doing. Such a simple question and she'd barely been able to answer.

*Fun. Pleasure. Enjoyment.* Those words had disappeared from her life and she couldn't pinpoint exactly when it had happened. Could it really be as far back as childhood? Numbers, work and taking care of her mother had been her life, her shelter for so long she didn't know any other way.

In the barn, he'd said that she confused him. *I confuse him? Lord, he doesn't seem confused.* He didn't stutter in her presence. Instead, he did things like pin her with that steely gaze of his and call her gorgeous. She was the one who was completely flustered. She'd nearly left the house this evening with two different shoes on.

She so wanted to enjoy the evening, bringing with it Katie's invitation to dinner at the main house. Miranda had liked the woman immediately and the idea of eating with someone kind and warmhearted was much better than spending another Friday night alone. And she had to admit, she was curious about Katie and Javier. He seemed part of everything around here at Brockman Farms, but in a subtle way. His face carried such wisdom. And she might be slow when it came to most social cues, but it was pretty obvious his heart belonged to Katie.

The market was tiny and charming. It was painted a deep cobalt blue, its small windows trimmed in white with white shutters. Several terra cotta planters stood outside the door with bright pink and purple petunias spilling over the edges. A little girl with black hair pulled into a long braid sat on the step petting an old mutt who made a pleased noise at her touch. Miranda recognized her immediately.

"Oh! Ms. Miranda!" Ana jumped up and hugged her. "You look so pretty. I love your dress. I can't wait to grow up and wear pretty dresses and look beautiful. This is Romeo. You can pet him." Ana pointed to her mutt, whose gray muzzle betrayed his years. He barely lifted his head from the step as Miranda leaned down to scratch behind his ears.

The little girl's face danced with amusement. Calm for an instant, Ana quickly jumped up and pulled Miranda into the market. "Mama! Mama! It's the lady, Ms. Miranda, I told you about." Ana let go of Miranda and ran searching for her mother.

Miranda gazed in awe. For its tiny size, the market was packed with all kinds of stuff. There were grocery items, crates full of lemons, limes, oranges, and apples on display, beautiful fresh flowers in tin buckets, tall brightly colored candles with the Madonna painted on them, a wall full of coolers with soda, beer and water. And up by the counter were glass jars full of candy. Colorful, vibrant, bright. Miranda fell in love.

A beautiful woman with deep brown skin, long dark, curly hair and the same caramel-brown eyes walked out from the back with Ana.

"Ahh, the lovely accountant, Miranda. Hello. I'm Roxanna," she said. "Ana, José and Javier, well, everyone's told me all about you. Now I finally get to meet you." Roxanna took Miranda's hands in hers.

Miranda felt the other woman studying her. In turn, Miranda couldn't stop staring at the stunningly gorgeous Roxanna. Rich curls flowed around her shoulders, her skin glowed with health, her smile practically lit up the whole place and she was enormously pregnant. She looked radiant.

"We're going to have a baby," Ana said with her arm around her mother's waist.

"Yes." Miranda smiled. "I can see that."

"Go out and keep Romeo company and give him his biscuit if he wants it. Papa should be along soon," Roxanna said to her daughter.

"What can I help you with?" Roxanna asked turning back towards Miranda.

"Flowers," Miranda said. "For Katie. She invited me to eat with her tonight and I wanted to take her something. She's gone out of her way to make me comfortable since I've been here."

Miranda hadn't left herself much time before dinner or she would have stayed longer to stroll along the colorful aisles, but she was drawn towards the tall purple, reddish-brown and yellow irises. "These." She gestured. She picked one of each and as she turned towards the register, she noticed a small stone-carved bullfrog. Smiling, she ran her hands over the smooth surface. "I'll take this too."

"Perfect. Katie loves irises. Can I wrap them in tissue for you?" Roxanna asked.

"Thank you. That would be lovely."

Roxanna gently drew out some lime green tissue and purple ribbon and within a few minutes had them wrapped.

"They look beautiful. Thank you."

"You're very welcome," Roxanna said. She took Miranda's money and walked her to the door. Roxanna stopped abruptly at the entrance, placed one hand on Miranda's shoulder to steady herself and another on her large stomach. "I'm sorry. This baby is playing soccer in there."

"When are you due?" Miranda asked.

"In four weeks. Not soon enough." Roxanna laughed. "Oh, I love being pregnant, but I'm tired. Tired and cranky."

"Mama!" The little girl jumped up and wrapped her arms gently around Roxanna's stomach, and Miranda was touched by the warmth and love between the child and mother.

"Shh, *bebé*, rest now. You'll be here soon," Ana cooed to her mother's stomach and smiled her cute grin at Miranda again.

"Would you like to feel?" Roxanna asked, as if sensing Miranda's curiosity.

"I…yes." Miranda answered. Ana took Miranda's packages, set them down and, taking Miranda's hands in her small ones, placed them gently on Roxanna's belly. Together the child and mother covered Miranda's hands with their own and the three women stood together feeling the tiny movement beneath Roxanna's stretched skin.

"Wow." Miranda's voice was hushed as she stood in awe in this moment of intimacy with these beautiful people.

"That was a foot, I think. Pretty amazing, isn't it?" Roxanna said. Her whole face lit up in smile.

Miranda might have stayed there all night if some people hadn't come into the market, breaking the link between the women. She thanked them, took her gifts and headed back toward the Brockman house, feeling as though she had been touched by something magical. Everyone here was so connected, so warm with each other. The people, the animals, the land, such community. Miranda was struck by how empty her own life was, but felt for the first time in a long time that maybe she could do something to change that. She only wished she knew what that something was.

# Chapter Twelve

Arriving at the porch, she felt silly with her gift. Roxanna had said that Katie loved irises, but surely no one had ever only given Katie Brockman three flowers. She probably never got less than a dozen. Well, it was too late to turn back and anyway, she didn't want to eat dinner alone. Eating with Cruz last night had made her feel warm, a warmth she didn't want to let go of.

The beautiful screened-in porch faced the flower and vegetable gardens and housed a small round table set with a beautiful but simple white linen tablecloth. It was thin and had an edging of eyelet lace and small embroidered red flowers. One small lamp and several votive candles on the window sills lit the porch with a soft, flickering glow.

She set the bullfrog down and ran her fingers over the embroidery on the tablecloth. At the sound of footsteps, Miranda turned to see Cruz step onto the porch from the house. The un-tucked, short-sleeved black shirt he wore sharpened his features and surprise appeared on his face when he found her there. A small fresh cut over one eyebrow added a dangerous look to his already dark expression. And he smelled amazing, clean and with a hint of cologne. It felt like a drug to her senses.

"Hello," he said, and smiled that blazing smile. "It's nice to see you."

"It is? I mean, your mother...ah, *Katie*, invited me for dinner." She could hardly speak around him. Every time he was near, she made a fool of herself.

"I'm glad," he said as he took a step toward her and smiled. "I should have invited you this morning after the tour. I guess you could say I was distracted."

"Oh," Then there was the way he did that, walked toward her as if he wanted to devour her again. She lost all power of speech.

"Looks like we have the same effect on each other," he said.

*How does he do that?* He moved closer without her even realizing, probably because she was too busy drowning in his presence. All of a sudden he was right there, his presence consuming her. "You cut your head," she said and started to raise her hand up to brush aside the hair on his forehead, but pulled back abruptly. What was she doing? She'd nearly caressed his face. She wanted to touch him, yet she knew she shouldn't.

"It's nothing," he said, his voice clipped, his eyes going dark.

"Right, I..." She'd angered him. She could feel it, all that energy aimed towards her, but she certainly couldn't figure out why. Maybe she should have taken some classes in college to help her figure out brooding men instead of spending all her time on numbers and formulas. She'd thought things were more comfortable between them since they'd shared dinner last night and with the friendly walk back towards the house this morning after he'd showed her the farm. He'd held her hand and she hadn't wanted him to let go. It had been the nicest walk she'd ever had. He'd been funny and kind and relaxed. She had no idea what had happened since then.

"Oh, Miranda, you look lovely." Katie stepped onto the porch. "Cruz, why don't you pour Miranda a glass of that wine you brought? Unless you'd like something else, Miranda?"

Miranda let out a breath as Katie and Javier came down the steps, carrying plates of food. She looked towards the woman and, unlike the whirl of emotions on Cruz's face, she saw only warmth. "Wine sounds good, thank you."

"I'm so glad you came," Katie said, turning back towards Miranda.

"I brought these for you." Miranda handed Katie the irises. "I'm not sure now why I only got three. They seemed to go together."

"My goodness, they're lovely. A girl can never get enough flowers, can she?" Katie looked like a child who'd never had a gift given to her in her whole life.

"I don't…uhm…" Miranda wasn't sure how to answer. No one had ever brought her flowers before. She tried to cover her quiet by glancing towards Cruz, but looking at him did nothing to settle any emotion inside her.

Cruz stood in silence. He'd been surprised to find Miranda standing on the porch when he arrived, and frustrated at the way he had spoken to her simply because she'd drawn back before touching him. Coming up on her unexpectedly and acting like a jerk were habits of his lately. And it had nothing to do with her.

When she'd reached towards the cut on his face and abruptly pulled away, he'd felt like a wounded animal waiting for her balm, and instead left empty. He wanted her to *want* to touch him, to be near him the way he wanted her. He couldn't stop wanting her, which frustrated him, because he'd never been affected like this by a woman before. It felt so much more profound than simply attraction and friendship. And he didn't know if he even had the capacity to handle what that meant.

Casual relationships he was really good at, relationships with no expectations, relationships he could easily walk away from. Yet with her he felt like it would be so much deeper, with nothing casual or easy about it, and oddly enough, he wanted that with her, even though he knew in his gut that he'd never be good at that kind of relationship.

"This is for you." Miranda interrupted his thoughts and held out the obese grumpy bullfrog towards Cruz. "For the garden."

"Cruz." Javier smacked him on the back. "The lady gave you a gift."

He looked at the bullfrog, knew it well from Roxanna's and Miguel's shop. It was the same one little Ana liked to talk to when she was pretending it was a prince. He took it out of Miranda's hand, letting his fingers rest on her wrist for a few seconds longer than necessary. "A frog?" He raised one eyebrow at her, but he was smiling, trying to ease the tension he knew he'd created by practically jumping down her throat when she didn't touch him.

"They say there's a prince inside each one." She smiled back, but moved slightly away around the table.

*Is she flirting?* Totally unexpected. He liked it.

"Cruz, pour us some wine. I'll get a vase for these flowers. Then we can eat," Katie said.

"That was kind of you, to bring my mother something." Cruz broke the silence as he stood by the table and poured the wine. He looked up from the glasses in time to catch Miranda quickly move her gaze away from his. She'd had that puzzled expression on her face that changed her from hard and guarded to flustered. And flustered on her looked absolutely cute.

"Miranda?" Javier held out a chair for her.

Cruz tried not to watch her every move. Her hair was up in a loose ponytail and she had on a white sundress, simple but attractive, tied around her neck, leaving her shoulders bare and smooth as the soft light from the porch shimmered over her skin.

While Katie lit the candles on the table, Javier dished out the salmon, potatoes and salad. Miranda sat and took a sip of her wine.

Cruz ate in silence for a few moments, hoping to let go of his tension and confusion. He could get through a simple meal and get his mind back on track. Somehow it was getting harder and harder to remind himself that she was here to do a job, a job that could ruin him. She would finish her audit, move on to the next job, and they would be left behind in the dust.

"Cruz, you're awful quiet tonight, dear. Is everything okay?" Katie put her fork down and took a sip of her wine.

"What?" Cruz looked up, startled. He smiled at his mother. "Everything's fine." He caught Miranda watching him and stared down at his food. "Salmon's fabulous, Mom." He wasn't about to explain to his mother that he had been both fantasizing and worrying about Miranda Jenks. "Great catch, Javier."

"It is wonderful, Katie," Miranda joined in. "It's better than many of the fancy restaurants I've eaten in."

"Do you prefer fancy restaurants?" Cruz asked.

"No...I..." She seemed caught off guard again by the way he aimed his gaze directly at her. "I usually go where my clients prefer or I eat in my hotel room. I can't remember the last time I had a home-cooked meal with people." Miranda inclined her attention toward Katie. "It's wonderful, and kind of you to invite me."

He hadn't meant to sound like he was interrogating her. When she'd said fancy restaurants he'd naturally pictured her on dates, with men. He didn't like thinking about her with other men. He knew so little about her, where she came from, who was in her life.

With an attempt to loosen the edge from his voice, he tried again. "Is Houston your home?" Cruz couldn't believe that a beautiful woman like Miranda didn't have people waiting for her somewhere—*parents, siblings, a lover?* Maybe he really was losing it. They'd shared a perfectly nice dinner the night before, spent the morning touring the farm, walking and talking, getting to know each other. He'd worked himself up into a jealous fit over the thought of her with someone else.

"Yes," she said. "It's more like a home base. It's the house where I grew up. I...ah...live with my mother, when I'm there. She was sick for a long time and had a live-in nurse. I've never really thought of it as my home, though."

"Home can sometimes be a difficult place to find," Javier said. "And sometimes it's right in front of you."

Cruz was stirred by Miranda's words, and not in a way he expected. She sounded as though she didn't really know what home meant. Deep inside he knew what she was talking about when she described that cold feeling. He'd never felt connected to this house. But he'd always loved the land, the people and the town of Graciella, and more importantly, he'd always felt warmth and love from his mother. He didn't get that sense when Miranda spoke of her own mother.

When he listened to her, Cruz found he could once again see through the cool reserve to layers and layers underneath. There was more to her words than what the surface exposed. As her voice drifted to him, he thought he would enjoy uncovering all her layers, every last one.

"Katie," Miranda said touching the older woman's hand, a look of concern now on her face. "Katie, are you all right?"

"Katie." Javier grasped her hand and put his other gently on her cheek.

Cruz snapped out of his thoughts in time to see his mother. Her face was ghost-white and beaded with sweat.

"It's just a migraine." Katie barely got out the words in a whisper. She tried to push back from the table, but as she rose, she fainted back in her chair. Javier carefully folded her body over so her head was between her legs. "Steady now. Take a deep breath."

"Mom." Cruz put his hand on her back. "Mom, can you hear me?"

Snapping into action, Miranda ordered, "Check her pulse and her breathing. I'll call an ambulance."

She started to run towards the kitchen when Javier's strong, calm voice stopped her, "No, Miranda."

"Shh, it's okay now," Javier said gently to Katie as he carried her to the settee on the porch. "You're okay. I've got you." He looked at Cruz, and said, "She's had them before. Sometimes they are very intense, but she'll be okay. Miranda, thank you, but we don't need an ambulance. She has medicine at our house to help with the pain. I'm going to take her home, all right?"

"Can I help? I can drive you," said Cruz.

Javier nodded and said in his soothing voice to Katie, "*Mi amor*, we're going home. Cruz is going to carry you to the car. I'm right here with you."

"I'm so sorry," Katie started to say before both men hushed her.

Cruz lifted his mother. He glanced at Miranda, who gently squeezed his shoulder, then let them go.

# Chapter Thirteen

Miranda stood, stunned in the silence that was left after Cruz and Javier had taken Katie home. The evening's sounds gently brought her back, crickets beginning to play, the branches in the orchard rustling together in a dance on the breeze. She could almost smell the salty sea scent as the air drifted in through the screens.

*Well, this job certainly feels like a series of initiations.* First time ravaged by a kiss in the client's library while working. First time feeling sexual tension and flirting with a client. First time being invited to dinner by client's mother. First time left alone in client's house without a soul. She let out her breath as the adrenaline in her blood calmed down. They probably thought she was a crazy lady, jumping up to call an ambulance for a migraine. She'd gotten so used to her mother's medical emergencies that it had become second nature to respond like that. She shook her head to clear her thoughts. Too much thinking when she'd much rather be busy than dwell on what her life had become, and the fact that she was really great at jumping into action during an emergency without really feeling anything at all.

Cruz stirred emotions in her, ones she hadn't known she was capable of feeling. She was finding it impossible to keep her eyes off him. Her body was incredibly aware of his, the hint of his spicy cologne, the way fireworks lit up her skin her every time he touched her, the boiling tension that rolled through him.

She was losing it, buying that bullfrog for him, her silly attempt to flirt. *Definitely losing your mind, lady.*

Miranda looked at the beautiful table and decided she could at least help by cleaning up. She'd lost her appetite, but there was no reason to waste good food. When she stepped into the kitchen, she felt warmth and comfort and could instantly tell why they all preferred this room, why they gathered here and on the back porch. The white country kitchen cabinets, the pale butcher-block countertops, one whole wall of windows looking out onto the back porch and the garden beyond. There was a large island in the middle with old wooden stools. Someone had placed white pots in front of the window and green herbs spilled out of them as if showing off their luck and happiness.

There was even a happy mess of ingredients left on the counter, a cutting board with a knife and the remains of some garlic, the pans left on the range as if there wasn't a care in the world to when they would be cleaned up. This was home. She hadn't wanted to tell them that she didn't have a clue where her home was, that she wasn't ever really wanted at her home. And that whenever she was there, she felt the loneliness creep upon her with difficult memories and her mother's sickness.

She certainly didn't want to tell them that her mother had so recently died. Even thinking about it felt surreal.

Miranda found an apron and got to work. Cleaning up was something she was good at. Tonight, she actually enjoyed putting the food away and cleaning the pots and pans, starting the dishwasher. This was a happy space and she didn't mind doing a favor for Katie who, in only a couple of weeks, had made her feel more welcome than her own mother ever had. The last thing she did before she left was put the vase of irises on the counter with a note to Katie.

*I hope you're feeling better soon. Miranda.*

Cruz flipped on the lights in the kitchen over an hour later when he returned. He'd come back to clean up before he eventually had to go down to the barns later tonight to see if they needed help with birthing the calves that might be making an appearance soon.

Everything was cleaned up.

These last few weeks since he'd returned, he, his mother and Javier had cooked Friday night meals together here at the farm. Sometimes Adam joined them. For some reason this kitchen still held happy memories for them all and after a long week on the farm, this seemed the place to be together. After dinner, Adam would head home. Katie and Javier would sit and sip wine on the porch or in the kitchen with him while he did the dishes. Sometimes they'd put some Louis Prima on and dance.

Tonight was different. He'd had no idea his mother had been suffering from migraines or for how long. The guilt dug into him. There were so many things he didn't know any more about his family, this farm. He'd done some amazing things in his life, but coming home after his father's death, to handle the estate, he'd faced one of the steepest learning curves of anything he'd ever done. And he was faced with the guilt that had built up over the ten years he'd stayed away.

He stood at the sink and looked out of the windows towards the cottage where Miranda was staying. There was a glow from the porch light and he could see the movement of the porch swing. They'd completely walked out on her and she'd cleaned up and put everything away for them. Cruz was worked up and restless, full of guilt and stress energy, and he realized he was hungry. A smile warmed his tired face as he got an idea.

Half an hour later, he was back and she hadn't stirred from her sleep. *Stunning and vulnerable,* he thought as he looked at Miranda. She lay asleep on the porch swing under the warm, muted light of the small lamp. All her worries gone, her façade no longer up. Her papers were scattered on the table next to her laptop, and she still had her glasses on, as if she'd only intended to rest for a second. He wanted to get lost in her, forget all the stress from the evening, from the last few weeks, from what was surely to come. For a minute he imagined bending down and taking those lips while she slept, taking in her scent, but with all the willpower he could find, he turned to go.

"Cruz," she said as he started down the steps.

He turned back as she sat up. Her hair was loose and her cheek was flushed from where she'd been resting on it. He didn't know if he could turn away again. Everything in her called him towards her.

"I didn't mean to wake you. I thought you might be hungry," he said holding up the picnic basket he'd brought over.

Her stomach rumbled before she could speak. "I guess I am. How's your mother?" Her face was serious once again.

"What?" All he could think about was her smile.

"Your mother? Cruz, are you all right?"

He shook his head to clear it, brought the basket over and placed it on the small table as he sat next to her. "Yes, she's much better. I had no idea she'd even been having migraines, and we left you there on the porch. I'm sorry. You shouldn't have cleaned up, I...I stood there acting like an idiot and you jumped into action like you knew exactly what to do — are you always so calm in an emergency?"

"Cruz." She covered his hand and stopped his words. "It's all right."

He took a deep breath and let it out. "Salmon?"

"You were hungry." He smiled as she finished her plate and set it on the coffee table. "The house felt lonely when I returned," he said.

Confident, happy, sure of himself, even rude, those were the words she would use to describe Cruz Brockman, she thought. Definitely not lonely. He appeared as if nothing could bother him. Well, that wasn't entirely true — likening him to his father could bother him. She remembered the rough scratch of his five o'clock shadow from that one amazing kiss in the library. Her face flushed with the memory and she was grateful for the dark.

"It's big, your house. It must be wonderful when it's full of people, maybe not so lonely then?" she asked. His world must be full of people, too, wonderfully warm and friendly people, family. People like Cruz Brockman always had a crowd around them.

"I can't remember the last time there was a crowd of people at the house when I was here." Cruz pushed his plate away. There was an edginess to his voice. "The most people I've seen here since I was a child was for T.D.'s funeral a few weeks ago, and almost everyone there was an employee of the farm. And I'd bet my life most of them showed up to make sure the bastard was really dead. My father didn't have friends, Miranda. He had no one, save the people in his life he bribed or hired.

"It hasn't really bothered me much since I've been back. I've never felt attached to that house and I've been too busy to do much besides work, eat and sleep, but tonight, after my mother…it was as if all the ghosts of growing up in that house were gathering there waiting for me."

"Were there many ghosts?" She was baffled by him, by this conversation. There were more layers to this man than she'd thought possible.

"Enough to make a kid leave home at eighteen and never look back."

"Never, not even for your mother? But you all seem so close to each other." *So comfortable, so loving.*

His face changed in an instant—even in the low porch light she could tell. He'd gone from nearly relaxed to taut as a bow.

"More wine?" he asked. His words had that clipped tone again.

There he was, all anger again, cased in politeness. And again Miranda didn't know what had just happened. "Cruz, I'm not even sure what I did, but you're angry at me again. I—"

"No, I'm sorry, Miranda." He stood, let out a long breath and paced the length of the porch. "It's not you I'm angry at. It's me. For over ten years I've been gone. I've kept in touch, I've been back to visit Miguel and

Roxanna and see my mother, Javier and Adam for a few days at a time. Selfishly, I've mostly been absent. Instead of being here, I've been pursuing a career, letting the ghosts of a horrible man chase me away, and all this time something could have happened to her, to my mother. Tonight the guilt came to pound on me and I took it out on you."

"Oh." She let her breath out slowly. He was beautiful even when he was angry. *How easily he lets everything show.* "I wasn't judging. It surprised me. You seem so warm and connected to one another. It's a connection that doesn't go unnoticed. It's enviable. And migraines aside, Katie looks healthy and happy to me. She doesn't seem to me like someone who needs taking care of or someone who would use guilt against you."

"No, you're right. She's not and she is happy. That's partly why she never left Graciella. Her heart was always here with this stretch of land and the people. It's my own guilt. I can't explain it. She's my mother and seeing her collapse like that tonight and not knowing what was going on, it made her seem so vulnerable. I felt helpless. I don't like feeling helpless, Miranda. I got used to being away, I guess, and being away, it's easier to imagine everything is fine." Cruz sighed and sat next to her on the swing again.

Miranda's emotions were all stirred up. She wondered if he knew his words hit so close to home—and how lucky he was to have love and warmth from his mother, even with all the guilt and hopelessness he felt.

"Then T.D. did something that surprised us all. He made me executor of his estate, dragging me back whether I wanted or not."

"You didn't want?"

"Actually I did, but I've been traveling for so long, at such a fast pace, I hardly thought this time would come, when I could come back to a place without T.D. present. I knew I'd never really come home until he was dead. I thought I'd have to wait a lifetime, was willing to."

"What kept you traveling?" She wanted to know more about him. Once they saw through their assumptions of each other, it was almost easy, this thing called conversation, especially here on the dark porch with a bit of wine warming her thoughts.

"My work. I'm a professional photographer. I travel all over the world taking pictures for magazines and newspapers."

Something clicked in her memory. "Wait, *you're* C. Cooper?" She sat forward, startled at the knowledge. "The photograph here, the one of the girls at the river." She set her glass down and grabbed his hand. "I have one of your photographs in Houston, of the mama elephant and her baby. But you're famous. Your work is amazing. You've won the Pulitzer!"

She barely registered the fact that she'd grabbed his hand until he'd taken control of the situation and started caressing her finger.

"You're beautiful when you let your guard down, Miranda," he said and smiled. He rubbed his thumb over her palm. "You're beautiful when you're angry too, but this is different."

Warmth and embarrassment seeped through her. She covered her eyes with her free hand. "It must be the wine. I never drink."

"Miranda, it's not the wine. You've hardly finished a glass. I like it when you let your guard down. I'm egotistical enough to think it's because of me. I *want* it to be because of me."

Before she could respond, she could feel him close in. He moved her hand. His face was right there in front of her. She couldn't breathe. His eyes, so intense, were alight with desire and they dared hers to hold his gaze. Like a dark, mysterious midnight pool she could drown in.

"No award has ever made me feel as proud of my work." His voice played its own game of seduction on her body. He twined his fingers through hers.

He gazed at her mouth.

This time his kiss was gentle, yet no less torturous on her senses. His mouth was warm and demanding, but slow, like a dancer luring the audience along for the story. She opened for him and he deepened the kiss. Letting go of her hands, he pulled her towards him. His touch on her bare shoulders set her skin aflame with a beautiful fire she'd never felt before. Without a thought, she brought her hand to his face, needing to feel him as he touched her.

"Miranda." He said her name again as he stopped kissing her, but didn't pull away. His voice was deeper. He rested his forehead on hers.

Oh, she didn't want him to stop, not ever. And without a careful study of the situation, she put her other hand around his neck and pulled him towards her, back to her mouth, to her body, to all the passion she'd been craving her entire life.

It felt like he wanted to ravage her. She wanted him to. He was igniting her mouth, her senses, her entire being and still it wasn't enough.

Cruz kept her close and, with his hands on her bare shoulders, deepened the kiss and plundered her mouth with his. He kissed her as if he couldn't get enough of her.

For a second, she was in agony as he left her mouth, but before she could cry for more, his lips were on her neck, the skin behind her ear. Who knew skin could be so amazingly sensitive — how could she never have known? Then he was kissing her shoulder. His lips were like a fire she would gladly walk into. All she could think was, *Everywhere, touch me everywhere.*

"You taste like wildflowers and wine, Miranda. I love the way you taste."

"Cruz," she pleaded as her hands tangled in his hair, pulling him closer, wanting to never let go. He brought his hand over her shoulder and trailed his fingers down her body, across her back. She loved his warmth. He toyed with the tie of her sundress at her neck and savored her skin with his hands along her collarbone. Then his lips followed the path of heat his fingers left. When he rubbed his thumb under her breast, the shock hit her and she reared back.

She pushed up and away and took a deep breath. She'd been about to throw every rational thought out of the window and the fear shot through her like an arrow. It was like coming up for air and, *oh*, how she wanted to keep drowning.

"Miranda," Cruz whispered, his own breathing ragged. He stood up next to her and her waist. "I feel like I should apologize again, but I'm not sorry, Miranda. I want you. If I'm not mistaken, you want me too. Tell me I'm wrong and I'll walk away."

She put her hand on his chest. "I can't, I can't..." His warmth was all-consuming. "You're a client. I completely overstepped bounds."

Cruz took her hands. She tried to pull them away but he kept them, kneading them. "I overstepped as well. I've never enjoyed overstepping bounds more in my life." He brought one of her hands to his lips.

She looked up to meet his gaze. He truly wasn't sorry. It should have shocked her what she'd been about to do, what they'd been about to do—her entire career nearly tossed out of the window by sleeping with a client—but instead her heart leaped into her throat, giddy at his words.

She saw desire in his eyes, desire for her.

"As much as I want to stay, to convince you to let me stay, I have to go, Miranda. I need to be at the barns tonight." He kissed her neck again, and slowly backed her up against the cottage door. "Think about me."

"What could you possibly have to do at the barns so late at night?" *Talk*, she told herself. Talking would keep her calm, would slow her pulse that felt like it was going to beat out of her skin.

"Babies." Cruz feasted on her lips one last time, his body pressed up against hers. And with that, he turned and left.

"Babies?" she called in a whisper after him. She stood there nearly shattered and cold without him touching her.

"It's calving season and we have a few mamas in labor tonight. One is having twins," he called back into the darkness. "Adam and I try to be there to help the men in case of complications. Sweet dreams, Miranda." His voice was rough with what she could only hope was desire.

She put her hand to her heart and felt it pounding. Spring on a farm. *It's like a cliché*, she thought as a laugh bubbled up her throat. She leaned against the wall of the screened-in porch as he walked away. *Animals having babies, love in the air.* She was a cliché.

*Sweet dreams? Ha!* She'd be lucky to fall asleep. It might take her forever to wipe the silly smile off her face.

# Chapter Fourteen

Organizing the papers and past accounting of the farm had taken up most of Miranda's initial two weeks on the audit. Trying to understand everything in front of her was hurdle number one. She still hadn't found anything to signify tax fraud, but that didn't make her feel any better. More often than not, it could be the absence of a paper trail that meant wrong had been done. Today was Saturday, most people's day off, but with a deadline like this one, there was no such thing for her. Every day was a work day.

There was one difference for her this morning. She smiled at the memory again. Cruz, his kisses, the touch of his hands, his rough voice last night in the quiet. It was all so clear in her memory, on her skin, warming her insides.

What it was, was a huge distraction. She couldn't quit replaying every moment in her mind, from the moment she'd woken on the porch swing to his penetrating gaze, to the sound of his voice trailing off in the night as he left to go birth cows. And every second in between. She'd been kissed before—okay, maybe not that many times— but honestly, after last night she might as well say she'd *never* been kissed before. Not like that. Ever. She was buzzing, her entire body still humming with the sensations he'd made her feel. And she'd kissed him back. Her blush crept all the way up her face. She'd wanted to do so much more than kiss him back. Her heart kept doing flip-flops in her chest.

She glanced back at the papers she'd been reading from one of Brockman Farms accounts, completely at a loss to what she'd been doing. *Damn!* If she kept this up, she'd never finish this audit. At the moment she could barely remember how to add. She'd forgotten that she'd even been *attempting* to add.

*Miranda!* she reprimanded herself, as she rested her head on her papers. *Get a grip. At least get some coffee.* She could smell coffee. Coffee had to help. She wandered into the kitchen, where someone had made a fresh pot.

As Miranda filled her mug, she heard voices. She leaned against the sink and took in the sight in the garden. Katie was sitting in one of the oversized Adirondack chairs with her sunglasses and sun hat on, laughing. Cruz and Adam looked like they'd been through battle with their mud- and bloodstained jeans and sweatshirts. They were shoveling compost into the new raised beds that they must have built that morning—they hadn't been there at six a.m. when she'd walked over to the main house from her cottage. She was hesitant to interrupt them, but her curiosity won out.

"Ah, Ms. Miranda." Adam smiled at her. "If you're smart, you won't come near us. We smell worse than we look, but we have two new healthy calves to show for it."

*Ahh, now the blood and dirt make sense.* "Babies," she said, looking right at Cruz. She nearly laughed out loud at the stunned look on his face. Instead she flashed him a smile. It was automatic. She decided not to worry how unlike her that was and enjoy the feeling instead.

"I think I'll take your word for it," she said. "Katie, how are you feeling?" Something made her reach out towards the woman and, without hesitation, Katie took her hand. It was the kind of gesture, the quiet easy touches, the hugs, the pats on the back that Miranda had come to notice between the people here. She wondered if they knew what it was like not to have such comfort, such intimacy, such warmth between family members and friends.

"Much better, thank you. I'm so sorry for last night, for such an inconvenience and putting you out like that. I don't make a habit of inviting people to dinner then leaving them in the lurch. You must think we have terrible manners. Here, sit with me for a minute and take a break."

Miranda sat in the matching chair next to Katie. "Please don't apologize for last night. I'm so glad you're okay." She looked at Adam and Cruz. "Do they usually go right from birthing calves to building raised beds and planting gardens?"

"They're treating me like an invalid today, won't let me lift a shovel." Katie tried pouting, but her smile gave her away. "They won't rest either, the two of them, but they thrive on it, all the work around the farm. And I'm so happy to have them both here that I'm trying not to kick both of them out of the garden so that I can start planting."

"They don't look put out at all," Miranda said. She settled into her chair, although settled was the last thing she felt as she watched Cruz over the rim of her mug.

*Disgusting,* she thought as she looked at his clothes. *Magnificent,* when she looked at his face. Over a day's beard growth, dirt smudged on his forehead — he looked like a man who could ravage her. His muscles bunched as he shoveled the dirt. How she wanted to put her hands on them again. Fatigue shadowed his eyes, even through the laughter and happiness, and something almost predatory shone in his gaze when it raked over her.

"No, indeed, they both look happy. All I could ever hope for my boys. All three of them," Katie said.

"Turner?" Miranda asked, looking at Katie. "I read the will."

"Yes, he left on a full-ride scholarship right after graduation and he hasn't been back since. Adam's the only one who could never pull himself from this place. Cruz and Turner needed to leave for many reasons. I knew Cruz would come back some day, but Turner's a different story." She looked at Miranda. Love and pain shadowed her face. "Sometimes I worry he'll never stop running and that it's my fault he ever felt he had to. Forgive me for being too candid. I'm sure that's way more than you expected. I feel very comfortable talking to you."

"No one's ever said that to me before," Miranda said. *Closed off and cold I've been seen as, but comfortable talking to, never.* "I don't mind it at all." She looked at the brothers as she said it. It seemed easier that way to admit something so personal.

Cruz tried not to stare at Miranda while she spoke to his mother. All his thoughts were on last night, how he'd acted, how he'd wanted her. As soon as he'd kissed her, he hadn't been aware of anything but her. The scent of her had assaulted his senses. The night had called for gentleness, but his emotions had been raw and his mind lost. All he'd been able to do was feel as he feasted on her mouth, her skin. He hadn't even bothered to talk himself out of wanting her on his walk to the barns.

She looked happy this morning, more than happy, with pure feminine glow. He'd put that there. He liked that. Now, if only it wasn't so maddening being this close to her without being able to touch her.

"I should get back to work. Can I get you anything?" Miranda asked Katie.

"No, please, these clowns are waiting on me hand and foot, and as soon as they leave, Javier will be here to do the same. A woman could go mad."

Miranda laughed as she got up. She gave the men a wave and headed back inside the house.

"Miranda, wait," Cruz said as she stepped into the hallway. He stopped where he was as she turned from the doorway into the library. She sipped her coffee again to hide her eyes, but he could catch the humor in them as she looked him up and down. He knew he looked atrocious. She looked stunning.

"It's Saturday."

"It is," she said, smiling openly now.

*When did that happen, that switch of places?* Now she looked like the confident one while he felt nervous and unsettled.

"You're working."

"Cruz, I have to." She straightened and the smile was gone again.

"No, I know. I have work too, I..." He'd completely lost the ability to talk in front of her. Where had his confidence gone from last night, his normal bravado? He took another step forward—he wanted to get closer to that scent. She'd left a trail behind her and he wanted more. He'd follow her around like a love-sick puppy.

She took a step away, but at least her smile was back. "Your brother was right. You do smell worse than you look, and you look like you fought tooth and nail through a battle to hell and back."

"Twins are hard on the mama. We had to turn one of the babies."

"Are they all okay? I don't even want to picture what the mother and babies look like if you and Adam look like you do and you were only helping."

"Everyone's doing fine." He grinned at her. "I'm sorry about last night. For leaving so abruptly. I'd like to make it up to you if you'll let me." All of a sudden, all bets were off. He didn't care if he *shouldn't* be pursuing her.

"You don't have anything to make up for. Really, it's—"

"I want to. I want to be with you. Let me take you to dinner. I'd like to show you a part of Graciella that has a bit more warmth to it than this huge, empty, cold house."

"Dinner sounds nice, Cruz, but…"

"Come to dinner with me, Miranda." He couldn't hide the want in his voice and he ran his thumb over her lips. She preened at his touch and let out a breathy sigh she let out.

"All right," she said.

# Chapter Fifteen

The invitation from Cruz and the gentle caress of his fingers had transformed her into a blooming flower. Her insides were alive, waking up after a long, heavy sleep. And although somewhere in the back of her mind her conscience was giving her warning signals, Miranda ignored them. She hadn't tried that hard to get out of dinner, hadn't wanted to. She could think of nothing else but spending the evening with him, especially with him touching her.

She could have searched her mind for excuses. There were plenty of good ones, but the truth was she didn't want to. He desired her. When had anyone ever desired her?

And she remembered what he had said about kissing her, that he wasn't sorry for it. His simple declaration that he wanted her. Words that mirrored her own feelings. A link had been forged. It was a feeling of closeness that went beyond the kiss. It was something she couldn't define, and in a way that felt like shedding a skin, she honestly didn't care.

And the combination of the physical and emotional swirled together to warm her entire body from the inside out. She hadn't realized how cold and lonely she was until he wasn't touching her, probing her with his intense eyes, reading her thoughts. It had nothing to do with the temperature outside, but with an emptiness in her life, her heart.

She pulled on the black dress with the lacy-edged flowing skirt and the tight bodice with a boat neckline that she took with her everywhere, but it wasn't enough tonight. She wanted to look different for Cruz. On the small back deck, Miranda bent and picked a deep red camellia blossom from the bush to tuck behind her ear. It might be silly, but it made her feel more feminine, pretty and sensual. And, she realized with her nerves already beginning to hum, she wanted Cruz to see her that way.

Miranda was sitting on the porch swing when he pulled up in his vintage truck, which was painted black with cream leather seats. She saw the word *Apache* in silver letters attached to the door. The black paint was shiny and new-looking, as if it too had gotten spiffed up for tonight. Suddenly she was nervous, a butterfly emerging from her cocoon.

"Hi," she said as she walked down the steps to the door he held open. "New truck?"

"Yes, No, I mean…" He practically stuttered his words, but the look of surprise and hunger on his face told her all she wanted to know. "Wow! You look amazing."

"Thank you." Miranda hoped he couldn't see how nervous she'd become. Nervous and feminine at the way he'd lapped her up with his eyes when she stepped down from the porch. That gave her a smile along with some courage. Right now, she needed all the courage she could get, because she honestly didn't have a clue what she was doing.

Cruz helped her up into the truck, his grip gentle on her arm as he lifted her. As she sat down she breathed in the scent of new leather mixed with the musky smell of Cruz as he climbed in on his side.

Miranda sat with the window down and the warm evening air brushing against her skin. *It's only dinner,* she told herself, trying to calm the flutters in her stomach, *and we've had dinner together twice now, even last night.* And look where that had ended up. She closed her eyes and breathed in that hint of the sea that always seemed to be wrapping itself around her. Over-thinking things was not something Miranda usually did. She went about her days knowing exactly what needed to be done at work and at home with her mother, neither of which required much emotional input from her. This place, Cruz sitting next to her, the sea — everything here had her feeling emotions she'd kept neatly tucked away for a long time.

"You're quiet," Cruz said.

"Sorry. It's so open, so vast, here. I can't get over the rugged beauty. It's like I'm drinking it all in." She gestured out towards the land again. "The deep greens and blues and the fresh sea air almost make it look pristine, but with the rocky coast and those enormous rocks jutting up out of the sea, it feels ancient at the same time. A person could get lost."

"Have you never been to the Pacific Northwest before?"

"I have a few clients in Seattle and Vancouver but this is so different, especially without the city surrounding you. Tell me about the restaurant."

"My friend Miguel's family owns El Cielito Lindo, one of the best Mexican restaurants on the west coast. It's in town, not too far. I think you'll like it. They have live music. You said you liked listening to music."

\* \* \* \*

The restaurant was dark with lots of candles and low lights as they entered, with musicians getting ready to play, mostly men and a few women dressed in the traditional costumes of Mariachi bands. The men wore large sombreros. Their gray-blue pants were intricately embroidered down the side of the legs. More embroidery stood out on the short jackets which were worn over vests. The women wore long skirts in similarly brilliant decorations.

The tables were covered in white cloths with a red votive candle and small bud vase of flowers on each one. The benches, booths and chairs were a deep, rich burgundy color. Every detail, Miranda thought, was exquisitely seen to. Sensing something sparkly above her, Miranda looked up. The ceiling was adorned in a shimmery royal blue fabric with tiny little lights. A perfect starlit sky. It was magical.

"Miguel, good to see you," Cruz said to a tall, striking man with a huge smile.

"Ah, Cruz, you finally decided to grace us with your presence." Miguel spoke with warmth and teasing. He gave Cruz a hug and stepped back to look at him. "You look good. Graciella looks good on you. Finally decided that to inherit all of this wouldn't be so bad, eh?"

Cruz laughed. "I came to steal your mother's tamale recipe, or at the least bribe her into making me some."

"Ah ha! At least you haven't lost all your good sense. And who is this lovely lady?" He took both of Miranda's hands and kissed each one. "And what are you doing with this rogue? Oh wait, you're Miranda. My lovely Roxanna and my kids have told me all about you."

"Miranda, meet Miguel, one of my oldest friends."

"Oldest, ha! I'm your only friend. Come, let me take you to your table."

Miranda sat down in the booth against the wall at El Cielito Lindo. Cruz slid in right next to her, his thigh touching hers. The touch hummed through her body. She swallowed and tried to calm her senses, but then he leaned his head in close to hers and she lost all power of rational thought.

"When the band plays and sings, everyone sits or moves their seats to where they can watch them." He gestured towards the stage as the lush midnight-blue curtains, also sparkling with sequin-like stars, opened. He leaned close to her ear. "I didn't know if you spoke Spanish, and I thought you might like me to tell you the words in English when they sing."

"I would," she said, meeting his eyes with hers. He could whisper whatever he wanted in her ear and she wouldn't care. She was falling fast.

# Chapter Sixteen

It was startling at first. The warmth of his breath sent shivers through her body. *Sensual* was the word that entered her thoughts as she listened to the songs in Spanish and him translating the words into English. His voice, although quiet, was deep and thick. A wonderful warmth slid into her and she relaxed next to him. This was the most romantic thing anyone had ever done for her.

Never in her life had she felt so awakened, so raw, so on fire as he seemed to speak from his heart to hers. He wasn't repeating words. He was sharing something passionate with her. The way he whispered the words into her ears told her so.

It was the music that broke through the barrier neither one of them seemed able to fully conquer, the music that both melted the awkwardness and allowed them to enjoy their awareness of each other, the music that drew them down a spiral together, inviting them into a sensual, intimate space.

Their margaritas and ceviche arrived and Miranda was grateful for the chill of the glass between her fingers, hoping it would cool the heat that burned through her body. She took a sip of her drink, holding the glass with both hands, afraid that she might drop it, and let the tequila mix with the foreign things her body was feeling. Foreign, but like she had been waiting forever to feel them.

Without missing a verse, Cruz dipped a tortilla chip into the ceviche and handed it to Miranda to taste. Her senses were more awake than ever as she savored the delicious flavors of lime, fish, onion and tomatoes. She stole a glance at Cruz as he sipped his own drink and the music ended for intermission. He certainly didn't look as flustered as she felt, especially when he looked at her, as if he could see the battling emotions inside her.

"Do you like tamales?" Cruz asked. "It's customary for us to order dinner during the intermission. And El Cielito Lindo has the best tamales you'll ever taste."

"I've never had tamales, but I'd love to try them."

He looked more relaxed than she had ever seen him at the farm, and for a moment she wondered at the complexities of this man. The sharp lines on his forehead had softened and his mouth formed into an easy grin as Miguel and Roxanna came to greet them.

"Roxanna," Cruz said, standing. "You are as beautiful as ever."

"I'm fat, Cruz. I feel like a beach ball, but you can keep lying to me." She kissed him on both cheeks.

"Hello," Roxanna said to Miranda. "It's nice to see you again."

"You too. How are you?"

"Good." Roxanna smiled at her husband. "My love got a babysitter and brought me to dinner. That's a lovely camellia, perfect for your black hair, Miranda." Roxanna reached up to touch the flower. "*Es muy romantico.*"

"Thank you." Miranda found herself blush at Roxanna's compliment. She'd forgotten about the flower.

"He's busy tonight." Roxanna took Miranda's hands and placed them on her belly. Miranda had never seen a pregnant woman so flushed and happy and at peace.

"Ready for another one?" Cruz asked.

"Who are you kidding?" Roxanna patted his arm. "I was born ready."

"Yes, you were." Cruz smiled at his friends.

"Let's get you off your feet, my love." Miguel took Roxanna's hand.

Roxanna turned back towards them, "Cruz, why don't you bring Miranda to the family cookout tomorrow night? The kids would love it. All Ana can talk about is her new friend, the beautiful lady, Miranda."

"We'll see if she can put up with me after tonight." Cruz looked at Miranda.

Miguel looked between Miranda and Cruz for a moment then took Miranda's hand and said, "Don't believe for a second that this man is a jerk. He's a good man. He doesn't want anyone to know it." And with a wink at her, he turned and led his wife back to their table.

Miranda watched them go, Miguel's arm around the small of his wife's back, the way he pulled her chair out for her and kissed her before she sat down. *Longing.* There was a deep longing in Miranda. She wanted to belong to someone like that and for someone to belong to her as strongly. She turned back towards Cruz as he sat down next to her again.

"They are some of my favorite people," Cruz said.

"They're lovely. And so much in love."

Miranda was completely charmed by his friends, the obvious love they had for each other evident in their faces. *Love and family.* Cruz had grown silent, but his face was a whirlwind of emotion. She'd never seen someone say so much without words. One minute he looked relaxed and open, the next, angry. Then she would see desire flash. She nearly asked him about him but the waiter arrived with their tamales.

She followed his lead to unwrap her tamale and tasted. Pork and chilies, garlic softened by the corn. Her taste buds were alive. Food had never tasted this good, she was certain.

"What do you think?" Cruz asked.

"This is one of the best meals I've ever had." Her smile was genuine.

"Having a good time?" he asked. With one look he stunned her, as though he wanted to devour her kiss by kiss.

"Yes. I'm having a lovely time."

"You use that word a lot," he commented. "Lovely." His body adjusted so that he was closer to her. He lifted his arm and draped it across the booth behind her, toying with her hair and the bare skin on her shoulder as she ate.

Unraveling, that was what he was doing to her. He was slowly, carefully unraveling her with each light touch, his compliments and open longing. She took another sip of her drink and studied him. "There's something about you here, Cruz, something different."

"You mean different from rude and ill mannered?" He laughed.

"Open, at ease." *Except for the moments you look as if you want to ravage me.*

She was finding it hard to concentrate or speak while he caressed her shoulder. It was definitely harder to keep reminding herself that this man was essentially a client and she was here to do a job.

But she wanted him. And with that admission she was suddenly more afraid than she'd ever been in her life. Not afraid of him, but afraid of herself and her desires. Perfected through years of unconscious practice, her walls began to rise back up. How easy it would be to let them—but she was tired of living behind them.

"I don't think it's this place. I think it's you. Who are you, Miranda Jenks? And what are you doing to me? You've bewitched me."

She knew his questions were rhetorical, but without knowing why, she felt a need to open herself to him, to let her guard down and tell him who she was. "I'm not a coldhearted accountant, Cruz."

"Miranda, I'm sorry. Those comments were way out of line that day."

"No, I didn't mean to make you feel guilty about saying that. When I'm nervous, I sometimes start talking in the middle of what I'm trying to say. I want to tell you who I am, why I keep my barriers up."

"Miranda, I'm embarrassed that I was so rude to you."

"Shhh." She touched his lips with her fingers. "I grew up poor, Cruz, always scraping by. I don't want to dwell on what it was like, because it was so long ago, but the scars stayed with me. Some girls dream about becoming a ballerina or a veterinarian, I dreamed of a steady job with a good paycheck, to never be poor again.

"And accounting's something I'm good at. I've always been good at numbers. I used to enjoy it. Or I thought I did. It got me out of the house, out from under financial stress, which was freedom to me.

"My mother was sick for many years. My salary paid for a live-in nurse for the times I needed to be away for work. I wanted to use my knowledge to help people who couldn't afford it. But then my mother became ill and I spent all my time working to pay for the medical bills to keep us out of debt. It's not all of who I am, Cruz, someone who's only concerned about money. I mean, I have been concerned about money, but there isn't any other way for me right now."

Abruptly she stopped talking. *Wasn't.* She'd meant to say, there wasn't any other way around things. Her mother was dead. How long before that would sink in? How long before she would tell someone? How long before she realized she had her own life to lead now?

Feeling awkward now in the silence, Miranda sensed she'd said too much. She'd completely rambled on without a thought. She'd wanted him to know she wasn't greedy, that there was more to her than that, but she'd exposed herself and in doing so had made him uncomfortable.

"I'm sorry, I'm sure you didn't want to hear all about my family drama."

"Don't. Don't pull away. I do want to hear." Cruz moved his arm from around her shoulders and took her hand. He held her gaze. "I was thinking what a royal jerk I am, Miranda. I pried into your personal life as if it were any of my business. I made you uncomfortable and hurt you, which I never intended. I'm glad you told me."

She trusted the intense look in his eyes, and she felt that maybe it had been okay to share all that with him, although she never had with anyone before.

"A live-in nurse must be expensive. Was there no one else to help you?"

"Nope, only child, and my parents were both only children. My mother had a hard life with my father. They never could make ends meet. They had me, then she had three miscarriages. After that, she seemed to project all her sadness onto me. I reminded her of all her suffering. Unlike your mother, Cruz, my mother, well, she didn't really want me there..." Now the way he focused on her was almost too much to bear. She felt completely exposed. "It's over now, so it doesn't matter." The last words were out before she could stop them.

"Over? You mean... When?" he asked, his voice softened to a near whisper.

She looked back toward the musicians as they got ready to play again. "The week before I came here."

Cruz put his hand on her neck and pulled her close. He brought his lips down to rest on her head. "I'm sorry, Miranda. Jesus, I nearly came undone when Katie collapsed last night with a migraine and you've recently lost your mother. That's a grief I can't imagine."

His words were simple but honest. He hadn't tried to change the subject like some people had when her mother died. He hadn't said he knew how she must be feeling, like others. He'd accepted and given her comfort. Even though she'd never felt loved by her mother, the pain of loss was still there like a rock in her chest. Perhaps it was a kind of grief. Grief for what she'd never had and now never would, or maybe grief that it was finally over. Miranda hadn't realized how lonely and empty she'd been until she felt his arms around her and his hands kneading the skin amazing of her neck and shoulder. She'd begun to crave his touch.

"Cruz, I..." She lifted her head up to look at him. "You do something to me too, Cruz." She echoed his words from the night before. "From the very beginning when you shook my hand. Your touch..."

Before she could finish her explanation, Cruz leaned in towards her, tilted her chin and kissed her gently. His mouth was soft but confident and he lingered for a few extra seconds, as if letting her know that he wanted more. When he pulled away, he grazed his thumb over her lips, causing her to shiver all over again.

"I thought maybe my touch made you uncomfortable. Last night, well, I couldn't think rationally last night, but you wanted me to stop."

She smiled at how easily they could misinterpret each other's reactions and feeling bolder than she'd ever felt before, with the flicker of light dancing around them, Miranda put her hand to his cheek and said, "You do make me uncomfortable. 'Uncomfortable' is putting it mildly. But I didn't want you to stop. I thought we *should* stop, because I work for you, but I don't know if I can stop, Cruz. I know I don't want to." And she brought her face to his and kissed him again while the music played around them.

If they hadn't been in the middle of the restaurant he would never have stopped kissing her, especially when she kissed him back willingly. Something had opened inside her, releasing her shyness, her concerns, her inhibitions. He felt them slipping away from her.

As the next song began, the Mariachi music reminded him that they were surrounded by people. He pulled his lips away but sat close to her as he began to translate an old love song. She took his hand in hers, connecting them in those intimate moments with touch, something that had been missing from his life for a long time.

He barely remembered finishing the meal or the rest of the music, so enamored was he of watching her, being near her, listening to her. Now the night was over, and upon leaving the glow of the restaurant, it was as if he were overcome by a sudden awkwardness, a desire not to screw anything up, confused at how to proceed on this fragile new path.

They didn't speak as he headed back to the guest house, but he reached over to take her hand and reignite the link between them. There was a chill in the night air and they sat in silence, both lost in their thoughts and feelings. He'd been wrong about her. She wasn't coldhearted at all. He'd seen the vulnerability written all over her face when she'd spoken about her mother. It angered him that she had spent her life taking care of a woman who didn't want her, and that, even in the end, during her mother's death, Miranda had been alone. More than anyone, he knew what it was like not to be wanted by a parent, to live with that burden, to carry it always—that invisible pain of T.D.'s rejection that he'd buried deep, but never fully gotten rid of.

He wanted her, but more than that, he wanted to bring her pleasure. It wasn't pity he felt for her—it was anger at her circumstances, awe at how she'd handled it and a purely physical ache of desire.

Sitting in the quiet, thinking, drifting through the feelings she'd stirred in him tonight, part of Cruz longed to return to the closeness of the restaurant, to the awareness that surrounded him with intoxicating sensations, the love songs, the warmth of her. Now, here they sat alone, with no one else around them, but there were choices to make, lines to cross.

Miranda rolled her window down and the crisp spring air washed over them. He tuned out all sound and breathed in the scent of the land, the damp fields from a quick rain mixed with the heady, seductive perfume of blossoms coming alive. It was her scent that wrapped around him and he'd never been so aware, so awake before. She'd done that, whether she knew it or not. She was peeling away a part of him, the part that kept intense, personal emotions at bay.

"Cruz." Her voice stirred beside him in the truck.

He glanced at her in acknowledgement, feeling the power of her gaze.

"I don't want to go home, back to the guest house, not yet." She clasped his fingers closer in hers. "Will you take me to your home? I want to be with you." She couldn't hide the desire in her voice from him and it sent his blood simmering. He'd never wanted anyone as much as he wanted her.

"You're sure?"

"Amazingly."

He brought her hand to his lips and kissed it, and with her words burning inside him, Cruz turned the car around and drove up into the cliffs to his small secluded home overlooking the beach and the ocean beyond.

# Chapter Seventeen

"It's lovely," Miranda said. His small house stood against the towering fir trees, like black knights guarding the night sky. The moon and stars shone, glittering over the ocean she could see in the distance. He took her hand and helped her down from the truck. Cruz held on to her and walked her to the steps of his front porch. The sounds of crickets and frogs echoed through the night. In the distance, waves danced onto the shore.

"Cruz." Her voice was a whisper. Her body, heady with anticipation. All her senses seemed so alive, so acutely aware of the night, of him. Like a guide, the sea air spoke to her, seduced her.

"You're breathtaking," Cruz replied, pulling her to him, the hunger in his eyes betraying his desire.

She looked up at him then and put her hand on his chest. She wanted that heat — she wanted all of him. Miranda was tired of seeking approval for what she did. She wanted someone to love her, but even more than that, she wanted to love someone. She closed off her thoughts that told her she shouldn't be here doing this.

For once she ignored the shouldn'ts and focused on her wants. She wanted to give her heart to someone who would cherish it. And it might have been the most foolish wish she'd ever had, but she wanted that someone to be Cruz. Foolish or not, having admitted that to herself, she suddenly felt free and alive.

"Miranda," he said, his voice harsh with need. Wrapping his arms around her, he carried her up the porch steps and leaned her against the door to his home. The heat of their bodies simmered into each other. Miranda was dazed and floating, giddy and alive at the same time. She could feel everything, the solidity of the wood door on her back and the heat of his gaze as he drank her in. Before she could speak, he claimed her mouth with his, and her entire body with his warmth.

Cruz's lips caressed hers, gentle at first, as if he were trying to hold back the strength of his desire. His mouth on hers, his tongue teasing, asking, a need to explore further, deeper. She opened to him and a soft moan rose up inside her, begging for more. Her senses were on fire. She let herself go completely, let the fire take control. And what a beautiful fire it was.

As if jolted by her response, he pulled away a fraction so she could still feel his breath on her skin. "Miranda? He braced himself with his hands against the door on each side of her. "Are you sure?"

This time she wanted all of him, and she knew she'd have to be the one to tell him.

"Mmm," she responded wrapping her hand around his neck and pulling him back. "I'm floating and sinking at the same time. Take me inside, Cruz. I'm hungry. I can still taste those tamales." She brought his head back down to hers and, with a boldness she never knew she possessed, she traced his lips with her tongue.

"Delicious." And as the laugh escaped her throat he feasted on her neck.

"Not nearly as good as you taste," he said and dove in. He pinned his body against hers, every inch of her feeling his muscles. He kissed her deeper as he brought one hand to her hip then grazed his fingers up her body till they rested at the wispy short sleeve of her dress. He toyed with it, slid it off her shoulder and brought his mouth to her collar bone. "I like you here, up against a door. It seems to be a habit with us."

Her skin tingled. His voice was deep and husky and warm with an intimate humor. He trailed his fingers up and down her body and she lingered in the sensation and the gentle seduction. He toyed with her nipple through the thin material, causing it to harden and eliciting another purr of pleasure, this time from that deep hidden place inside her that had been too long locked up.

"Cruz." Her voice was deeper and laced with passion and want. She tightened her arms around his neck. She couldn't bring him close enough. He was rock hard against her inner thighs, pulsing with desire.

"God, Miranda." He pushed the door open, stepped into the house and slammed the door behind them with his foot.

The feel of his leg between hers, nudging her into his home, brought pleasure rippling through her body. She slipped out of her heels and had to stand on her tiptoes to keep her lips on his. Now that she had touched him, she didn't want to ever let go.

He held her like that and moved against her while he explored her mouth with his. His pleasure seeped into her.

With both arms around her, he unzipped her dress and guided the material off her shoulders down the entire length of her body. Both his dark eyes and his rough fingers caressed her body on the way down.

"Sweet Jesus, you're not wearing a bra," Cruz said as his eyes savored her skin. Her nipples swelled at his gaze.

Miranda hadn't thought to be embarrassed until now. She'd never been with a man like this before. All of a sudden, her inexperience came rushing into her mind. "Oh," she said with a start and brought her arms up to cover herself. She had never been well endowed in that department, but it hadn't been that big a deal until now. "I don't really…I mean the dress…I don't need one with this dress."

"Shh," he said gently taking her arms away from her body. "I wasn't complaining. You're perfect, Miranda." He touched her skin gently with his fingertips. His fingers grazed her cheek, then along her neck and down, first over one breast, then the other, and the fire seared back into her. "You're stunning and beautiful. Let me show you how beautiful you are." He ravaged her lips then picked her up again. Cruz carried her through the house to the bedroom in the back, never taking his lips from hers.

He left the light off, allowing the full moon to cast its sensual gleam over the room. Carefully he laid Miranda on the bed and trailed his mouth lightly down to her breasts, teasing one nipple with his tongue until it hardened again. Miranda dragged his head closer as her body arched up to meet his mouth.

"Oh, Cruz!"

He tasted the other nipple while his hands roamed over her body. It felt as though he was marking her with his touch. She was drowning in pleasure as he lifted her farther up towards the pillows and leaned into her, feasting on her mouth again as if he might never get enough.

His clothes grazed her, the rough fabric bringing every inch of her skin alive, sensitive and tingling. But she was desperate to feel his skin on hers, all of it, without anything in the way.

Miranda fumbled with the buttons on his shirt and finally freed him of it. Her hand found his heart and felt the racing, beating rhythm that matched her own. He kneaded her skin with strong, insistent hands and teased her nipples in and out of his mouth. Her body moved towards his, arching again and again. She'd never been so out of control. It felt wonderful.

"Cruz." She pushed his pants off, revealing a body hard and ready. She'd never known she could have that effect on a man.

Cruz groaned and took her hands away from his body. He kissed each one and laid them down beside her. "I'm lost in you, the way the moonlight bathes your body, so sensuous in its light. Let me pleasure you, Miranda. I want you to feel what you do to me." His voice was ragged, his breathing harsh.

He dragged his body down hers and drew her black lace panties off. He parted her legs with his hands, gently touched the soft skin between her thighs, and a glorious sensation rippled through her. Her eyes shot open, shock, pleasure and want electrifying her.

Miranda struggled to brace herself against the firestorm that seared inside her. She had never been this high, rising higher as Cruz tasted her, darting his tongue in and out, while he explored her thighs and the sensitive skin of her belly with his rough hands.

Cruz dove deeper, teasing her with his lips, his teeth, parting her. Oh, the feel of his tongue on the most sensitive part of her body. He touched and caressed a part of her that had never been touched before. It made her feel swollen with need, as though she was ready to dive over a cliff. Without warning he took her over the last edge and she screamed his name as her body exploded with sensations.

"Cruz, Cruz, I...wow."

"Wow is right, Miranda. Jesus, do you realize how beautiful you are when you let go like that? The most beautiful thing I've ever seen." He kissed her belly and roamed his hands over her body as she drifted down from the high.

"Was that real? Did that really happen?" She nearly whimpered with joy.

He slowly made his way up her body, devouring her with his kisses. She loved the feel of his naked skin against hers, and even though she had just climaxed, she grew aroused again. *Is this what I've been missing all these years?* Again. She wanted to feel that way again. And she wanted to touch him, this amazing man who'd brought her the most intense pleasure she'd ever felt. She ran her hands over his back as he drew up and studied her face, and all she could see was a desire that matched her own. He laced his hands in hers, rose over her and covered her body with his. He lingered for a moment, allowing them both to feel that erotic sense of anticipation. His body teased the wet warmth between her legs, already tingling again, and his eyes were smoky and full of need. "I want you, Miranda."

"You have me." She writhed against his hardness, unable to wait any longer. She watched him roll on the condom, his body magnificent in the moonlight.

He entered her with passion unleashing his desire. For an instant, the pleasure turned to pain

"Miranda." He suddenly stilled. He cupped her face, as he started to pull back. "I didn't know…"

She shook her head as the pain eased into an erotic need. "Don't pull away," she whispered. She held him to her, willing him to see deep into her desire for him. She was almost pleading, desperate for the feel of his length in her. She rocked her body up to his. "Don't stop." She kissed him, deeply, greedily, as he had her. "Please want me."

"You have no idea how much I want you," he said. Slowly he pushed his way back in, moving as she moved. He began to ride, taking her higher, taking them both higher. He kissed her, making that deep connection. Her body took him, surrounded him with hard, strong pulsing motions. Never had she felt so raw and aching and unbelievably amazing at the same time. She reached up to pull him down to her, to feel every inch of his body on fire with hers as they rode the wave faster and faster.

Miranda lost all control and her body reared as the climax poured through her, and as it did, it took Cruz over the cliff as well, both of them rocking as one, sweat covering their bodies, their hearts beating together.

Their breathing calmed and Cruz gently kissed along her jaw and back to her lips. Slowly he eased off her, gathering her to him, the length of his body touching her back. He ran his fingers over the soft skin of her belly, her arms, her breasts and listened to her murmurs of pleasure.

"Miranda, why didn't you tell me? I hurt you," he said. He nibbled on her ear and hugged her to him.

"No." She shook her head. "I wanted to be with you. I didn't even think about it being my first time. I wanted you. It felt right, and," she whispered, "I was afraid you wouldn't have wanted me."

She slayed him with her words. *So honest, so raw.* He nuzzled the skin around her ear. "Want is such a mild word for how I feel about you, about your body, Miranda. But I could have taken more care." He moved her hair out of the way and planted kisses along her nape.

"Cruz."

"Yes," he said, his hand on her belly.

"I've never felt anything that incredible before."

"Neither have I," he said, propping himself up on one arm to appreciate her body with his eyes as he turned her to face him. He trailed over her skin with his fingers till his hand rested on her hip. His voice, completely relaxed was playful.

She put her hand on his to stop him. "Don't tease. I don't think I could bear it if…"

"Miranda." He'd hurt her. He brought his hand up to her face. "I'm not teasing. You are incredible. You make me feel incredible. I mean it. Your body is part of that beauty. Don't you believe that about yourself?" There was that look again, a memory of pain. He wanted to know what had caused it. "Did someone hurt you?" He didn't even need her answer—he could tell by the shadowed look on her face. "Tell me," he said tracing her cheek with his fingers, drinking in her flushed look.

"Cruz, it's not what you're thinking," she said covering his hand with hers.

"Tell me," he said, gentler now. He could feel her hesitation. "Let me in, Miranda."

She studied him for a moment before she began. He loved it when did that, all that intensity focused on him.

"It was when I was in college and right after I graduated," she said. He kept her fingers laced with his and watched her as she spoke.

"To say I was shy is an understatement. I studied a lot, kept my head down. I went home most weekends to take care of my mother, so college wasn't exactly a party for me. It was easier to keep myself closed up. Then senior year I met and dated a classmate in accounting, Eli. People said we were perfect for each other, good at accounting, top of our class, both of us driven, you could say. He was from money. I wasn't, but not many people knew." There was no emotion in her voice as she spoke and his heart clenched for her.

"Then after graduation my mother had one of her bad strokes, so I went back to Houston with my job, and he went on to Chicago. He left me a message the next week. Said it was nice while it lasted but he'd found someone new, and now I was free to do the same, as if he were releasing me or doing me a favor. Left the message on the machine."

"He was an idiot," Cruz said, his voice ragged with anger and confusion for her.

"I wouldn't call what we had passionate. We dated, we went to dinner, we kissed. It was all so neat and tidy. I was so ignorant. I thought that was how it was supposed to be. It's so pathetic." She buried her head in his shoulder for a moment. "I found out a few weeks later from a coworker that he'd been sleeping with someone else on the weekends when I was home taking care of my mother. Apparently he was getting all the passion he needed from someone else."

She shrugged as if trying to make light of it, but he saw the pain in her expression. "It's not important anymore."

Cruz wrapped his arms around her and pulled her close. "Dammit! Miranda, someone made you feel that you weren't worthy of being wanted, of feeling passion."

*Love.* He'd been about to say, worthy of love. He brushed the word away. He'd only just met her. He knew people who fell that quickly. Miguel and Roxanna had fallen in love immediately and ferociously. One could tell by looking at them, married ten years now, that they were as much in love, if not more so, than ever. But him, Cruz Brockman, in love? It was the one thing he feared in life. Love was... How the hell could he be in love? He was confusing it with lust. She was amazing and beautiful and she occupied his thoughts more than any woman he'd ever met, but it couldn't be love. He couldn't disguise the shiver that ran through his body as his skin touched hers.

"Is something wrong, Cruz?"

He was determined to let nothing ruin this night for her. Maybe it wasn't love, but he felt something intense for her, and because he was incapable of fully giving his heart to someone didn't mean he had to show her that, or that they couldn't enjoy each other's company. He eased her back towards the bed and fit himself on top, claiming her under him.

"No, I'm angry that some jerk could make you feel undesired." He followed the line of her body to her toes and back up to her face. Then he smiled, a slow smile full of desire. "I think it's my duty to help you see that not all men are as stupid or callous, Miranda, to show you how much I want you."

He pulled himself down to her feet and kissed his way up her body, beginning with her toes. "How much I want every part of your gorgeous, sensual body." He drew up slowly from her feet along her calves, to the tender skin behind her knees, paying special attention to each one. He smiled against her as she trembled under his mouth and fingers. *Pleasure.* He could give her pleasure, make her feel as beautiful as she was. Placing his hand on the dark patch of hair between her legs, he probed his thumb into her, teasing and caressing, enough to make her cry out. He realized suddenly she might be sore, so he eased off the bed, kissed her long and hard and said, "Wait here," before he turned and walked away.

"Cruz?" she said, "What? Where are you—"

"Shh, let me take care of you, Miranda," he said when he returned. He lifted her up and carried her into his master bath, where he'd started the water in the tub. He helped her in and climbed in behind her so she was resting with her back against his chest. He grabbed the soap and caressed her body with the suds, making it relax into him.

"Mmm, Cruz, I feel amazing, like I'm floating." She rubbed against his body like a cat as he washed her. He let the soap slide away and pulled her closer. He circled one nipple with his fingers, then the other, and nearly came listening to her breathless moans of pleasure.

"I can't keep my hands off you, Miranda, and now that I've had you, all I can think about is how I want you again," he whispered into her ear. Then his tongue was on her neck darting and tasting and driving her wild while his hands stroked her body, moving lower until he found her clit and teased her.

It was like torture, sweet, fascinating torture. He'd known that making a woman feel such pleasure could arouse equal excitement within him, but never with such intensity. Watching her long, graceful body tremble and snake beneath his hands, he was rock hard again, when only minutes before he didn't have enough strength to move off her. He listened to her pleading, heady cries for him, the way his name sounded in her soft, husky voice. She tightened around his fingers and burst into a climax so sweet that it was beyond anything he'd ever imagined.

# Chapter Eighteen

Sun poured in through the two glass doors leading from the bedroom to a deck and danced over the bed. She was covered with a sheet, alone in Cruz's room. She turned over onto her side to face the spot where he had slept next to her in the king-sized bed. She pulled his pillow towards her to breathe in the leftover scent of his masculinity.

Last night unfolded in her mind and she hid her smile in the pillow. They had made love until both their bodies were delightfully sore.

And finally, when she'd begun to drift into sleep, he'd curled his body around hers and they'd slept entwined, unable to break the connection that touching each other gave them.

Miranda had never had a night like it. She hadn't even known her body could do some of the things they'd done, that she could feel the amazing sensations Cruz had sent through her over and over again. She still tingled in places that had never been touched in her life. And she blushed when she thought of the effect she'd had on him. They would barely be rested when Cruz would be on fire again, tasting her, claiming her. And she had matched his desire and arousal. She wanted him even now.

Her body ached with pleasure, but something else inside of her felt heavy. Was it regret? *No,* she thought and smiled again. *I will never regret this as long as I live.* The growing emotions scared her with their strength, and even though she had never truly felt it before, some instinctual knowledge spoke to her. It was love.

She had fallen in love with him. And although last night had pushed her over the edge, her feelings for him had started earlier, perhaps when she'd seen him with the calves, or possibly that first day when he'd wiped that tear from her cheek.

*Now what are you going to do?* Her mind questioned as she came more fully awake. "I have no idea," she spoke aloud.

"Talking to yourself?"

Miranda turned at the sound of Cruz's voice. "Hi," she said, a smile spreading across her face. He was carrying a tray and he came towards her with nothing on except pajama bottoms hanging very low on his very sexy hips. Her eyes filled with the sight of him in the daylight, his taut muscles, strong arms and those hands. His hands made her body feel amazing.

"What were you saying? You seemed deep in conversation with yourself."

She rose and, pulling the sheet with her, leaned back against the pillows. "Oh, nothing." She wasn't about to tell him what she'd been discussing with her conscience. "What are you doing?"

He sat down on the bed next to her and pulled the tray with him. "Making you breakfast. There's something about watching you eat, Miranda." He looked like a pirate this morning, with a sly dimple in his grin. "Coffee?" He handed her a cup.

"Mmm," she said. "This smells wonderful. You cook?"

"Don't look so surprised." He cocked an eyebrow at her. "I made you one of my specialties, huevos rancheros with a bit of cilantro and sour cream."

"What about you?"

"I thought we could share." Holding up a forkful for her, he said, "Trust me?"

She stared back at him, wondering if he were referring to more than trust in his cooking. "I do," she said, taking the bite and never taking her eyes from his.

"Not bad, eh?"

"Mmm," she moaned. "I didn't know eggs could taste this good. Where did you learn to cook?"

"Oh, here and there." He leaned in and kissed the side of her mouth. "I love everything about this mouth of yours. I can't seem to get enough of it."

Then he flashed that grin and the flush crept up her cheeks.

"I love the way you blush too, Miranda."

She looked down at her plate, trying to shake off the intense emotions nearly boiling over inside her.

"You have a nice way of changing the subject whenever I ask you a question about your life, Cruz."

For an instant he shuttered his eyes, then he was open again and the grin was back. "You really want to know about my life, huh?"

She nodded.

"I learned from my mother, and Miguel's mom. When I was little, whenever I could sneak away from our house, I spent my time at Miguel's. He has five brothers and one sister. They lived in this tiny bungalow on the hill in town. It was packed with people and stuff and noise and chaos. And I loved it.

"One of my favorite things was helping them cook. The tamales we had last night are his mother's recipe." He brushed her hair behind her ears and trailed his fingers over her cheek, his touch warming her skin.

Miranda listened carefully to the happiness in his voice when he spoke of the Hernandez family, as opposed to the ice in him when he referred to his own father.

"Come on, let's go sit outside, where we can hear the sound of the waves." He held up his robe for her and took her hand to lead her to his back deck. "Have a seat. I'll get us some more coffee."

In the night, his house had looked small, towered over by the trees, but she realized how much more space it had as it spread into the back, and this rambling deck was amazing, with a view down to the water.

"Tell me about your own family, Cruz," Miranda said when he came back, steaming mugs in his hands. He sat in the Adirondack chair next to her. "I like learning about you. They're a part of you." She rubbed her hand down his arm and took his hand.

"Well," he said, playing with her fingers. "You've met Adam. Adam's the easy one—not simple, but straightforward. Adam loves the land, working it, tending it, taking care to see that everything thrives. He always wanted to work with the crops and the animals but T.D. wouldn't have it. Said we weren't to lower ourselves to the hired help. We could learn all the tasks but we should never love the labor. It was a Brockman's duty to be in charge, to own, not to fall in love with the job. Called Adam a sissy. He tried to beat it out of Adam. But by then Turner and I were big enough to protect him.

"After a few times, T.D. never tried it again—said it wasn't even worth his time to beat sense into him. But he was rotten to Adam, hurling insults at him, mocking him, trying to make him feel small.

"Katie took Adam and left when he was fifteen. Packed a suitcase and walked out. She filed for divorce and T.D. signed the papers. He didn't care about any of us anymore. All he cared about was power and ownership and money, obviously—it was always about more money for him."

She was beginning to understand why people who were only concerned with money angered him. "What made Katie finally leave?" Miranda asked.

"I wasn't here, but I suspect it had something to do with Javier. He came to work for my father, to work with the horses about that time. When I left I was so mad at her, mad that she stayed with T.D. all those years, mad that she let us be brought up by someone so mean and spiteful. I stayed good and mad for a while, a young man ignorant of so many things in the world. When I finally asked her a few years ago why she stayed, I was actually shocked at some of the things I learned. I always thought she must have stayed out of fear, fear for herself and fear for what he could do to her sons, because no matter how bad it seemed at times, T.D. could always be meaner if pushed."

"But it wasn't?" Miranda nudged him on.

"In the beginning it was part fear, and her heart was here in the land. It was her land and was supposed to go to her when her father died, but once she married T.D., if she left him she would get nothing. She had had a few years of nursing school and had always known about herbal medicine from an employee of her father's when she was growing up. T.D. never allowed a medical clinic to be built for the migrant workers, wouldn't pay them if they missed work because they were sick or injured. Katie started to take care of them in secret, bringing them medicine, vitamins, simple things like toothbrushes. She snuck food to them whenever she could."

Miranda sat back in her chair and drank her coffee. "Like a modern-day Florence Nightingale? Why did, I mean I'm confused — I've seen the will, as part of my job to learn about the assets and the inheritance — but Adam got nothing?" She pushed up and looked at him as she realized.

"Correct," Cruz said. "The farm should have gone to him. But T.D. cut him out completely."

"Oh, Cruz, that's horrible."

"It is. It's also exactly like T.D. to divide everything up, and to leave Adam nothing. We're going to fix it — as soon as Turner shows up, we'll change the ownership to represent all three of us."

"Where is Turner?"

"Turner's a mystery. The last time I spoke to him a few months ago, he was working in Berlin, trying to drown his guilt for the way our father treated Adam and me."

"What do you mean?"

Cruz leaned over and kissed her gently before he continued. "My father was disappointed in and embarrassed by Adam, but me, well, he's hated me since the day I was born. Never tried to hide it. He treated me like crap, spoke to me with venom, beat me when he could get away with it, and made it plain that he despised me.

"But not Turner. T.D. never laid a hand on Turner. For T.D., Turner was the brilliant one, the strong one, the perfect child to be groomed to take over Brockman Farms. He was smart and talented. He's named after my father, Turner Duke. But that's the only thing they have in common."

Miranda listened, thinking it odd that the second son was the one named after T.D, instead of Cruz, the firstborn.

"Turner always had a wild side in him. T.D. appreciated that quality, but what T.D. refused to acknowledge was that Turner also had a gentle, loving heart. And it nearly killed Turner to see the way T.D. treated Adam and me. As soon as he graduated from high school, Turner left and he hasn't been back since. He swore he'd never come back unless it was for T.D.'s funeral.

"I hope he comes back to see how much potential is here with this land, the farm and the town now that T.D. is gone."

*So much potential in you too, Cruz,* she thought.

"You are a good listener," he said. "You know more about me than most people would ever learn." He pulled her up and led her to the railing, where he wrapped his arms around her. "Do you like the land?"

"It takes my breath away, Cruz. It's simple, earthy, rugged and magnificent at the same time. Almost magical in its beauty, how the fir trees rise up and how the flat wide beach stretches out to that water. I love the water."

They stood watching and listening to the waves for a while, lost in the moment.

"You still haven't told me the most important part," Miranda said later. She turned in his arms.

"About?"

"You. Why did T.D. hate you, Cruz? The oldest son, strong, intelligent, successful." She brought her hands up to his face. "And if he hated you, why leave you the corporation?"

He looked down at her, fresh and happy from their night together, that flush in her cheeks, the way she looked at him as if she wanted to see all of him. "It's not important," he said, and hugged her. Would she look at him the same way if she really knew everything about him?

"It is, Cruz. I can see when you talk about it, a storm comes over your eyes." Leaning up to him, she brushed her lips over his forehead, the edges of his cheekbones and finally to his lips. "Let me in, Cruz." She echoed his words from the night before. With a simple touch of her lips she stripped down some of his worries.

He looked toward the sea — his sea. This place was his now. Did he still have to hide who he was? He could tell her part of it. That would have to be enough for now.

"My guess is he was trying to drag me back here to spite me. I made it seem to him that I never wanted to come back, but he knew if he left it to me I would be forced to return because he knew my love for the people and for keeping this place running would win out over my own wants and needs."

"He sounds horrible, Cruz. And his hate for you? Where did that come from?"

He searched her eyes. Those eyes of her seemed to hold a haven for him, but he wasn't willing to tell her everything, that two fathers, not just one, hadn't wanted him.

"I think I'd rather take you back to bed and kiss every part of your body," he said, teasing her ear with his lips.

"Cruz, I —"

He took her mouth to silence the words. For a second, she hesitated under his lips and he stood, gently caressing her mouth with his, trying to seduce the serious conversation out of her mind. When she kissed him back and wrapped her arms around him, he felt as if he'd been found.

Her touch, so soothing and delicate, loosened the grip Cruz had on his deep hatred for his father. The tension seeped out of him as he poured it into the kiss. For so long he had been consumed by it, but now, here in her arms, he was finding something so much stronger. Any control he had left withered as she opened her mouth to his, inviting, asking him in.

He answered her the only way he knew how, with his body.

# Chapter Nineteen

Rushing to get dressed before the barbecue at Miguel and Roxanna's, Miranda was flustered. In what felt like a past life, or one she'd merely watched through a screen, she never rushed — she was very careful about planning every step of her day. But today was different. She couldn't seem to concentrate on anything but Cruz and the way he'd made her feel last night.

She fumbled around like a lunatic, first with the zipper on her dress, as she attempted not to paint mascara all over her face. And her hair — she simply couldn't make it do what she wanted it to. Looking into the mirror, she tried to talk herself into a place of calm. "Fine, leave your hair down, Miranda, it'll be okay. The world will not end if you don't have your hair neatly tied back." She looked closer and grinned. He thought she was beautiful. He made her feel beautiful. When she'd told him she wanted to be with him, she'd had no idea how amazing it would all be.

As she put her shoes on, her smile faded a bit, because there was another part that confused her. There had been those few moments when he'd closed himself off to her. Not in words, or actions so much, as he'd practically devoured her his body and everything he'd said to her had been magical, seductive and open. It was more what he hadn't said. She'd caught that shadow coming over him right after she'd told him about Eli, and although he'd attributed it to being angry for someone treating her like that, she'd sensed it was something else.

When she'd asked him about his family, he'd been so free with his words as long as he was speaking of others, but when it came down to opening up fully about himself, he'd stayed silent, and silenced her questions with his mouth. And she'd let him seduce her back into bed rather than pry. She wanted to find the right time, because her heart told her it would be worth it to have Cruz open himself fully to her.

His truck pulled up and, tossing her worries aside for the time being, she ran downstairs to meet him.

She walked into his arms as he came up to the porch. He kissed her and played with her hair, hanging loose down her back.

"I missed you," she whispered in his ear. It had only been a few hours since he'd dropped her off to get some work done, and shower and change for Roxanna and Miguel's.

"Mmm. I know. I missed you too. It's too bad we have somewhere to be or I'd take you right back inside and keep you to myself all night." He pulled himself away from her then, but the lust remained in his eyes. "I'll just have to wait until later."

"You could certainly use your imagination until then," she said, bringing his hand to her mouth and kissing it before she hopped into the truck.

"Torture," he moaned. "This evening might be pure torture." He leaned towards the open window and kissed her one last time before he walked around and climbed into his own side.

It was one of those precious late spring nights along the Pacific Northwest coast, when the air was dry and light and the sky a deepening perfect blue. Even the few clouds were thick, white and unthreatening. The evening was beautiful and, as they neared the last few acres of the farm, Cruz turned down a charming narrow hill into the old village.

The street was lined with wild shrubs and fir trees, intensely green in the evening light. Miranda looked ahead and was awed by the sun setting over the water, casting orange and lavender and pink across the horizon and shimmering on the surface of the ocean.

"Tell me more about Miguel and Roxanna," Miranda asked, watching his profile from her seat beside him. She wanted to know everything about him, and even though he might not realize it, getting to talk about the people who were important to him opened a part of his heart to her.

He smiled at her then looked back towards the winding hill. "I've known Miguel since we were boys. In fact, he tried to beat me up when we met." There was a trace of a happy memory in his voice as he continued, "I threw a rock at his sister Bianca because she wouldn't marry me."

"Cruz!" Miranda laughed in shock, loving the humor in his voice as he recounted this story for her. "How old were you?"

"I think seven or eight, maybe. She was beautiful and she was taller than me and I was in love."

Miranda punched him playfully in the shoulder.

"Hey, be kind. I had my heart broken at a young age." Cruz grabbed her hand and held it as he drove. "Anyway, as soon as Miguel was done defending her honor, he asked if he could try out my bike and we've been friends ever since. I spent more time at his house with his family growing up than I did in my own home."

"And Roxanna?" She liked listening to him talk about his past, the things he loved, his fears and worries and dreams. "She's so beautiful and glows with happiness. I think I want to be her when I grow up."

"We were seventeen," Cruz began, "Miguel and I, when she moved to town with her grandparents. Both her parents had been killed trying to cross the border, along with her siblings. She lost everyone except her grandparents and cousins. She was already here in America. The 'lucky one', we call her, because she wasn't in the van with her family when they died."

"God!" Miranda exclaimed, all humor gone from her voice.

"Yeah, it was awful. She was sixteen and pissed off at the world, had every right to be I suppose. She actually spat on us when we dared to talk to her, and cussed us out pretty good. That girl had a mouth on her." Cruz laughed at the memory and Miranda drank in the sound.

"But Miguel had fallen hard and fast from the moment he saw her and he never gave up. He kept trying to talk to her and he'd think up little gifts to give her and things to help her with.

"I think she secretly liked him as well but had too much anger and grief inside her to see anything else. Finally, one day, after she quit yelling at him to leave her alone, he handed her some flowers he'd picked for her and she stared at him. Before we knew what had happened, she threw herself at him kissed him, burst into tears and ran away all in about ten seconds."

Miranda laughed, picturing the young people in such a charming story.

"Miguel was too shocked to do anything until she was gone. He was like, 'Wait.' In this weak voice. It was several days before she let herself be seen again and I don't think they've been apart since. Although I left the next year." His face lost some of its warmth.

"But I kept in touch with them. They were married when she turned eighteen and they have five kids now, with another on the way, as you can tell. She always wanted a big family to make up for all that she lost."

"And Miguel, did he want a big family?"

"Oh yes, and he's a great dad."

*And you,* Miranda wanted to ask. *Do you want children?* But she couldn't vocalize the words. The image of him with Ana and José at the barns played through her mind, but something held her back from actually asking him. She wanted to give to him, not take, not demand. She'd been peppering him with questions about his life and his family, but the topic of kids was an entirely different level of intimacy and she didn't want to scare him away.

That afternoon, with her entire being feeling alive, Miranda felt as though she noticed everything. The scent of rain in the distance, the earth, the sweet apple blossoms and that salty air again. A girl could get seduced by that air, so she let herself be giddy in the moment. If all she had was right now, she would take it.

They passed the workers' cottages Cruz had showed her last week.

"You said the guest cottage I'm in was here first, but it doesn't look as old, Cruz?"

"The guest cottage has had updates over the years, and initially it was the main house before T.D. built the massive house. Those" — Cruz pointed towards the workers' cottages before he turned and followed the old streets through the downtown — "were built to house small families or one or two workers. They're simple and small, but well made."

They arrived at a beautiful white home, a mixture between bungalow style and an old Spanish mission, with a large yard and wild flowers as far as Miranda could see, at least in front. The front door was painted cobalt blue, like the market Miranda had been in, and bougainvillea vines climbed up the house on either side of the door, their bright pinkish-red flowers beginning to show.

"When T.D. died, my mother and our friend, Liliana, who owns her own construction business in town, got to work refreshing the guest cottage for Adam or Turner, but Adam's still in his rental, and there's still no sign of Turner. They resurfaced the floors, opened up the back wall to the French doors to let in more light, my mother got new furniture and decorated. It was always cozy, but all the light and beauty there today is because of those two."

"A woman with her own construction business. Hmm I think I like her already," Miranda said.

"She's pretty amazing. Speaking of..." Cruz swung open his door and grabbed a lady in an enormous hug, twirling her around on the lawn.

"Cruz, put me down," the woman said, laughing as Cruz kissed her with a loud exaggerated smack on the lips. He kept her hand in his and walked around to open Miranda's door.

"Liliana, this is Miranda, our accountant, my friend. Miranda, this is Liliana, my bratty little sister all grown up."

Liliana rolled her eyes at Cruz. "He only wishes he had a sister as cool as me. Although we might as well be related."

*Exotic princess* was what came to mind when Miranda got out of the car and the woman took her hand to shake it. Darkly tan skin that looked like it was lightly sprinkled with gold dust. Gorgeous brown eyes perfectly decorated with bronze shadow and a thick coat of mascara. Wild, curly, long hair and a body to die for, one with curves. Miranda had always wanted curves. She tried to bite back the shot of jealousy that kicked her in the stomach.

"Hello. It's nice to meet you, Liliana," Miranda said.

"Call me Lily. Great dress. I'd kill for green eyes like yours. They go perfectly with that shade of sage. Please tell me you'll share where you got it and that you're not one of those women who keeps shopping secrets."

Her smile and voice matched the exotic princess image, but Miranda couldn't help but like her immediately. All her tension eased away. "My dress? I made it."

"Stop!" Lily said. "Wait, do a spin. I need to see the back. It's gorgeous. Serious talent. We need to talk." Lily wrapped her arm through Miranda's and strolled away with her towards the back yard.

Miranda glanced over her shoulder, winked at Cruz then turned back to listen to Lily's chatter.

"Welcome." Miguel hugged them a moment later and ushered them into the back. Miranda couldn't help but smile. The yard was beautiful. Several trees lined one side, interspersed with lilac bushes. Towards the back was a fenced-in vegetable garden, the short fence painted all colors of the rainbow. A swing-set sat up against a taller fence near the house. The yard, full of shade and life and color, spoke of joy and comfort.

All at once, several children caught sight of them and ran towards Cruz, vying for his attention. He introduced them all to her and she loved the sound of their names — José, Ana, Juan Carlos and Bianca.

Cruz pulled a bag of sour candies out of his pocket for them. They ran around the yard chasing each other for the best flavor, all except for José and Ana, the oldest. José climbed up Cruz's body, as he'd done with Adam in the barn — as if he were a jungle gym — all the way till he sat on Cruz's shoulders. And little Ana took Miranda's hand and intertwined their fingers.

"Twins," Cruz said, smiling at her. "Can you believe it? They tend to stay very close together."

A large hammock in the back corner under the shade of an old oak tree rocked, and Roxanna climbed out of it in a beautiful fuchsia sundress and bare feet, her hair pulled back in a messy pony tail. She came towards them slowly, one hand pressed on her lower back. It was plain to see Roxanna's discomfort, and yet the woman still had that radiant smile, that glow about her.

"Lily, Cruz," Roxanna said kissing them on both cheeks. "And Miranda. I'm so glad you brought her, Cruz. Look at you, Miranda, you look lovely." Roxanna took one of Miranda's hands, twirled her around and hugged her as if they were dear sisters.

Caught up in the laughter and family warmth, Miranda hugged her back.

"Quit staring at the women and help me get the food ready to grill, Cruz," Miguel said as he elbowed Cruz in the side and turned him towards the kitchen.

"What can I do to help?" Miranda asked Roxanna.

"Nothing," Roxanna said. She took Miranda's and Lily's hands in hers. "Come and sit here next to me, ladies. Relax and gossip with me. The men are doing the cooking tonight."

They sat on gorgeous teak furniture with plush green cushions. Roxanna put her feet up on the coffee table. "I'm sorry, but my feet are so sore and swollen. I hope you don't mind."

"Please don't apologize. It doesn't bother me at all."

"*Cervezas*?" Miguel held out beers to Lily and Miranda.

"What about me?" Roxanna asked.

"For you, my love, all my love." And setting down a large glass of lemonade, Miguel kissed her with his hand on her belly. Across the deck Miranda met Cruz's gaze, their own passion for each other simmering below the surface.

"And now the grill calls to me." Miguel kissed Roxanna's hand with a flourish and went to help Cruz.

"How many weeks left?" Lily asked Roxanna and patted her belly.

Roxanna closed her eyes and smiled. When she opened them she said, "Three weeks and five days. I'm counting down. It feels like someone keeps riding a lawnmower across my back, but for the most part, I love being pregnant."

"It shows," Miranda said.

"But it's time someone else around here started having babies," Roxanna said and winked at Lily.

"Don't go there, sister," Lily snorted. "Work is my baby. Besides, I haven't had a date in months." She leaned back and sighed. "Ahh. I can't even remember what a date is like, or a kiss, a really steamy melt-your-toes kiss, or sex, or sex in the shower."

"Liliana!" Roxanna smacked Lily's shoulder.

"It's true!" Lily laughed. "We all have droughts, well, except you. You've never had a sex drought."

It was Roxanna's turn to smile. She rubbed her enormous belly. "True."

"No need to gloat." Lily smacked her back.

"Let's ask Miranda if she's in a drought," Lily said.

"I...ahhh..." She glanced towards the kitchen inside, where Cruz stood with Miguel.

"Wait, what?" Lily started to giggle. "You and Cruz? Good for you, girl!"

A flush heated Miranda's cheeks. She covered her face. She might have been completely mortified instead of only partly, except these two women made her feel at home, included, welcome. "Is it that obvious?"

"I wondered when I saw you two at the restaurant. You couldn't take your eyes off each other," Roxanna said. "And you're all shimmery today. Besides, you're gorgeous and smart, exactly what Cruz Brockman needs."

"I bet it was your eyes that did it. He fell right for those sagey, gold-flecked beauties, didn't he?" Lily asked. "How come no one's told me about this? You're supposed to keep me posted on all things romantic, Rox."

"You've been out of town," Roxanna pointed out.

"For three days, jeez. Okay fill us in, Miranda. You and Cruz. That man hasn't had anyone special in forever," Lily said. "Is he a good kisser? I bet he's a good kisser. I bet all those Brockman brothers are good kissers." She sighed.

Miranda blushed completely and smiled again.

"I knew it!" Lily said. "So, who are you and what are you doing here? Tell me everything, I need details."

"She's shy, isn't she?" Miranda quipped to Roxanna, and took a sip of her beer.

Roxanna's belly laugh sounded through the air.

"I knew I liked you the minute you stepped out of Cruz's truck in that dynamite dress," Lily said, "but a sense of humor too. That's exactly what Cruz needs to stop brooding over the past. He's so ready to move on from T.D.'s shadow. He needs someone to shove him off the cliff."

"We just met," Miranda said. Now she was embarrassed.

"Mmm hmm," Lily said over her beer bottle. "The look you two have for each other doesn't say 'just met'."

"I've never seen Cruz Brockman like this, so taken with a woman," Roxanna said. "He's never brought one home to visit, never brought one to our Sunday cookouts, ever. You're in love, aren't you?"

At the startled look on Miranda's face, Roxanna continued, "Oh, I'm sorry. I didn't mean to pry. I mean, of course I do. It's what I do with friends. Forgive me. Miguel told me to behave, but I know what it's like to try to deny it. Believe me, I was furious when I realized I was in love with Miguel."

Lily patted Roxanna's hand.

"I didn't realize it was that easy to tell," Miranda said quietly. *Do I have it written across my forehead for everyone to read?* "I'm trying to understand everything. I don't want to pressure Cruz, in case he doesn't feel the same."

"You haven't told him yet. I wondered." Roxanna touched Miranda's hand. "And you're afraid because it's so fast. That too I understand. When I met Miguel, it was so forceful, the feeling that hit me. Like I said, I was mad, well, mad at the world really. My entire family was gone and I had sworn to myself that I would never ever love anyone again in any way. If I didn't love, then I could never be hurt." Roxanna rubbed her hands over her stomach in light caresses as if comforting the baby within.

"How did you know?" Miranda asked in a soft voice.

"I'm not quite sure, except that something in me broke open. I thought nothing else inside of me could feel anything but grief, but this other feeling took over. And once I got over being angry and afraid I let myself open to it. Although I'm not really sure I had any say in the matter. The man wouldn't leave me alone."

The women laughed again.

"It's tricky," Miranda began.

"Love's only tricky when you don't know you're in it," Roxanna said, reaching out for her hand.

"I mean I'm auditing his books. Essentially, I work for the man."

"You sure are auditing his books." Lily giggled.

"Lily!" Miranda was both shocked and couldn't help doubling over into laughter with the two women.

"So are you going to tell me, or do I have to beat you up to get you to talk to me about her?" Miguel asked Cruz.

"Tell you what about her?" Cruz used the tongs to turn the chicken on the hot grill.

"Are you really that dumb, or are you pretending? Come on, man, I'm your best friend. I can see it written all over your face. And I have to say it's quite amusing." Miguel chuckled.

Miguel was right. They were best friends and Cruz knew he couldn't lie to him. He wasn't sure he was ready to accept what Miguel was talking about. "I'm not sure what to do, Miguel."

"Ah, so it is true." Miguel changed his tone to a serious one now. "What do you mean what to do? There's only one choice. Tell her. That's what you kept telling me all those years ago when Roxanna moved here and moved right into my heart."

"You're right, but it was different with you two."

"How?"

"I'm not sure she feels the same way." It was a lie. Cruz knew it as soon as he spoke it. He could feel her love for him like nothing else he'd ever felt in his life. He watched her across the yard talking and laughing with Roxanna and Lily. When she looked at him, her face practically bloomed. It was then that he saw her feelings, a mirror of his own. Maybe she felt the same. *But does it really matter,* he asked himself. They could never have a future together. His only future was this place, and this farm. Hers was a world away from here, helping clients with their money.

"Oh, and Roxanna spitting on me and cursing me to hell was how you could tell she felt the same about me? Are you crazy, man?" Miguel smacked him on the shoulder. "Look at her face." Miguel gestured towards Miranda. "She's absolutely glowing when she looks at you. That lady better not hope to win a poker bluff anytime soon. Her emotions light up her face. Be honest with me. Tell me what this is really about, Cruz. Roxanna and I are your friends. We want you to have the kind of happiness we have. It's out there, Cruz. Not every relationship is like your parents'."

Miguel was probably the only person besides Cruz's brothers who really knew about his parents. "I know. I'm …" He had to tell someone what was going on and he knew he could trust Miguel with anything.

"You're afraid?"

"Maybe, but it's more than that, Miguel. I'm not sure I'm good enough for her. It's not T.D., it's my biological father too. Christ, neither one wanted me. She deserves a man who can give her everything she wants, everything she deserves. I don't know if I'm that man."

"Bullshit! That has got to be the stupidest thing I've ever heard. You can't use that excuse. T.D. was a bastard. He couldn't see what an amazing son you were. He didn't have the ability to recognize good in anyone. The man didn't care. And your biological father, you told me he left before he even knew Katie was pregnant. But even if he 'didn't want you,' as you say, I still call bullshit. The rest of us—your real family—know your worth, Cruz. Don't insult me with that 'I'm not good enough.' Don't be afraid, or be afraid, but don't let the fear stop you from finding something wonderful in this world, someone wonderful to share your life with, if that's what you want. You may be able to convince everyone else in your life that you'd rather spend your days alone, but you can't fool me."

"There's more," Cruz said, watching the women across the yard while he spoke to Miguel. "The farm's been under investigation by the IRS. That's why she's here, to perform an audit to find the suspected evasion. Seems T.D. hasn't been paying taxes, or worse, for years now. Best-case scenario is that we are leveraged with a huge fine. If it's bad enough, they could shut us down and take everything. All those years I've waited, Adam's waited, hell, I like to think Turner too, all those years and now we may not be able to keep the farm."

"You're kidding?" Pure bafflement swam over Miguel's features. He put the basting brush down and closed the grill.

"Nope."

"That bastard!"

"As if it surprises you," Cruz said. "And there's no way I can make promises until I know what's going to happen after the audit. We could be ruined. I wouldn't have anything to offer her then."

"If she loves you, none of that matters, Cruz."

"I want to believe that, but she scraped herself and her mother up from the poorhouse. It took her years to get to a place where she felt safe and where she didn't have to worry about finances. I can't ask her to go back to that. She's amazing, Miguel. She deserves better."

"So do you, my friend," Miguel said.

The two men stood in silence, drinking their beers while they finished grilling the meat.

"Did Cruz tell you how we met?" Miguel asked Miranda with a chuckle. They had finished their meal and put the children to bed. Now the adults sat on the deck in the candlelight, drinking coffee and wine.

"He did," Miranda said. She smiled at Cruz, who sat next to her, playing with her fingers.

"Did he tell you he threw a boulder at my sister?" Miguel raised his eyebrow, pretending to be serious.

"It was a pebble," Cruz said, covering his heart in mock pain.

"A boulder." Miguel opened his arms wide to illustrate the size of the boulder. "And it's a good thing his aim is bad or he would have seriously hurt her."

"And thankfully you were there to defend her from such a horrible man," Roxanna teased her husband as Miguel rubbed her feet, which rested in his lap.

"It was, and," he said with a big grin on his face, "I got to ride Cruz's new dirt bike after I beat him up."

"I think the rock gets bigger every time you tell that story, my friend," Cruz said. He poured more wine for Miranda.

Cruz had angled Miranda's body on the small love seat so that her back was against his chest. Wrapping his arms around her, he pulled her closer and kissed the top of her head. Miguel and Roxanna sat across from them on the double-wide chaise longue. These people were wonderful, kind and funny and so full of love. She envied Cruz in a good way, as she had never had close friendships like this, and she felt privileged to be a part of it, if only for one evening.

"It never gets old, coming here," Lily said. "But now I must drag myself home to bed so I can get up early for work. Goodnight, everyone." Lily blew kisses and carried her strappy sandals in her hand. "Hope to see you again, Miranda. Good luck with the audit." Lily smiled, winked at her and walked off.

"Are you tired, *mi amor*?" Miguel asked his wife, and when there was no answer, he glanced at her sleeping form. "Is she the most beautiful pregnant woman you've ever seen?" Miguel said as if speaking to himself.

"She is that." Cruz rose and lifted Miranda up with him. "We should go, my friend. Thank you for dinner."

"Yes, thank you, Miguel. I had a wonderful time. Thank Roxanna for me when she wakes, will you?" Miranda said.

"I promise. She likes you, by the way." Careful not to wake her, Miguel moved her feet, stood briefly to hug Miranda then sat back down next to his wife.

Cruz took Miranda's hand and they walked out of the backyard, both of them glancing back briefly as Miguel began singing a Spanish lullaby to Roxanna.

\* \* \* \*

"I think I'm in love with them." Miranda sighed and sat back in the seat as they started the drive back to the farm.

Cruz smiled at her. "They're pretty hard not to like, aren't they?" He twined his fingers in hers again.

Now that they'd made love, he was always taking her hand, always touching her somewhere. She wondered if he was even aware of that, or of what it did to her, what it said to her. After last night, it made her feel as if he couldn't get enough of her, never wanted to be apart from her. Knowing that he felt that way was a power she'd never even known about before. Or maybe it had never been there until she'd met Cruz. It was glorious to feel that kind of power, that kind of beauty, that kind of link to someone else. Especially when, as Roxanna had said, she was in love. It was like being high and delirious and, surprisingly, it hurt. She'd never expected falling in love would be painful.

She didn't know if it was because with the knowledge of being in love came fear, or if it was because he didn't love her back. Either way, her chest and, her ribs ached deep. Power, love, this bone-deep ache—these were all so new to her and she wasn't quite sure what to do with them.

They ran from the truck to the cottage in a downpour that was blowing across the coast. It exhausted itself as quickly as it came, and they stood on the porch kissing as the sound of rain drifted from a pounding to quiet drops in the leftover puddles. They were soaked and all she could think about was how delicious he smelled in the rain, covered in rainwater, his hair wet, even his long, dark eyelashes dripping.

"I find it very difficult to believe there was a time when I would have given anything to be back here on the farm helping with the birthing in the spring," Cruz said as he pulled away, took her face in his hands and looked at her. "And now I would give anything to stay here with you tonight, Miranda. Birthing calves is the last thing on my mind right now."

There he was making her feel strong with that power again. All she could do was accept how she was feeling and hope for more.

"Go," she said. "Rescue your brother. He's been there for over twenty-four hours."

"I know you're right. Knowing Adam, though, he'll probably stay and sleep in the barns to be sure his cows are okay."

"Want a towel?" she asked.

"Thanks, but I've got extra clothes down at the barn office. Miranda." He wrapped her hands around his waist and tugged her close. "Has it really only been a few weeks since I met you? I said you bewitched me and I was right. I feel like the last few days, it's like I've known you forever."

*Is it really so difficult for this amazing strong man to accept his feelings?* His words were intimate, warm and special. But he looked scared to death.

She stood on her tiptoes and kissed him. "Yes," she said. It was all she could get out, her heart overcome with emotion.

"I'm leaving tomorrow for a few days to go to an agricultural convention in Portland, and take care of some business. The timing sucks, when I want to spend every second with you. I'll find you when I get back?"

She nodded and kissed him one last time.

Once again, she found herself standing at the porch door watching him walk away. *Miss me,* she thought. *Miss me even a tiny bit of how I already miss you.* She watched long after he'd disappeared. By the time she turned to go in, the rain had started again.

Miranda climbed into bed, wonderfully exhausted. This was a dilemma she had never imagined. She'd never walked headfirst into someone like Cruz, who'd tipped her world over into this heady place of emotions and want. She'd never thought about a future with someone. Looking forward had always been about her next paycheck, and keeping up. She breathed in the fresh rain scent and listened as it watered the earth around her. There wasn't time for her mind to worry as she fell into a heavy, wonderful sleep.

# Chapter Twenty

There was something about mornings that Miranda loved, the quiet before everyone was up, the way the light changed over the land, dramatically at first then smoothing out into the day. But this morning, her emotions were in turmoil. Her entire body had been ravaged over the weekend. She was both exhilarated and deliciously tired. She felt as giddy as a schoolgirl, but she also felt foolish. Not for spending the night with Cruz, but for those few precious moments when she'd lost all thought. When hope and dreams had snuck in and she'd momentarily believed that what she had with Cruz was more than lust and attraction – a quick affair. And, oh, how she wanted it to be more for both of them.

But did she really know about things like that, about true love? And could she really even be entertaining a thought like that with someone she was conducting an audit for? It was the morning when thoughts became crystal clear, like the one throbbing in her head right now. She'd slept with someone she was in a business relationship with, something she should never have done. She'd never done anything unethical in her life—she barely even swore.

One amazing weekend together and she was ready to give up everything for him. But it was more than that. For sure the attraction and desire were there, were real, but she'd been getting to know him. He'd shared parts of himself with her she knew he'd kept hidden from others. He'd even shared his best friends with her, and he wanted to get to know her. Her mind and heart were a tangled mess of emotions. She'd woken earlier than usual and sat in the library working even before dawn.

While she sipped her coffee and focused on the tax return she was reading, something nagged at the corner of her mind. She might have completely missed the line item if she hadn't been touring the farm with Cruz earlier in the week and listening to him talk about all the upgrades and equipment they needed.

Stopping, she backed up and read some of the expensed items. Robotic milking machine purchased last year for over two hundred thousand dollars. Row crop tractor, front loader tractor, tiller, skid loader...

Some didn't have names, just numbers. All had been purchased in the last two years. But Cruz had said they wanted to replace their ancient tractors. And she certainly hadn't seen any new-looking equipment.

All the items she saw looked like items that a farmer would need—nothing out of the ordinary, nothing at all except it looked like T.D. had expensed items for the farm that he'd never actually purchased. It was an all-too-common scam in order to see larger tax refunds, and it looked like T.D. had nearly gotten away with it. Actually, he had since he was dead. It was the ones left behind who were going to have to deal with the fallout.

Now she needed to go through the tax returns for the past few years line by line and check to see if each item expensed was real or fake. She couldn't do it by herself, because she had no idea if what was on paper actually existed on the farm. She'd need Cruz or Adam to help her.

*Maybe I'll see if I can catch either of them before they leave for Portland*, she thought, as she walked toward Cruz's office at the front of the house. She practically ran right into him as he and Adam were walking out.

"Whoa, hi," he said, grabbing on to her arms.

"I..." She looked up him and practically gulped at the way his gaze, dark and full of desire. Her body warmed to his touch. She wanted all of him touching all of her. It was a good thing he steadied her so she wouldn't melt.

"Morning, Miranda," Adam said from behind Cruz, bringing her out of her haze. "Cruz, I think you can let go of her now."

"What? Oh, right." Cruz set her back and put his hands in his pockets. "You're in a hurry?" he said.

"I found something this morning in T.D.'s taxes and I thought I might catch you both before you left."

"You get to work early," Adam said. "The sun's not even up yet."

"I'm a morning person," she said. She wasn't about to explain that dreams of Cruz had woken her far earlier than she was used to. "I know you both need to go, but I came across something that puzzled me, and unfortunately it's a puzzle I'll need one or both of you to help me solve. Cruz, when you gave me the tour last week, you mentioned some of the things you wanted to buy for the farm. I might have missed this save for that conversation. Here," she said and pointed to the list she'd typed up for them.

Cruz and Adam glanced over the list.

She didn't know how to say it, didn't want to be the one to say it, even though this was the real reason she was here. "Those are items T.D. has expensed over the last two years on the farm's tax returns."

"Expensed," Cruz said. "You mean, he claimed he purchased them, but —"

"He never did," Adam finished for him. The humor and warmth were gone from their voices as they looked to Miranda for answers.

Wow, did she never want to be on the wrong side of an argument with those angry males that stood before her right now. "Exactly. I'm guessing based on what Cruz told me about some of the new equipment and things you need for the farm. I need you two to go through the list and tell me which, if any, of those things he actually did purchase." They stood there brooding as they read through the list. They might look physically different from each other, but they were very similar they were in other ways. Their stance, their concentration, the energy rippling off them.

"You can take it with you if you need to," she said, breaking into the long silence.

"We don't," Adam said.

It was the only time she'd seen Adam without a playful, relaxed smile on his face.

"We don't have any of these items on the farm. T.D. never purchased anything on this list for the farm."

"Okay," she said, feeling rotten about doing her job. "I'm sorry."

"It's not your fault, Miranda," Cruz said. "You knew when you came that this kind of thing was what you were looking for."

He was right, but it didn't make her feel better. Nothing about this situation was good. And Cruz, his words were so different from his tone. It was disgust she heard.

Adam must have noticed it too as he softened his own tone. "Miranda, is there anything we need to do about this right now?"

"No. Having your answer helps me to keep working on the audit. I am sorry. I know this isn't good news and I know you have to get going."

"Cruz, I'll give you a few minutes and meet you in the truck. Miranda," he said and smiled at her on his way out.

"I am sorry, Cruz," she said to him as they stood alone in his office. *What an empty apology.* But he was so quiet she felt like she had to say something to fill the horrible awkward silence.

"Stop." He held up his hand. "I'm not mad at you, Miranda. I'm angry at T.D. and this brings the reality back. I knew, I know why you're here, but it's been easy to forget the sordid details of T.D.'s behavior. I'm sorry you have to see this."

This was why people said never get involved with co-workers, because emotions changed everything. She'd lost all objectivity, because she was hurt by his tone. He walked behind the desk, putting distance between them, practically dismissing her from the room, from the entire situation. And it was obvious he thought she was some fragile idiot, which in turn made her angry.

"Believe it or not, this is what I do for a living, Cruz. I've been doing this for years. I'm stronger than you give me credit for. I'm not going to crumple at your feet."

"That's not what I said, or meant, Miranda."

"Then what did you mean? You very neatly, very rudely put me in my place. I *am* sorry to deliver bad news, Cruz, sorry to have discovered it at all, but you're right. It isn't my fault, and I do not deserve to be treated like crap. Thank you, though, for confirming my concerns about getting involved with someone I work with." She turned and walked out.

"Miranda." He caught her before she got down the hall. She stopped but didn't turn around. She wasn't sure she could hold back the tears, but she'd do her best not to let him see her cry.

"Miranda." He said it again softly. He stood right behind her. "I'm sorry, I'm a jerk. I don't think you're going to crumple. I see how strong you are. I don't know how to explain it. That any part of T.D.'s disgusting nature should have to touch you, right then in that moment it was like a punch in the gut, a punch of shame. Rationally, I know you're not going to fall apart with the real knowledge of T.D.'s tax evasion, but my feelings for you aren't rational. You are so beautiful and amazing. Already you've become something precious to me, and I don't want anything of his to be remotely near you, near us together."

Her anger melted away.

He took her hand. "I'm sorry," Cruz said.

She put her other hand on his face. "Cruz, it isn't your shame. You are not T.D. Brockman. You are not responsible for any of this."

He wrapped his arms around her. "Shame isn't rational either."

"I know, Cruz. I still have shame from having grown up poor, even though I know it wasn't my fault."

"We're a piece of work, the both of us, aren't we?" he said. "Can I still find you when I get back from Portland?"

"I was hoping you'd want to."

He reached behind her and pulled the clip out of her hair, allowing it to flow.

"Cruz," she said with a wry grin.

"I wanted to run my fingers through it one last time before I go. And I love the way your eyes go all dark when I do." He kissed her then, a gentle brush of his lips as he watched her. Then, with a last squeeze of her hand, he turned to go.

Putting her fingers to her lips, she tried to feel him still there. She'd never known one person could kiss so many different ways. Every time it was new and different, and it made her crave him. Miranda forced herself to think of profit and loss statements as she walked to the library before someone had to mop up the puddle she'd become.

# Chapter Twenty-One

The steady rain continued outside, but inside the house was quiet, too quiet for Miranda. Everyone except Elena, the housekeeper, was gone and she never made a sound. Or maybe Miranda noticed the quiet because of the folder she had discovered on T.D.'s private computer. It was well camouflaged, but when she found it, Miranda sensed immediately what it was. Time and again people thought they were being sneaky, opening foreign bank accounts, hiding money where the IRS couldn't see it. *And, wow! One point five million dollars is a lot of money.* Having a foreign account wasn't the problem. The problem came when people didn't file the correct paperwork to report the income. And she'd bet that T.D. hadn't reported his little cushion.

As if the false farm expenses she'd found earlier in the week weren't bad enough, Cruz's reaction was worse. It still bothered her, how he'd gotten so cold, and even though he'd apologized and she knew he meant it, it definitely brought the questionable nature of their relationship to the forefront of her mind.

Since she'd begun to get to know these beautiful people of Graciella, a small part of her had hoped that the claims of tax evasion were false. For their sake, because with a corporation this size and the amount the IRS suspected that was owed in back taxes—not to mention penalties for withholding taxes in the first place—it could completely ruin them. "Dammit! Everyone keeps telling me you were a bastard, T.D.," Miranda said aloud. "They were right."

Then there were her personal selfish reasons for wanting it all to be untrue. If she wasn't here to discover tax fraud, she never would have found herself in a relationship with someone so closely connected to this account and gotten tangled up with him while potentially uncovering the very thing that could destroy him. 'Tangled' was a good word to use. She knew she shouldn't have anything but a business connection with him, but oh, how she didn't regret anything they'd done, how he'd made her feel, how he'd looked at her as though he wanted her to belong to him.

Miranda felt as if she'd never worked so hard in her life—or maybe no account had meant as much to her before—but despite the long hours she put in during the week, there was still no sign of the proper reporting paperwork for the foreign bank account by Thursday afternoon, leaving Miranda raw with stress and fatigue. And she missed Cruz. She knew she didn't have a right to, knew those were exactly the kinds of emotions that were going to get her into trouble.

After a long walk, a shower and a change of clothes, she took her rental car into the post office in town to send some mail. The rain had stopped and everything was brilliant with color. So much was already blooming as she strolled through town—purple and orange pansies, bright yellow daffodils, red and white tulips bursting open. Magnolia trees lined one of the main streets. The buildings were old and looked well built, with lots of character. Old-fashioned street lights stood throughout the town. It was a shame that several—more than several—of the businesses stood empty.

The town seemed too quiet, as if it had been asleep for a long time. The small library was open. There was what looked like an old abandoned hardware store, a small bakery and the post office. The town needed a bookstore, and a good pub with a small place in the back for live music. Miranda let her mind drift again as she waited in line—a few other restaurants, a wine tasting room, a theater...wait, a theater. Miranda came out of the post office and spotted the old marquee across the street and down a few stores. She smiled. "Perfect."

Just as she said it, Lily came out of the theater, walking right in Miranda's direction.

"Hi," Miranda said as Lily crossed the street.

"Miranda, hi. You look like someone who's from here. Ready to move to Graciella yet? What do we have to do to convince you? Tell me you didn't make this gorgeous pink sweater too or I'll have to kill you and invade your closet."

Miranda laughed. "Lily, it's nice to meet someone like you who doesn't hold back or sugarcoat anything."

Lily's smile was bright. "So, did you or didn't you? Make it, that is?"

"I didn't. And I'm even at liberty to tell you where I bought it."

"That-a-girl," Lily said. "What are you up to?"

"Nothing. Taking a break from my work. I came into town to go to the post office."

"Mmm hmm, I bet auditing those books is exhausting, isn't it?" Lily fanned her face.

She had a way of lifting people's spirits, of poking fun without being rude. "Stop it. You're horrible!" Miranda said, but smiled.

"I'm sorry, you hardly know me and I'm teasing you. It's only because I have to live vicariously through my friends who are in love and have certain sleeping arrangements that I am sadly without at the moment. Speaking of which, where is your *amor*, Cruz?"

"He's in Portland all week, I think."

"Well then, that settles it. I bought groceries to make shrimp scampi linguini and I have enough to feed an army. You are coming with me so we can cook, eat, drink wine and gossip. Come on. I have to drop this in the mailbox. You can follow me. It's not far."

"Are you sure, Lily? I mean, I don't have anything to bring," Miranda said.

"Stop it. Do you like food?"

"Yes. Is that a trick question?"

Lily laughed. "Do you like wine?"

"Yes."

"That settles it. Besides, I bet you're dying to see my house, aren't you?"

Miranda laughed again. "I'd love to come."

"Good, then you can tell me more about you and Cruz." Lily took her arm again like she'd done the other night. *Maybe there's something in the water here.* Miranda had been surrounded by warm, friendly, open people since she'd arrived. She'd never met so many generous and kind people in her entire life. Maybe she hadn't been looking. How did a nasty man like T.D. Brockman survive in a place like this?

At Lily's, Miranda pulled her car into the muddy driveway, got out and simply stared. Set among the trees, with a large yard, was a house of stucco unlike any Spanish-mission style Miranda had ever seen. It wasn't the traditional-looking white with red tile roof. Instead it was vibrant, rich and beautiful. Two stories in an almost rosy terra cotta color, with a charcoal colored tile roof and windows slightly rounded at the tops, some with lacy-looking black wrought iron grills. The large arch leading to the entrance surrounded a thick wooden door with an enormous dragonfly carved into the wood.

"Well?" Lily asked standing next to Miranda. "I'm impatient. Miranda, you're so quiet. Do you like it? Do you hate it? Say something."

"Why do you ever leave?" Miranda said in awe. "I'm stunned."

Lily, arms full of grocery bags, let out her breath and elbowed Miranda, "You are good for my ego."

"Ha, I get the impression your ego doesn't need any help," Miranda said, teasing, but when she looked at Lily gazing over her own house, Lily's eyes were shimmering. "You really were worried what I'd think?"

"I put my entire heart into it. I do, in all my work, but this was different. This was all of me."

Miranda took one of the grocery bags out of Lily's hands. "I can tell," she said and nudged Lily back. "Do I get to see the inside?"

Lily blinked and grinned at Miranda. "Come on."

The inside was such a perfect mix of styles, starting from the blue and white Spanish tile in the entryway which opened up into a large open-floor plan. Then down a few steps into the combined living room and dining room and through to the kitchen, where dark but warm wooden cabinets and stainless-steel appliances were set off by a barely pink marble countertop. Bursts of color, burst of Lily were everywhere, from the fat white vase of red, yellow and orange tulips on the kitchen counter to the books scattered on the coffee table.

"Want to see my favorite part?" Lily opened the French doors to a sprawling teak deck.

Miranda pointed to the pool surrounded by a simple cement deck and bright, gorgeous landscaping. "That looks like the cover of a spa getaway magazine."

"Nice, isn't it. Heated too, with underwater lights and speakers."

"Are you kidding me? You may have to kick me out when you want me to leave."

Lily looked up at the sky. "If it wasn't about to pour again, I'd say let's go dive in. You'll have to come back. I guess we'll have to have wine instead."

Miranda sat at one of the leather bar stools and chopped scallions while Lily sautéed the shrimp in wine and garlic. They snacked on olives and salamis and drank a buttery Chardonnay.

"So," Lily said. "Accounting, huh? I can't see it. I mean, you obviously have the brain, but don't you get bored to death? I mean, I would be bored to death. Where's the creativity? No offense. You've obviously figured out by now that I sometimes speak before I think to stop myself."

Miranda laughed. "No, you're right, there are parts of it that are boring, can be boring, and it's definitely not the most creative career. Initially I was attracted to it because I'm good with numbers, and I could work by myself mostly, which is good for us introverts. Not that you would know anything about that," she teased.

Lily grinned.

"And it's good money, really good money." She glanced at Lily as she took the shrimp out and added shallots to the pan. "We didn't have any, money that is, growing up. I guess I wanted it. Money was definitely a lure.

"But the part I like, is solving problems, fitting the pieces together until the picture forms. Although for the past few years, my position has been to uncover inconsistencies or tax evasion. And that can wear a person down, always seeing the greedy side of humanity. Which, now that I said all of that, makes me sound like a hypocrite." Miranda swallowed her discomfort with a sip of wine.

"Don't say that." Lily tossed the shrimp and scallions with noodles then poured the entire mix into a large serving bowl. "Money's not a bad thing. We all want money. I love money. It's what we do with it, how we act with it that matters. Here, let's eat in the nook. It's one of my favorite spots."

Lily piled their plates with scampi, topped their glasses off and sat across from Miranda. "Plus, without money I wouldn't have this amazing house, and I don't know how I'd take care of my father."

"Take care of your father?" Miranda asked.

"He's in the nursing home here in town, in the late stages of Alzheimer's. He was diagnosed a few years ago so I came home from living abroad to help him, but eventually it got to be too much for me to handle at home, especially since I couldn't be there all the time."

"I'm sorry, Lily. My mother was ill for a long time. You're right about the money. We had a live-in nurse for years because I had to travel often for work. Money does help."

Lily looked up in surprise. "It sucks! It absolutely sucks, doesn't it? We're too young to be taking care of our parents. And my papa — when his mind was whole — was the best, funny and kind and so full of life. He always told me I could do or be whatever I wanted. I believed him. It's hard when they're here but not really here. Sometimes I think it might be easier if he'd move on to that peaceful place, you know. I'm sorry, I really am an insensitive bitch. Do you miss her, your mother?"

She loved how Lily said whatever was on her mind. "Honestly, I don't know. She's only been dead for about three weeks now and — "

"What? Miranda. I'm a bigger idiot than I thought. Please forgive me. I was devastated when I lost my mother. Wait, you're laughing. Are you laughing or crying?"

"Laughing." Miranda could barely get the word out. "Now I'm crying, but it's from laughing, I don't know why I'm laughing. It's not funny at all. I'm having a moment."

Lily stared.

Miranda wiped tears from her face. "I mean my mother died three weeks ago. I don't know if I miss her, because even when she was alive, she never wanted me, or loved me. I was an obligation to her, a burden. And in the end we shifted places and she became an obligation to me." She stopped laughing and gulped down some water. "I'm sorry." She waved her hand and started laughing again.

"I think you need more wine, friend." Lily said. Miranda put her hand on the table and Lily put hers over it. "That's a bigger burden to carry in your heart than taking care of a sick parent who loves you."

Miranda took a deep breath. "It almost seems like someone else's life when I look back. I mean, I was there, for years, but I got so good at closing off my emotions that I wasn't really present. God, when I think about how many years I've walked through life not really being present. Now I'm really depressed."

Lily laughed. "You don't seem unpresent to me, here, since I've met you. Is unpresent a word? Don't mind me.

I like to make up words." She waved her fork and got herself a second helping of scampi. "More?" She asked.

"Please, it's delicious, Lily."

"Don't forget butter. There's plenty of butter in there, to make your skin glow, although I'd say you don't need any help in that department. The shimmer that was on your face at the cookout the other night is still there. I don't know you that well, but I'd say Cruz is good for you. And the more I do get to know you, I'm confident you're good for him. In fact I think you're exactly what he needs. I'm wondering if he sees it yet. The man can be stubborn. Lord, all the Brockman brothers can be."

"Where'd you learn to make such delicious scampi?"

"Don't try to change the subject." Lily waved her fork at Miranda. "For your information, I can out-stubborn all three Brockman brothers put together. So tell me how it's going."

"I don't know. I'm so confused, Lily. I'm a successful accountant who's been all over the country and handled multi-billion-dollar accounts, but I've never been in love before." Miranda put her fork down and picked up her wine.

"You'd know if you'd been in love before. It's massive. It flips you over or flips your world over — or both — until you don't know which way is right side up anymore." Lily spoke with her hands as much as her mouth, gesturing, moving.

"Does it hurt?" Miranda asked.

"From what I remember, yes. And I've only been there once, a long time ago. But it was unrequited, so maybe that's why it hurt."

Lily made it so easy to feel at home. She accepted the way Miranda was. Miranda couldn't remember the last time she'd had dinner with a girlfriend.

"Here, let me make some tea and we'll go sit outside on the covered part of the deck. We'll take blankets and listen to the rain, and I can annoy you with questions about your love life. I'll take mental notes for the long lonely nights ahead of me."

"Only if you let me do the dishes," Miranda said and walked over to the sink before Lily could stop her.

"Deal."

It had stopped raining by the time they got outside, and a thick fog had settled in, which made everything quiet and muffled. The chamomile tea was fragrant and hot.

"So, does he make you go all gooey?" Lily asked her. "Can he kiss? Does he dive right in or do that whole gentle tease that goes on forever and ever? Mmm hmm, you don't even need to answer. I can see it written all over your face. I am so jealous right now."

"Stop. You're going to have me crying from laughter again. How do you do that, welcome me in and make me feel like we've been friends forever? Get all of my secrets out of me?"

"Like you're so difficult to hang out with." Lily rolled her eyes and had Miranda giggling. "We're pretty simple around here. If you're friends with someone we love, then you're our friend too. Maybe we were meant to be friends. I think you were meant to come to Graciella. Plus, if I butter you up enough, you'll make me a dynamite-looking dress similar to that one you had on the other night. Maybe in a shimmery bronze to highlight my eyes." Lily batted her eyelashes.

"You have no shame, do you?"

They laughed and drank their tea.

"What am I going to do?" Miranda asked, serious again.

"About Cruz? What do you mean? It's not like you can decide you're not in love. Unfortunately, that I know to

181

be true. Do you want to be in love? I have so many questions."

"Hello, me, accountant, Cruz, boss. There's that for starters."

"Technically the estate or Jake is your boss, or your bosses are your boss. Obviously it's not important. Next," Lily said.

"As you and Roxanna could so obviously see, I fell hard and fast, Lily. That must make me weak or fickle or something."

"Oh please!" Lily sighed. "Anyone who's had to deal with what you've had to deal with in life and come out as successful and put together as you isn't weak. And I'm not only talking about your relationship with your mother. I know what it's like to be a woman in a typically male profession. And falling in love fast doesn't make you fickle, especially when it's someone as good as Cruz. He's a good man, Miranda. Trust me."

"When you say all of that, my words sound ridiculous, but I can't help thinking or worrying that something's not right. Maybe I'm afraid he doesn't love me back or, even if he could, that I might not be what he wants. I don't know what he really wants, if he wants to be here in Graciella, or to get back to traveling and taking photos. He holds back a part of himself when we're together."

"Hmm, I don't know what he's told you about his past," Lily said.

"He told me about how abusive and mean T.D. was to him and Adam, and how manipulative he was in dividing up the estate the way he did."

"Well, that's huge, the fact that he opened up at all about that. I'd bet there are only a handful of people on the planet who know that information and you're one of them. Whether he'll admit it or not, that man has scars from T.D. I bet he's scared to death to love someone like you, or to admit it. You have to be patient and keep opening your heart to him."

"You make it sound so easy, Lily."

"Maybe not easy," Lily said, "as I've loved someone who never loved me back. But worth it, don't you think? You have to say, 'Yes,' you know, because I am living vicariously through you right now and I choose to believe in happy endings."

Right then, sitting on that beautiful back deck with a new friend and love in her heart, Miranda wanted to believe in happy endings too.

# Chapter Twenty-Two

By the weekend, she still didn't have the answer she was looking for. "Damn IRS! Do they want their money or not?" She and her contact in Washington had been playing phone tag for two days and it wasn't something she could discuss over messages.

"You sure go in deep when you're working, don't you?" Cruz's voice yanked her out of her thoughts. He stood in the doorway, leaning up against it with his hands in the pockets of his charcoal-gray dress pants.

"You startled me," she said with her hand on her chest.

"Sorry," he said, but he was laughing at her reaction. "You really did look lost in there and very serious, especially with those glasses on and talking to yourself. You looked like you were giving someone a very serious lecture."

He walked over to the desk, kissed her on the lips and took her glasses off. "Hey," he whispered, and kissed her again. He pulled away only to press his forehead against hers.

"Hey." She couldn't prevent the smile from spreading over her face.

"I missed you." He pulled her up so she was standing next to him, against him. He kissed her temple and ran his hands up and down her arms.

"Mmm," she murmured. She couldn't think when he was touching her. He took away all her thoughts, her worries, for him, for her, for anything in front of her.

"Where have you been all week? Where have *I* been? Why haven't I been here doing this?" He trailed kisses down her neck.

"How was Portland?" she asked between sighs.

"Mind-numbing. Going to agricultural conventions, I must say, is not my favorite part of farming. Two entire days of meetings." He brought his hands up to her head and released the clip to run his hands through her hair. "I feel like I've been in meetings since the beginning of time."

"That's awfully dramatic," Miranda said, teasing him.

"You laugh, but I could have been here, kissing you." He teased her with his mouth, lightly brushing her lips with his while he spoke. "And my head hurts." He kissed her again. "Make it feel better." This time he took the kiss deep, pulling her in closer.

Gone was the chill that had surrounded her when she'd been lost in worry over the audit. Her entire body grew warm at his touch, his kisses. She loved the feel of his body up against hers, how intimately she felt his touch.

"Better?" she asked when they finally pulled apart. *Better is such a good word,* she thought, giddy with the shimmers he sent through her body. *She* certainly felt better.

"Almost." His voice was seducing her and his hands kneading her head and neck were like sweet agony. She wrapped her arms around his neck and he plundered. He turned her so she leaned against the desk and he roamed the sides of her body with his hands, never leaving her mouth, as if he couldn't get enough. Stepping closer, he nudged her legs apart with one of his. He started to kiss her neck and down, one hand braced on the desk and the other reaching up under her blouse. When his fingers touched her skin, the shock of warmth nearly undid her.

"Cruz, stop." Miranda put her hand on her chest. "We can't here."

He stopped, but he didn't pull away. "Miranda, Miranda, what you do to me. I nearly took you right here on the desk in the library." She felt his smile against her neck. His breathing slowed and he rested his chin on her head.

She started to chuckle. She tried to stop it, but couldn't help it.

He leaned back and looked at her. "And you're laughing. I'm so glad my torture is your pleasure."

"I'm sorry, Cruz, I can't. I thought, what if Elena had come in while you and I were..." She recovered enough to continue, "She'd have gone running with embarrassment, or maybe she would have reprimanded us." And she doubled over in laughter. Tears were pouring down her face while Cruz stared and smiled at her.

He stood back and watched her. "Ms. Jenks, you startle me with these bawdy thoughts. Certainly puts a whole new spin on the idea of housekeeping, doesn't it? Wanna risk it?"

"Stop, Cruz." Tears were streaming down her face from the laughter.

He raised one eyebrow at her. "You started it."

She rose on her tiptoes and kissed him gently with both hands on his chest. "*You* started it."

"Hmm, I guess I did. Shall we go somewhere where we can finish it?" He nibbled on her bottom lip.

"I would love to, but I still have a few things to get done tonight," she said and took a deep breath, remembering what she'd been worried about before he'd interrupted her. She wanted, needed to determine whether T.D. had ever paid taxes on the account she'd found this week. It was important she know before she told Cruz about it, and she had a bad feeling she wasn't going to like what she discovered.

"I could easily forget all my responsibilities around you." He rubbed her fingers in his. "But I have a few things to check on as well while it's still light out. Can I invite myself to your cottage with a pizza and wine around seven-thirty?"

"That sounds perfect," she said.

He squeezed her hands and she watched him walk away.

*Miranda, Miranda, how are you going to feel when he walks away from you for the last time? Will you be able to pick your heart up off the ground in the millions of pieces it'll be in?* Even though she'd never been in love before, she knew now what it felt like. And she also knew it would break her heart when things were over between them, when she would have to leave him behind.

"What are you going to think of me when I'm the one to deliver all this bad news to you, Cruz? Will you still want me then?"

No matter how much she wanted to find the answer right now, the answer she suspected was there, fate wasn't in her favor tonight. It was almost laughable how many times she had worked on audits where the IRS was involved and, no matter how badly they wanted their money, they still ran by such strict government hours and bureaucracy. Not to mention the time change didn't help. Three hours behind was a heavy weight on her shoulders tonight.

There was still plenty to do, and even as she flew through the numbers and the accounts, the one unsolved piece to the puzzle was the one frustrating her as she packed up her things for the evening. It was later than she thought when she headed out of the main house for her walk back to the cottage. The rain had come and gone again, the clouds had cleared out completely and above her was a darkened sky with stars and a hint of a slumbering moon.

She tried to talk herself out of it, this feeling she had that once Cruz—once they all—knew how bad things were, they would blame her. A coldhearted accountant with a thirst for dollar signs would destroy their lives and leave with a big fat paycheck, on to the next job and more money.

Stepping up onto the porch, she saw Cruz was already there waiting for her, his head resting on the back of the oversized wicker chair he sat on, his feet up on the table, arms crossed over his chest. He was so beautiful to look at. *Does he even know how he makes every environment he's in ablaze?*

"I was thinking about you," he said without opening his eyes.

"I thought you were sleeping."

"Dreaming of you."

She had to tell him, even though it was the last thing she wanted to do. He looked so relaxed and happy. Okay, maybe the look he gave her wasn't necessarily relaxed. He always looked like he could devour her with his eyes.

She put her laptop and briefcase on the coffee table next to the pizza box and saw the short fat vase overflowing with deep purple peonies. "Oh, Cruz, you brought me flowers." She buried her nose in the blooms. The sweet scent overwhelmed her. "No one's ever brought me flowers before," she said before she could think to be embarrassed by her admission.

He reached over and pulled her onto his lap. "Miranda," he said, burying his face in her hair. "I'm sorry it took me so long to think of it. It's been on my mind, bringing you flowers, showing you a little romance., I love your hair, the way it feels, the seductive scent. It's intoxicating. I wasn't asleep when you got here. I couldn't fall asleep with thoughts of you, thoughts of what I'd like to do to you on my mind—they've been on my mind all week."

She'd missed him. Running her hands through his hair, she let emotions take over and let everything else go as she poured all of herself into a kiss. Here and now was all that mattered. She would take and give everything.

"Don't let go," he said. He wrapped his arms around her and stood. Desire raced through her at his intense tone. She wanted him now.

She wrapped her legs around him as he carried her into the cottage. They nearly fell against the door as he leaned to shut it. "Clothes," she said on a ragged breath as he kissed her neck, her chest, his touch left her entire body wanting. "Why are there so many clothes?" She ran her hands up under his shirt to roam over his chest. His skin felt as hot as she felt, on fire with need.

"Bed." Cruz struggled to get the word out. She let go of his neck long enough to pull his shirt off. Her hands roamed everywhere. He made it up the stairs, fell with her onto the bed and ripped her blouse open, reaching under her bra to ravage her breasts, to take his fill.

She lost herself as he ravaged her, took her up and over the edge. His mouth left her breasts and he roamed lower, yanking her skirt and underwear down in one pull so he could feast on her there where she was throbbing, waiting, wanting. She came again, so quickly, so powerfully it rocked her entire body. Lost in the heady, desired haze of all that was Cruz and his lovemaking, before she could blink, he was over her, sliding on a condom. He gripped her hands with one of his and locked them over her head and in one strong motion thrust himself deep and hard into her. With his other hand, he pulled her closer together where power met power and together they dove into the fire.

He lay on top of her, his heavy breathing slowing. Her heart thumped against his, beat for beat. "Are you all right?" he asked into her hair. She loved how he was always nuzzling her neck and breathing in her hair. Such a tender gesture from such a fierce, amazing lover.

"Am I alive?" she asked and his body shook with a laugh. She wrapped her arms around him to keep him there. She never wanted him to leave. "Did we, am I…are we still on the planet?"

"Did I hurt you?" He shifted slightly to the side. He sounded genuinely concerned now.

"My body's never felt so wonderfully sore, Cruz. If that's what you mean by hurt. When can we try that again?"

"It might kill us both to do that again."

"I'm willing to try if you are," Miranda said playfully.

Cruz laughed. He got up to dispose of the condom them climbed in next to her and turned her so they faced each other. He threw one leg over hers and snuggled her closer. "I might need a few minutes to recover."

"You, Cruz Brockman, need a break?"

He pinched her thigh. "You weren't the only one ravished, Ms. Jenks. So much for romance. I lose my mind around you."

The way he looked deep into her melted her. "Felt like romance to me, Cruz." She'd never been ravished so completely before.

"I have an idea," he said, tapping her forehead with his finger.

"I like your ideas. Does it require movement or thought of any kind, though?"

"How about if we refuel with some pizza and wine and see what we can come up with for later, when I bring you back upstairs to bed?"

# Chapter Twenty-Three

She woke with Cruz's arm draped over her, his face buried in her neck. At some point last night he must have pulled the covers over them both as they'd fallen asleep. *More like passed out.* It was early, but the sky was already beginning to change, the midnight blue from last night easing into cobalt. Her internal clock told her it was after five a.m.

"Awake?" Cruz asked pulling her towards him so her back rested against his chest.

"Mmm-hmm," she murmured. "Look at the sky."

They gazed out of the large picture window facing the coast, skimming out over the tips of the trees. "It's almost as beautiful as you. They're going to be short a few men this morning. I told them I'd help out at the barns. Come with me. There's something I want to show you before I get to work."

"Let me take a quick shower and see if my brain cells recover."

He kissed the back of her head and got up. "I'll make some coffee."

"I thought we could walk," he said when she came downstairs twenty minutes later. She took the travel coffee mug Cruz gave her as he went to his truck to grab his camera bag. She'd finished putting on one of the old jackets and a pair of rain boots when Cruz met her on the back porch. "Chilly out this morning."

"Gorgeous, isn't it?" she said.

"Breathtaking," he said and smiled at her. "Gonna make for some great shots." He took her hand as they set off down the path. Overnight the sky had cleared, and with it the warm layer. The rains had left everything damp and shimmering. With the dampness and the crisp sky every scent seemed magnified — the wet earth, the fir trees, the sweet apple blossoms and the strong perfume of the lilacs. *So many wonderful scents.* She loved how nothing was covered up or blanketed by the intense humidity she was used to in Houston. Each smell was distinct and provocative. Houston, that place she'd lived for so long, seemed like a bad dream, one she was having trouble remembering and glad of it. Here and now was what she wanted to concentrate on.

"What are you taking pictures of this early in the morning?" she asked.

"*We.* What are we taking pictures of?" he corrected, squeezing her hand.

"Ha. I can't actually remember the last time I took a photograph of anything, if maybe ever," she said.

"I'll teach you. You'll love it, especially when you see the subject matter."

The path took them through the orchard over a few steep steps down the rocks. Cruz reached up and helped Miranda. She leaned into him for a kiss, then rested her head on his shoulder as he hugged her. Even with the surrounding spring blossoms lit up by the night's rain, the smell of earth and wet dirt and hay hit her, along with his scent. She breathed it in, male and spicy and always that lingering cologne on his sweater. With the earth and hay, it grounded her and made her heart flip at the same time.

He put his arm around her shoulders and led her down past a smaller barn and a field that stretched beyond. The horses were out, eating. As Miranda neared one side of the fence she saw her. *Sunflower.*

"Cruz." Her words were a whisper. "Look at her. Oh, there are more, two, three. Oh, my goodness." She climbed up on the fence and watched them. Two black foals, one nearly midnight with a black mane and silly white patches on her legs, another all black one and Sunflower with her rich mahogany coat. They were all eating, mamas and babies together as the sky changed in the distance, still dark blue but with some patches of pink and orange in the clouds. The foals were both beautiful and funny-looking with their too-long legs.

He stood a few yards away. He'd set up his tripod and was attaching his camera to it so it looked right in between two of the fence rails. She studied him as he looked through the lens and adjusted the focus. She wondered if she'd ever tire of watching him.

"Here," he said and positioned her to look through the lens. He adjusted the tripod gently for her height.

It changed things, what she saw, how she saw. It was like tuning an internal gear in her brain to focus differently. Cruz stood behind her. He leaned his body in close to hers and lowered his head to her ear. "Close your left eye." He took her hand and placed it on the lens to show her how to turn it to adjust the distance. Instinctively she placed her other hand on the camera, even though the tripod held it for her. Through the lens she watched the horses, the calm, tall, strong mothers and the small, gangly foals, the fence beyond and the grass and trees rising up the small hill in the background. Little patches of light danced off a few leftover puddles where the foals played. Everything looked soft in the early morning light.

"Go ahead," he said stepping away. "Take a shot whenever you think you're ready."

"I can't," she said, "there's so much going on. I don't know what to focus on, how to frame it." Even though the horses stood still for the most part as they ate, she couldn't get over the scene, the colors, the lines, the light and dark.

"Take several, then. Push the button whenever you want."

As she looked through the lens and tried to train her brain to fend off her other senses, Luna brushed her head down and rubbed it on Sunflower's head. Miranda took the shot. Luna reached back for more grass and Sunflower followed her lead. Miranda took another shot. She stood and looked over the camera and fence.

"Good. Let's take it off the tripod and move around. I'll show you how different the pictures look depending on where the light is." As the glow of the new day spread around them, gently changing the look of things, Cruz moved her around the fence and had her try different shots from different angles.

"Want to see?" Cruz asked. He nudged her gently aside and took the camera from her to look at the pictures. "You're a natural." He showed her the first shot she'd taken.

"Oh," she gasped in surprise. Luna and Sunflower were in focus and bathed in a soft golden light. She'd caught the shot as Luna touched her mouth to nuzzle Sunflower's head. It looked like love, like pure love for her baby. Luna's white body stood out in front of the dark fence. Sunflower's auburn coat added another layer to the photograph. And the sky beyond them? The colors were brilliant, blue and hazy orangey-pink fading out now even as they stood there.

She scrolled through the other photos, the ones he had taken before her, and came to one of Sunflower shaking her head. Drops of water whirled through the shot, shining like diamonds around her face. The contrast was lovely, the light amazing. There was another of Sunflower and the other two foals standing, long gangly legs holding up their strong bodies, brilliant light directly behind them putting the three in full silhouettes, dark against the glowing pink sky. "This is gorgeous," she said. "I've never seen any of your photos in color. I love this, the way you captured them in a pale pink spotlight."

He wrapped his arms around her from behind, fitting his hands to hers on the camera to show her how to change the photo to black and white directly.

"I had no idea you could do so much manipulating on the camera itself."

"It's convenient. The computer editing programs allow you to do pretty awesome stuff too. I still love a darkroom, but technology has made it much easier to get good photos much quicker, or at least be able to see immediately if it will be a good shot."

"Why do you do it?" Miranda asked turning in his arms to look back up at him. "I mean what do you love about it?"

"This," he said, taking her lips with his.

"I'm serious." She pulled away slightly, taking a mental photograph of his face, the deep blue of his eyes, the way his black hair curled, those strong lips and the set of his jaw. He could look so broody at times. And as gorgeous as broody looked on him, she wondered what had put the solemnity there right now.

"I like trying to capture that perfect moment, the emotions. Fear, love, pain, beauty, anger, desolation, triumph. I capture that one moment then move on to find another. It's the search I love."

She wondered if he was always going to be searching, if that need would always be in him.

"Look," he said, turning her back towards the horses.

Sunflower was nickering around her mother, dipping her head up and down as she trotted a few paces away and back again to shake her head at Luna, as if she was teasing her to play. Luna stood in the growing light, eating and swatting her tail at Sunflower every few seconds. Eventually Sunflower turned and trotted to play with the other foals, running and stopping and chasing.

"Like children. They look so happy and playful, frolicking," she said. She tried to let it go, the knowledge that as much as she wanted Cruz, she might not be enough for him, he might always be searching. How easily he could change the subject when she asked him something personal about himself. And yet, everything he showed her, this farm, the horses, his friends, his lovemaking, through all of it, he showed her his heart. *How can he not know that?*

He put his camera around his neck and poured them some coffee from the Thermos. "Your hands are cold," he said, putting the mug in her hands.

The scent of hot coffee traveled to her face with the steam. "Mmm, everything seems to taste and smell so much better here, Cruz."

He winked at her and moved around again to take some more shots.

"I guess I never really thought about it, but I can see why you wanted to come out here this early. The light is magnificent, every color deep as if it's been infused, like I'm looking at everything through a filter, and yet at the same time everything seems to be surrounded in a soft glow."

"I love the morning light, especially here on the coast after a good rain," he said.

She drank and watched him for a little while longer and, with regret, knew she had to get to work. It was as if the day agreed with her. The sun was fully up now and the dramatic change of color in the landscape as it rose over the eastern hills was done. The magic was gone. *Well, maybe not completely gone,* she thought, watching the new foals play and witnessing how graceful Cruz was in his element.

"You going to play all day or get to work?" Adam yelled from the doorway of one of the barns. He walked towards Miranda and took his gloves off. "Miranda, you look lovely as usual. Hey," he said to Cruz. "You teaching her to use that toy of yours?"

"You're jealous of my talent." Cruz walked toward them.

"Who said anything about talent?"

She watched the brothers tease each other and saw how easy and goofy they were. Adam put his arm around Cruz's shoulders. "Does your lady know who you really are then?" Adam pointed to Cruz's camera.

"She does," Cruz said and glanced at Miranda when Adam called her his lady, but she smiled at him as the sunlight warmed her face.

"I have one of his photographs framed in Houston," she said to Adam.

"Spectacular, isn't he? This is like a toy to me." He indicated the camera. "But in his hands, he seems to make magic happen with it."

"Stop. Go do whatever it is you do. I'm going to walk Miranda to the house. I'll be back to help."

"I'm fine by myself, Cruz. Get to work. I know you're busy," Miranda said.

"I'll walk you,"

"Cruz, I'm fine, I have been known to walk on my own before."

"Funny, aren't you? At least let me help you up to the path." He climbed up and reached for her hand before she could argue.

"Thank you, Cr —"

He pulled her in and kissed the words away. Rough and needy, his lips took hers, as though he could never get enough.

"Will I see you later?" he asked when he pulled away.

"I'd like that." *I don't want to spend a night without you until the end*, she thought.

He left her then, jumped down the ledge and jogged over toward the barn. *It's a good thing I'm walking*, she thought, watching him. "I'll need the walk to wipe the fuzz off my brain you put there," she said to herself. The man could kiss the balance right out of her.

# Chapter Twenty-Four

On Wednesday morning, a light fog settled over the farm, obscuring the ocean in the distance but playing tricks with the trees, hiding some and allowing others to peek through, like wispy strands of cobwebs shrouding throughout. It seemed fitting that Miranda was lost in thought. Cruz had left at sunrise. They'd spent every night together since he'd been back from Portland. Now, as she dressed, she thought of him, of this place, of her job, and she was utterly confused about what to do with her life. The fog fit her mood, beautiful and mysterious and troubled all at the same time.

She liked watching it through the large windows facing down to where she knew the water was, as though she was high above the clouds, floating in the cottage. The only problem was that she missed her walks to the beach. It struck her as odd that in barely three weeks she'd grown to love walking outside on the mulched path down to the water, that wide-open water, not crystal-clear blue like the Gulf, but dark and brooding—like

Cruz, in a way. *It's definitely too foggy for a walk down to the beach,* she thought as she stepped outside.

With the fine mist around her, blanketing everything in quiet, she walked over to the main house. Lost in the muffled world of the fog and thoughts of Cruz, the scent hit her, like a lover's caress, heady, musky, spicy. It flustered her. The part of her that wasn't confused felt awakened or stirred. It was an essence she'd been chasing for years. She took a deep breath.

"Wonderful, isn't it?" Katie said.

Startled, Miranda saw Katie standing there on the path.

"Is it roses? I've never smelled roses like that before. It's like what you read about in historic fiction or old romances, musky and a bit spicy. It smells like what you wish roses really smelled like, not like what you find in the grocery store or florist shop. I've indulged myself over the years with different rose lotions and soaps and shampoos, trying to find one with that perfect scent, but nothing's come close."

"Roses it is. Look," Katie said gesturing to a line of bushes, taller than both women, beyond the guest house and around towards the new garden. "They're planted all over the estate. When I finally left, it was what I missed most, the only thing I really mourned. After a rain or with the morning fog at this time of year, when the blooms are starting, it's quite amazing. I've been making up excuses every day to come over and wait for a morning like today. I think Javier sees right through me, but he indulges me."

"I don't think I've ever smelled anything so beautiful. It's like I can't get enough, like it's filling a place inside, a place that's been waiting for it." Miranda hugged her bag to her chest. "Well, that probably sounded ridiculous, didn't it?"

Katie smiled. "Not at all. It's exactly how I feel. I love it here, the land, the air, the people. I love every season, but I long for this moment every spring for the roses to cast their spell on me, like the beginning of so much growth for me. We all long for spring, for new life, for that promise."

They turned and walked towards the back porch. "Besides," Katie said, "You know roses are the flower of love and beauty, don't you? And you, Miranda, are glowing with both of those right now."

Embarrassment rushed up Miranda's neck to her cheeks.

"I'm sorry. I'm sure you probably don't approve of me getting involved with Cruz, with someone I work for."

"Stop." Katie put her hand on Miranda's arm. "Why wouldn't I approve? We all want love. Whether we're brave enough to search for it depends on the person. You're a remarkable, kind, intelligent, beautiful woman who looks like she's fallen in love with my son. And I don't see anything wrong with it. You're still going to do your job and do it well, I'm sure.

"More importantly, who am I to judge anyone? Regardless of my past — and we all have one — it's not my place to approve or disapprove. I like to think you and I are becoming friends, Miranda, and approval isn't what we should seek from our friends. I should have said, 'It makes me happy to see you happy.' It's lovely the way it shows all over your face."

"I used to be so good at hiding my emotions, Katie."

"I could sense that about you the day I met you, but then I saw you looking at the photograph in the cottage and I could also see you weren't happy keeping everything so hidden and closed up. I certainly understand the need for it at times in our lives. Believe me, I've been there. And it saved me for a time, but I'm so grateful that I'll never go back to that kind of place. It's lonely. No one should be that lonely."

"No," Miranda said, searching Katie's face. "You're right."

"Look, now I've gone and gotten us all serious and maudlin, when we were talking about love and how wonderful you look in it. It agrees with you, and it certainly agrees with Cruz. It warms my heart to see him so happy."

What was she supposed to say to that? This was his mother she was talking to. "I'm not sure Cruz is there on the same page, in love, if you will," Miranda said carefully. She glanced at Katie as they made their way towards the house.

Katie was quiet for a moment. "Did you know he's C. Cooper?"

"Yes, he told me, or I guessed when he told me what he did for a living."

"So you can see, Miranda, even though he might not realize he's also been searching for love, it comes through in his photographs. He's got more layers than most of us. Some he deliberately built up to protect himself. You have to be brave enough to keep peeling them away. It's there. He might not know it yet.

"Now, before I start digging in the garden here, I'm going to see what Elena's made this morning. Smells like her almond croissants. Speaking of love."

Miranda smiled and stepped into the kitchen with Katie. "And my hips are going to be feeling all that love."

"You and your hips could use a bit of that kind of love. Food's a way to nurture too, and you could use plenty of that, dear."

"Am I that desperate-looking?" Miranda practically snorted.

Katie laughed. "I didn't mean to insult you." She took Miranda's hand. "You don't look desperate at all. In fact, you look absolutely put together, but I can see underneath. A mother can see through many defenses. And every time I've seen you eat, you look as though you're tasting delicious things for the first time, feeding your soul, in a way."

"I really am transparent, aren't I?" Miranda said, but smiled. "But for your information, regardless of what kind of nurturing I might need, you people seriously know how to cook. Since I've been here, I really have had the most amazing meals I've ever had in my life, Katie."

"We do like to eat, don't we?" Katie said, with that dimpled grin that put a youthful look in her expression. "And don't let what I said worry you. We're all more transparent than we like to think."

"You certainly don't look lonely anymore," Miranda said as they sipped coffee and sampled the housekeeper's morning pastries. "You've got that glow about you as well."

Katie's smile lit up the room. "I was lucky. It took a while for it to come into my life, but when Javier rode onto the farm, I took one look and my heart flipped over inside. I don't think my heart had ever done that before, not even before T.D., with someone I thought I was in love with. Javier looked at me like he felt the same. His cheeks got all flushed and he could hardly speak. I mean, the man's quiet anyway, but every time he tried to talk to me, it came out all mixed up. But he found ways to be near me. I was down at the barns a lot, helping the men, bringing food and making sure all their kids had clothes and shoes and books, and he was always there helping me.

"He rented the small house we live in now. I took him a meal and invited myself in. I never spent the night in this house again. Came home the next morning, packed a few things, got Adam and left. Filed for divorce the next week."

"Wow. What did Javier do when you walked in with food and stayed the night?"

"Well, he completely lost all power of speech." Katie held her mug with both hands, closed her eyes and smiled. "Then he found other ways to use his mouth that night."

"Katie!" Miranda started laughing. "Look at you, talk about flushed cheeks. And talk about brave. What did T.D. do?"

"Oh, Miranda." Katie took a deep breath and put her coffee down. "It didn't feel brave. It felt like I had to do it or I couldn't survive anymore. The feeling was that strong. T.D. actually gave me the divorce. By then he had plenty of mistresses, he had his power, and with the divorce, he had the estate, which was what he'd always wanted, the only reason he ever married me. Me leaving meant leaving it all behind, everything and any claim I ever had on the place."

"Katie! No, how? Why?"

"When we were married, my father had a contract drawn up, a sort of pre-nuptial agreement that if I were to die or leave, everything would be T.D.'s."

"That's horrible."

"It was. I was twenty when I found out. I cried for days, but I was a teary mess anyway. Cruz was fifteen months old, Turner was a few months old and I had just found out I was pregnant with Adam. I had been forced into a horrible marriage with someone who hated me. I wanted a divorce right then, and he laughed at me, said I could leave whenever I wanted, but he would get everything, the farm, the money, my children. He didn't want me, but he wanted my inheritance and the appearance of me, the devoted wife, the perfect family. If I left I would get nothing. So I stayed."

Miranda watched the woman re-live her shock. It played out over Katie's face as she drank her coffee, but she shook it off and her smile was back. "I don't go back there, to that person, very often, but when I do it reminds me of how lucky I am now."

Tears pricked at Miranda's vision. "You gave up everything for Javier."

"None of this seemed to matter anymore. I mean, I grieved a bit for the land that had been in my family for generations, but Javier opened my heart and made it bloom, and suddenly I wanted that more than any piece of land or security or false life. It didn't feel like giving up, but going towards, finally taking what I wanted."

"That is so beautiful, Katie."

"Oh, look at us, crying into our coffee, the both of us." Katie started them laughing again as Lily walked into the kitchen.

"What has gotten into you two? Crying and laughing and it's not even seven o'clock in the morning. And wait, I smell Elena's croissants. Tell me you saved me an almond croissant." Lily grabbed a pastry and plopped down in the chair next to Katie.

"Katie was telling me about how when Javier came to town and she seduced him with a dinner," Miranda said.

"I like to think it was my beauty more than my cooking," Katie said.

Lily sighed. "I love that story. Gets me every time how you two knew as soon as you looked at each other and how he got all tongue-tied and how you left and gave all this up." Lily gestured around her.

"And got so much more than I ever dreamed of," Katie said.

"That's the kind of love story I want." Lily patted her heart. "Oh well, I'll have to go dream of happily ever after while I'm working. I stopped by to check with Cruz about some properties in town. That man never answers his phone. Are they back yet?"

"Yes," Miranda said. And she couldn't hide her smile every time she thought of him. "He's at the barns."

"Ugh. I'll go chase him down, but since you're both here, I thought it would be nice to pamper Roxanna a bit before the baby comes. She's been complaining about needing to get a pedicure since she can't see, let alone reach, her own toes anymore. How about Friday night at my house? Rox's cousin, Mary, and her daughter said they'd close their salon in Florence early and come down to give us all pedicures. I'll make fun cocktails and something delicious to eat. We can pamper and gossip?"

"As much as I would love to, I have a date," Katie said. She got up and put her coffee mug in the dishwasher.

"Oh, do tell," Lily said.

"Javier's taking me away for two nights to a bed and breakfast in the mountains." She fluttered her eyelashes.

"Quite the romantic, isn't he?" Lily said.

"He is." Katie's face lit up in a brilliant smile. "You girls will have to do without me, but I'll make some of my chocolate truffles for you. Can't have a girls' night without chocolate. Enjoy the day," she said as she sailed out of the back door.

"I like her," Miranda said.

"Isn't she wonderful? So, are you in for pampering and pedicures? Don't tell me you have a date too?"

"No, I don't." She didn't have a date. Since Cruz had returned, they'd spent their nights together, but it had been very casual. She didn't want to ask him what they were, because she was still afraid that he didn't feel the same about her. And if he didn't, she would deal with that at the end and not a minute earlier. "Are you sure? I mean, I'm not as close as you all are."

"Stop." Lily got up and waved her words away. "We'd love to have you. Remember, Roxanna and I have plans to make you fall in love with Graciella and stay."

*The falling in love is easy,* Miranda thought. *They all make it so damn easy.* Staying was another issue entirely. But a girls' night with some women she was getting to know and enjoy sounded like something she didn't want to give up. "I'd love to come. What can I bring?"

"Good answer. How about some wine? I'll let you know what time when I talk to Mary."

Miranda was late getting started with the accounts, but she felt much better than she had earlier that morning, sitting alone in the cottage kitchen with her worries. Katie and Lily had a way of making Miranda feel she was worthy, and that something like a business connection could be a flimsy excuse for hiding from love. Katie had been through so much. She'd survived a brutal marriage, raised three boys, helped countless others and had grabbed on to love when it fell at her doorstep, no matter the consequences.

In Katie's case, it had worked out. She was happy and she deserved it. Miranda wanted to believe that about herself.

And Lily welcomed her as if she were a long-lost friend. Friendships were another sacrifice of having spent all her time working and taking care of her mother. She wanted love, family and good friends. It was too late to go back to who she'd been even a few weeks ago, when her own wants and needs had been carefully buried.

She knew there could be repercussions, but she told herself she'd worry about those later. For now, she would enjoy these wonderful people around her, take whatever time she and Cruz had together and welcome whatever he would give. Katie was correct. It wouldn't affect the job she would do for them. If anything, it motivated her to do whatever was in her power to finish their audit as fast as she could, for them, so they could get on with their lives. If Cruz wasn't the one, she would deal with that when the time came, but she was never going back to that shell of a person she'd been before.

# Chapter Twenty-Five

On Friday evening Miranda pulled up to Lily's with wine, Katie's chocolate truffles and a small print of the photo she'd taken earlier in the week, the one of Luna kissing Sunflower. She'd asked Cruz to print a copy for her. She knew it wasn't fabulous photography or anything, but she thought Roxanna might like it, the way the mother's love for her baby shimmered through, and she'd wanted to bring her something special.

Before she could knock on the door, it opened and Miguel walked out with Lily behind him.

"Miranda," he said. "So good to see you again. And thank you in advance for spoiling my beautiful wife." He turned to Lily and kissed her on the cheek. "Call me. I'll come get her when you ladies are done. I have three teenage girl cousins staying the night and watching the kids, so I'm going to have dinner and male bonding time with Cruz and Adam."

"Outnumbered at home, aren't you?" Lily smiled at him.

"I've been outnumbered by gorgeous women my entire life." He winked at Miranda and walked off to his car. "Wouldn't have it any other way," he called over his shoulder.

"Come in. Come in. I'm so excited. Roxanna looks like she's in heaven." Lily pulled Miranda into the living room. "Miranda, meet Roxanna's cousin, Mary, and her daughter, Gabby. Ladies, this is who I've been telling you about." Lily was beaming. Roxanna laughed and Miranda was completely embarrassed.

"Lily," she said. "What have you been telling them about me?"

"Oh, nothing much, simply that you're here to steal Cruz's heart."

"And how much fun it's been to see him take the fall," Roxanna added.

Before she could be embarrassed, Lily took her things and Mary led her down into the leather chair, where they had a portable pedicure bath waiting for her feet. "It is very nice to meet you, Miranda. Rox and Lily have been gushing about you," Mary said.

"They already have your wedding already planned," Gabby added, laughing. "And if you and Cruz don't end up together, I'm pretty sure they're going to adopt you anyway."

Roxanna sat on the sofa, drinking a pink drink with a cocktail umbrella in it. Her feet were in another portable foot bath that was bubbling with something deliciously floral-scented. Lily returned with champagne glasses for the rest of them and said, "Cheers to all of my favorite ladies, and to our Rox, who's the best friend a girl could have and one of the best mothers I've ever seen. I want to be you some day."

"Stop, you're making me cry." Roxanna waved her hand in front of her face as they all clinked glasses.

"So," Gabby said with a bit of mischief in her voice as she rolled Miranda's jeans up and carefully put her feet in the hot massage bath. "Those Brockman boys look like they know how to kiss. True?"

"Gabby!" Her mother reprimanded her.

"What? Just because you and Auntie Roxy are happily married with someone to kiss you senseless, doesn't mean the rest of us can't dream of it someday. Isn't that right, Lily?" She winked at Lily.

"Exactly what I've been saying," Lily said. "And Miranda can't tell a lie, so even if she doesn't speak, the answer will be right there on her face."

Miranda smacked Lily on the arm as they all laughed. She sat back in the chair with her champagne and let Gabby rub the delicious honey scrub over her legs and feet. "I can't speak for Adam and Turner," Miranda said, smiling, "but Cruz, well, let's say the man's got talent."

"Ha!" Lily said. "Not embarrassed anymore, are you? Good for you, lady. You're among friends. You know that. Or we wouldn't tease you."

"Believe me, I'm still a bit embarrassed talking so openly about these things. I never had any of it to talk about before, but you all make me feel included and normal."

"Never?" Lily asked.

Miranda shook her head and took another swallow of her drink. The embarrassment was there then, creeping up her cheeks.

"Why didn't you tell us?" Roxanna asked softly.

"I hardly know you all. I mean, it doesn't feel that way now, but in the beginning, I didn't...well, the fact that I'm completely ignorant and inexperienced isn't something I go around broadcasting."

"The better question," Mary began when they all stopped laughing, "Is what the hell is wrong with the men of the world? Or the women? Not that I think a woman needs to have had many lovers to find the right man, but that you three beauties" — she pointed to Lily, Miranda and Gabby — "are still unspoken for. Stupid and blind is what those fools are. And that Cruz Brockman better step up and claim you soon before someone else comes along."

"I'll agree that there are some stupid ones out there, but I'm focused on my career now so it's fine," Lily said.

"Me too," Gabby said. "I don't need any complications at the moment, but I wouldn't mind some talented kisser to warm up my lips, or the rest of my body."

Relaxed, Miranda laughed with the rest of them, but she was glad the focus had gone from her and Cruz. A part of her was filled with doubt. She wasn't certain Cruz was going to step up and claim her at all. And, oh, how she wanted him to.

\* \* \* \*

"Cruz, you went all out on the accommodations, I see," Miguel teased as he walked into the barn.

They'd set up a folding table and chairs, and next to it on an overturned crate sat a cooler of beer and pizzas.

"Cruz? Adam?" Miguel called again.

"Over here," Cruz called from the back of the barn, where he and Adam were repairing one of the enormous doors.

"Finally. Can we eat yet?" Adam said shooting Miguel a grin. "Get lost, did ya?"

"Probably had a hard time dragging himself away from a house full of gorgeous women," Jake said from his crouch while he finished hammering in the last nail.

"They dragged you in too, huh?" Miguel laughed. "Got invited to play cards and here you are fixing a barn door."

"It's always something with these brothers, isn't it?" Jake stood up, wiped his hands off and shook Miguel's. "Good to see you. Proud father again yet, or still waiting?"

"Still waiting. Jesus, that'll make six. Six kids. I need a beer."

"You love it, the big family," Cruz said. "You can't fool us."

Miguel grinned. "I do love it, but I'm way past ready for some company. When are one of you idiots going to get hitched and start having kids?"

Jake put his hands up. "Don't look at me. I haven't had a date in months."

"Months? What the hell's wrong with you?" Adam smacked him on the back. "That's okay. Cruz'll be next. As soon as he realizes he's head over heels for Miranda."

The three walked over to the table and Cruz stood there in shock. Miguel turned back. "You look like someone knocked the wind out of you, Cruz. You look scared to death. Oh boy, you really are a goner."

"So how does it feel?" Adam asked.

"What?"

"To be head over heels, Cruz," Jake asked. "You didn't think your best friends were going to ignore that comment, did you?"

He grabbed a beer and drank long and hard. "I'm not," he said.

"Liar." Adam laughed. "It's a good thing, Cruz. She's drop-dead gorgeous, intelligent and easy to be around. She's lost in you, too, so what's the problem?"

*Lost in you too.* Cruz swallowed the words. He hadn't meant to fall, but they were correct. He was in deep, and she was right there with him. He'd felt it when they were photographing the horses, surrounded by the morning light and how stunning she looked with her face lit up in awe. His heart had fallen hard and fast, like a fist to the gut. He'd never planned on falling in love. And he knew he couldn't give her everything she deserved — a husband, kids, a family. Some people weren't built that way. It was in his genes and his upbringing, double strikes against him.

Somehow he'd always been okay with that knowledge, and he hadn't cared, as he'd traveled around the world on one assignment or another. He'd had relationships, but he'd never been sorry when they ended and he'd easily moved on, left things and people behind. He'd never hurt or been afraid like this in the middle of a relationship.

He felt stripped bare by his feelings for her, jagged and vulnerable. Cruz rubbed the ache in his chest. "There is no problem. We're enjoying each other's company. That's all." *It can't be more than that.* "Are you going to deal so we going to play cards? Or we gonna act like girls and talk about relationships all night?"

"Touchy, aren't you?" Adam said.

"That's okay, Adam, you can be the first to say, 'I told you so,' when Cruz finally comes to his senses," Jake said and finished his pizza.

"Do you think he's that smart?" Adam asked. "I'm not so sure, he seems pretty dense sometimes."

Jesus, now they were talking around him like he wasn't even there. "Deal," Cruz said, punching Adam in his shoulder.

\* \* \* \*

Later, the ladies sat on the back deck, the water of the pool shimmering with the underwater lights. "Lily, this was such a great idea," Roxanna said. "I don't think my feet were ever more in need of pampering."

"I have to admit it was purely selfish of me. My feet wanted pampering too and I have the hardest time getting up to your salon in Florence, Mary, even though it's an hour away," Lily said.

"We need one here in town," Roxanna said.

"Do we ever," Lily sighed. "I can't wait to see what's going to happen with all those vacant properties T.D. owned in town, now that Cruz and Turner and Adam are in charge."

"The one on the corner across from the library would be perfect, wouldn't it?" Gabby sipped coffee, her feet up on the chaise by Roxanna.

Mary smiled at her daughter.

"Wait, what?" Lily faced Gabby. "You're going to open your own place? That's amazing! Here in Graciella. Yes! I'll do the work for you. I'll make it spectacular."

"You better," Gabby said. "I want feminine and sparkly and classy. I hate waiting, but I can't do anything until the estate gets settled."

There really were a lot of people connected to the settling of the Brockman estate. More than she'd ever realized. Miranda looked around at the women. People in town, families, friends, a whole community. Well, good news or bad, her part would be finished two weeks from now. God, how she wanted them all to survive the audit.

This was the first time she'd ever really been close to the people involved, the first time she'd cared deep in her heart about what would happen to them after the audit was finished. And she wanted to belong to them, with them—she wanted to be a part of them thriving.

"Ladies, I think I'm going to get going," Miranda said. "I can't thank you all enough. My feet feel wonderful, Gabby."

"Hello," Miguel called from the front of the house as he walked through to the back deck.

"My love, did you win?" Roxanna asked as he helped her up.

Miguel kissed her. "I won a long time ago."

"Stop," Roxanna said, blushing at his words.

"And," he added with a wink, "I walked away with everyone's money tonight."

Miranda got her purse and sweater as the other ladies came in. "Oh, I almost forgot, Roxanna. This is for you." She handed her the present, wrapped in sparkly silver paper.

Roxanna's eyes welled with tears when she opened the photo and looked at the mother and baby horse captured in their tender moment. Miguel put his arms around Roxanna from behind and they looked at the photo together. "It's stunning. Is it one of Cruz's?" Her voice was heavy with love and admiration.

"Actually, I took it," Miranda said. "He showed me how and got the camera all set up, but I took it."

Lily looked over her shoulder. "Miranda, it's gorgeous. Now I might cry."

"It's beautiful, Miranda. And so special." Roxanna kissed her cheek and whispered, "Don't give up on him."

"Miranda, do you want us to give you a ride?" Miguel asked.

"No, I'm fine, thank you. I'm going to go to Cruz's."

"Mmm-hmm, I have to admit, having a man to go home to instead of a house full of younger sisters and cousins does sound lovely." Gabby sighed.

"You'll find your true love one day," Roxanna said. "I know all."

As Miranda drove away she wondered. *True love.* Was it really possible?

Cruz was asleep when she got to his house. He didn't answer when she knocked so she let herself in, thinking he might be on the back porch, but she found him on the couch, the baseball game on the television, and he was out. She sat down in his oversized leather chair and watched him while he slept. Her heart swelled. This man, this amazing, kind, passionate, driven man had shaken her world upside down, like Lily had said. And so much that was important to him was hanging on her work. That was a burden she'd never carried before. She closed her eyes to think and drifted off to sleep herself.

# Chapter Twenty-Six

Cruz walked to his bar to choose a wine for dinner. Tonight, he wanted to seduce her with more of his cooking. There was something about watching her eat. It was almost as sensual as making love to her. His mind strayed from the wine refrigerator as he pictured her naked in his bed, reaching up to him. And there she was walking up the porch steps, as if he'd conjured her.

He opened the door before she could knock and offered her a bouquet of dark orange tulips, beautiful and mysterious-looking, like her. There was that surprise on her face that he loved putting there.

"Cruz." She held them out to her. "You brought me flowers the other night."

"I know, but you told me no one ever had, and I kind of like being the one who does. I like the surprise and delight it puts on your face." He took her hand and led her inside.

"Hungry? Javier caught some trout. I was waiting for you so I could put it on the grill. White or red?" he asked, pulling out two bottles.

"Cruz." Her voice was so serious.

"What's wrong?" he asked setting the wine bottles down on the bar. He wanted to touch her, to take that horrible look out of her eyes, but she held herself away and it scared him. "Miranda?"

"Cruz, I need to tell you something about the audit. I need to get it all out. T.D. had hidden foreign accounts. I began finding clues to them when you were gone in Portland. Tonight I discovered that he never reported any of it to the IRS. It's substantial, over a million dollars. I don't know yet what the fines will be, but it's not good."

"Damn! That bastard!" He closed his eyes and took in a deep breath as he paced back and forth.

"I'm so sorry. I'll go and let you —"

"No." He pulled her to him and wrapped his arms around her. "Stay. Please."

She ran her hands across his back as his silence wrapped around them.

"I was hoping it wouldn't be there, but I knew it would be bad as soon as you and Jake mentioned the investigation. Typical T.D. When is it going to end? This sounds horrible, but I was so relieved when he died. I thought, finally, we can all take a deep breath and live now."

"I'm sorry he's still hurting you," she whispered, kneading the muscles on his back, sending shots of desire through him.

She took his breath away. He knew, even more now, that he would have to let her go. Maybe he could never have a lifetime with her, but damned if he wouldn't take her as his while she was still here. He knew better than most that taking advantage of each moment was all that mattered sometimes. He breathed her in where her hair brushed against her neck. He ran his fingers up her back and crushed her to him.

"Miranda." He brought her face to his, tried to will the truth of what would happen in the end into her, but she wouldn't see it, couldn't see it. He wanted to wrap himself in her warmth and forget where and who he was for the night. He brushed his thumb across her lips, open and inviting, then crushed his mouth to hers.

The pull of desire shot through him as she opened to him, his tongue tasting hers, trying to find the essence of each other. Their hands battled to get clothes off. She tugged at his belt. He ripped her skirt and lace underwear down and kicked them away, bringing his hand back to her, to her core. "You're wet for me, Miranda. You want me."

"Yes." She was breathless. He wanted her breathless.

He lifted her and brought his mouth to her breast, sucking and teasing through the thin fabric of her sweater while he caressed her soft skin.

Then his hand was back to her heat. He thrust one, then two fingers in, and teased her up and up, just shy of taking her over the edge. She cried out his name. He wanted to see her need. She writhed against his fingers and traced a path along his neck with her tongue.

He aimed to drive her mad, but she was the one with power over him, with her intoxicating spicy scent, the way she tasted, her soft skin, her blazing heat.

He fell with her to the couch and dragged her sweater up and over her head, taking her nipple with his mouth. If he could devour her, it still wouldn't be enough. He needed to make then one, make her see there was no one else. There never had been and there never would be. "Mine," he whispered.

She pulled at his shirt, bringing her hands to his chest, and he thought he might die with the caress.

"Tell me, Miranda, tell me you want me. You're mine." *Tell me you love me.*

She ground against him.

"Tell me," he rasped, stepping away to remove his clothes.

"Don't go," she murmured.

"I'm not going anywhere," he said as he slid the condom on.

He ran his hands over her body, making her writhe. Her eyes were sparks of fire. "Tell me."

"I want you," she said and he guided himself into her on her words. "Only you, Cruz."

Her hips rose to meet his need, over and over, creating their own frantic rhythm. He wanted to drive her over the edge with sensations.

"Tell me," he whispered, on edge, he ravaged her neck with his lips. "Now, Miranda."

"Always you, Cruz." And he lost himself, going crazy with all of her surrounding him. They rocked and crashed together, broken and laid bare.

She felt shattered. He'd called her his. Pain tugged at her heart, because he made her feel like a sorceress but still he kept a part of his heart locked tight from her. His fingers linked with hers, caressing even now. His embrace was like nectar, like a potion to her. What would she do without that magic? Later, Miranda would think about picking up the pieces of her heart and moving on without him later.

"You're so quiet, Cruz." Her whole world, body and heart, had been rocked to the core. Her skin was still trembling with the sparks from his touch, and yet she could sense the weight of worry on his mind. He'd made love as if the world were ending.

"You shattered me, Miranda," he said, pulling her to him as he sat them up. He nuzzled her face and neck with his nose. "I wanted to ravage you, needed to bury my anger. I used you, and you shattered me."

She wanted to believe that was all, that their lovemaking had shattered him and that was the reason for his worry, but she knew it was more. Why couldn't he tell her everything he was feeling? She wanted all of him too.

"How do you feel?" he asked.

*My body or my heart?* she wanted to ask. "I feel completely ravaged in the best possible way, Cruz." Her voice was like a purr, smoky and satisfied. "But I think I ruined your beautiful tulips." She could be light and easy if that was what he needed.

He looked around her at the destruction on the carpet, clothes and shoes and smashed flowers, and he laughed. "I'll bring you more flowers, Miranda. You should have flowers every day."

She knew the light tone was easier for him. What she didn't know was what to do with her own intense feelings. She wanted to tell him, but she was afraid it would push him away.

"Come," he said, taking her hand and leading her to his master bathroom. He turned the shower on and pulled her under the hot water with him. "Good?" he asked.

"Glorious." She sighed as the water calmed and comforted and soothed. Her limbs were languid. She let her worries go with the water for now.

She loved the way his eyes feasted on her, as if she were his artist's muse.

She closed her eyes when he washed her. As his fingers massaged her scalp she let out a moan. "That feels amazing," she whispered. Then his soapy hands were on her shoulders, her back. He caressed her breasts then moved lower with slow, seductive strokes. She swayed lightly and let him seduce her with his hands. The soap was gone and his hands were around her, pulling her up. He parted her legs with one of his and teased her, gently massaging her core. He was hard again and eager. She loved the feel of him right there before he entered her. *Searching.* Didn't he know, couldn't he see he'd found her?

Cruz came awake with a yell surrounded by the pitch black, his face covered in sweat. Miranda stirred next to him in bed. He got up and went outside, gulping in the cool air. He stared out toward the sound of the waves in the wind as they crashed onto shore. He let the rhythm soothe his memory, his ghosts. It had been a while since he'd dreamed of T.D. yelling at him, calling him a bastard, using his belt to whip him.

The first time T.D had beaten him, he'd told his mother, and later that evening Cruz'd stood outside her bedroom listening to the shouts, then the sound of T.D.'s hand slapping her face, then her tears. That was the only time T.D. had left a mark on her, a mark that anyone could see, as appearances were so damn important to the tyrant. Cruz felt it was his fault his mother had been beaten that night, all because he'd told her what T.D. had done to him and she'd confronted the bastard. After that, Cruz had learned how to hide, how to be secretive.

He'd gotten good at paying attention and knowing when to disappear. The beatings had happened less often as he got older and learned to fight back, and he'd never told his mother again for fear of what T.D. would do to her. He'd been afraid even to tell his brothers. The shame was too great. He could see how T.D. had treated Turner like a real son, and even though Turner had been Cruz's best friend as boys, Cruz knew they'd been treated differently. He might have gone his whole life without telling his brothers if he hadn't seen T.D. unleash his cruelty on Adam once. By then Cruz and Turner had both been big enough to at least attempt to fight back, to protect Adam. And Cruz had finally confided in his brothers. He'd been twelve and they'd vowed to always protect each other.

But the nightmares were still in him. He couldn't exorcise the memories from his mind. They would always be there, haunting him. That shame would always be in his heart.

He walked back to the bed and watched Miranda sleep in the moonlight, taking in every last inch of her to tuck away in his memory for when she was no longer his.

# Chapter Twenty-Seven

"Miranda, are you joining us for dinner tonight?" Katie stepped into the library.

Miranda closed her laptop as Katie walked in. "Yes, I'd love to."

"Do you still have work to do or would you like to help me cook? Or, if you like, you could sit, have a glass of wine and keep me company until the boys get here."

"I would love to help you, Katie. I feel like I've been sitting all day and I would love to get out of my head. I'll take my stuff back to the cottage to change then come help you."

"Perfect."

They walked towards the back door together. "I invited Lily too. She should be here any minute. And I hope you like lamb chops."

"I don't think I've ever had them," Miranda said.

"Well, I can promise you a delicious meal, and no disappearing act this time, either."

Miranda changed into some comfy skinny jeans and flats and a soft gray turtleneck sweater, and joined Katie in the kitchen. Lily was sitting at the island, opening wine.

"We were just talking about you," Lily said and kissed Miranda's cheek. "We're still scheming again on how we can get you to stay in Graciella when you're done with the audit. We've got lots of ideas."

There was that feeling of longing again, fluttering inside Miranda. If she could stay anywhere, it would be right here.

"Here's an apron, dear. Come over and I'll put you to work," Katie said.

Lily poured wine and put some music on and the three ladies marinated lamb chops, shredded potatoes for potato cakes and chopped mint to go with the peas. Katie and Lily teased each other and laughed. It was the warmth and the laughter Miranda would remember when she was gone.

She noticed him before the others did and their eyes locked onto each other. *Speechless*—he rendered her speechless.

"Ladies," Cruz said.

"Cruz, it's a good thing you got here when you did. We've been telling Miranda stories about you and your brothers when you were kids." Lily gave him a hug.

"Oh, no," he said. "Mom." He kissed her cheek while she cooked the potato cakes on the stove. Then he came up behind Miranda, put his arms around her and leaned over. "Hi, what are you making?"

"I'm chopping mint for the pea and mint puree. Your mother and Lily are teaching me a new recipe."

"You look nice. I like seeing you relaxed and happy with my family," he whispered into her ear.

Why couldn't this be enough for him? She wanted to stay here with him and his family. She wanted to *be* his family.

"Cruz, are your brother and Javier on their way?" Katie asked.

"Yes, they're heading over from the barns. I came from home."

When they sat down to eat, the hum of conversations continued. *Such a wonderful sound,* Miranda thought, after eating so many silent meals by herself with music or the television for company over the years. After a toast to family and friendship, she took a bite of her meal, potato on the bottom, then lamb and the pea and mint puree, with a bit of chopped shallot and tomatoes, all topped with a reduced beef jus. "Katie, this is divine. Am I drooling?"

"She's right, Mom," Adam said. "This might be the best lamb I've ever tasted."

"Miranda did most of it," Katie said. "I showed her what to do and cooked the potatoes."

"I never knew I could cook like this. This is gourmet," Miranda said. "You all seriously know how to cook. You should open your own restaurant."

"That is an excellent idea," Cruz said.

"Where on earth would I open a restaurant?" Katie said.

They all began to talk at once again, tossing out ideas, considering others. Katie laughed at them.

"Here," Miranda ventured when there was a lull in the conversation. "You could do it right here in the house." For a moment she was met with silence. They all stared at her.

"I'm serious. None of you live here in the main house. You don't even like the place—which I don't blame you for, as you can practically feel the ghosts hovering around — but you all keep coming back to this table to gather over a meal. Think of the possibilities. As opposed to an empty mansion none of you want to claim, it could be something beautiful. You could turn it into a restaurant or a cafe or a bookstore with a cafe, an art gallery, a bed and breakfast or all of the above if you wanted." They must think her mad — she'd spoken her daydreams aloud for all of them to hear. "You could make the house something to be proud of for all of you."

"Why would people come?" Adam asked. And he sounded curious, not teasing. He sounded as if he really wanted to know.

"Why do you love this place?" she asked them all. "Not the house exactly, but the rest of it, the land, the farm, the orchards, the sea?"

"For me, that's easy. My heart is here," Adam began. "I wake up to the sound of the ocean and smell it on the breeze, I get to work with animals and dig in the dirt all day. I've never seen a more beautiful sky in the morning or sunset at night."

"Lily?"

"All of what Adam said about the landscape, and for me it's the history, the people, the old downtown which I have dreams of restoring building by building. Family."

"Katie?"

"My heart is here as well. It's always been here — no matter how bad it, got I could never leave it. The roses coming into bloom in the spring, my garden." She grinned. "All of my gardens, the view, oh, the view."

"Javier?"

He took Katie's hand and looked into her eyes. The look said it all.

"Cruz?" Miranda looked at him. She could tell he'd been lost in his brooding thoughts again. Was he angry at her? Worried that she was offering ideas for a place that didn't belong to her? Why wasn't he saying anything? She still really knew so little about his plans after he settled the estate. Was he going back to his career as a photojournalist? Would he go on with his own plans for the farm after she was gone? Would he ask her to stay? Did he want a life with her the way she wanted one with him? Jesus, she wanted to grab him and demand answers to her questions. Why couldn't he talk to her, really talk about what was important in life?

When he did finally speak, he looked directly at her. "I've been all over the world and this farm is still one of the most beautiful places I know, the towering fir trees, our ocean, rough and calm, the land, our orchards, the light in the evenings, the way the fog rolls in and hides us now and again. I love the people here."

She met his intense gaze. "All of you described the lure. It's a magical place, the gently rolling farmlands and vineyards before you climb over the hill and down into your land, the rows of apple trees, that rugged drop to that wide flat beach and the deep beautiful water. There's community here. I see more of it every day. There's passion and love for this place and I know others would love it too." She looked around — they were silent again. "I'm sorry. I got a bit carried away."

"Not a bad idea," Javier said.

"Are you kidding. It's fabulous! Wait, we need more wine." Lily got up to grab another bottle.

Cruz tapped Miranda's forehead. "You've been busy?"

"How would we do it all?" Katie asked.

"I could help you. I could write a business plan or a sketch of some ideas and what you'd have to do to get it there. I'd need all of your thoughts as well, but, I mean if you want me to, I could help."

"You know," Lily said. "I've been dying to get my hands on the old workers' cottages as well. We could renovate those while we're at it and you could rent them out. It would be awesome, highlight the beauty of the area. The cottages are already there. People could come to relax and hide away or be a part of things, visit the animals and the orchards, go wine tasting down the road."

"When it's nice out, you could set up long tables in the lawn out back by the gardens before the orchards start and have farm-to-table dinners," Miranda added.

"I can picture that," Katie said. "Long tables set with white cloths. Jam jars full of fresh flowers."

"And lights," Lily added. "Lots of little lights or candles. It sounds warm and romantic and absolutely wonderful."

Opera music blared out of Lily's phone. "Anyone who would need to get a hold of me is right here in this room. Oh shit, my dad." She scrambled for her phone her purse hanging on the back of the door.

"It's Miguel." Her face lit up. "Yes, oh! Uh-huh. Oh, goody! And I'm here this time! We'll be there. Love you!" She slapped her phone shut. "Roxanna's having her baby! Let's go. We're all going to the hospital. Oh shit, I can't drive. I've had too much wine."

"I haven't," Cruz said.

"Me neither," Adam and Javier said at the same time.

"Good thing the men take care of us," Katie said.

"Come on, people, let's go. I get to be there when the baby's born!" Lily tossed jackets and purses and shepherded them all out of the house. "I've been gone for all the babies' births. Not this time."

\* \* \* \*

"Wait." The nurse stopped them with a hand and a large smile before all six of them barreled into Roxanna's room. "The baby's getting a bath, and Mama's getting cleaned up a bit. I'll send Papa out in a minute."

"She had it already," Lily said, as Miguel popped his head out, grinning and damp-eyed.

"It's a girl, I have another beautiful girl."

He was beaming, absolutely beaming. They all grabbed him and hugged him then, even the men. "We barely made it to the hospital in time. Her water broke about four hours ago. I never thought…" And he started crying like a happy fool. "I never thought it would be like this each time, that my heart would be filled with so much love all over again, and the baby, Serafina, she's as pretty as her mama."

Katie hugged him again. "Oh, you sweet, sweet man."

The nurse nudged him on his shoulder and nodded, holding the door so they could all go in.

Right away it struck Miranda was how beautiful Roxanna looked—tired, but beautiful, the baby asleep on her chest. Roxanna held out her hand and Lily rushed over and grabbed it.

"I can't believe I missed all the others being born. This is too special. She's absolutely precious. Look at her so tiny," Lily said.

Cruz took pictures of the warm scene, the baby on her mother's chest, the proud papa, little Serafina's hands.

Miranda held back a bit and watched as they all cooed over the baby, Roxanna and Miguel—all these people who loved each other so much, connected. That was family. She felt the tear, but before she could wipe it, Katie took her hand and pulled her close to the bed.

"What do you think?" Roxanna asked her.

"She's absolutely precious. Congratulations," Miranda said.

"Want to hold her?"

"Me?" Miranda smiled, "Can I?"

"Sure." Roxanna started to lift the baby, but Miguel was right there to help her. "Let me," he said. He took the bundle of love and carefully placed her in Miranda's arms. Serafina was swaddled in a soft blanket, a tiny knitted hat on her head, and sound asleep. Her eyes were closed tightly, as if she wasn't certain about being out in the world yet.

"She's so warm," Miranda said. "And so tiny." She looked up for a minute and caught Cruz watching her, and smiled at him, trying to will him to see what she wanted with him, what they could have together, if only he'd truly let her in and trust her with his heart.

# Chapter Twenty-Eight

Cruz was busy the next few days, which was good. It was practice, he thought, for when Miranda was gone. He was haunted by the way she'd looked in the hospital, holding Roxanna's baby. He'd raised his camera and taken the shot, and it was at that moment he knew. She'd never actually said she wanted marriage, kids, family. They'd never really spoken about those things, but he could see it in her eyes. The look in them was so open, so full of love.

And he'd felt sick. Of course she wanted it all. He'd known, even without her saying the words — there were hints and the way she was around his own family, so warm and comfortable. And he'd kept shoving the knowledge aside because he wanted to be with her. He'd been selfish. But he couldn't keep being that way.

Loving her wasn't enough. He knew he could never be a father and right now he could see it written all over her face that she wanted everything he couldn't provide.

She would be leaving soon and he would have to let her go. He couldn't expect her to stay. There were so many reasons. She had a career, an entire life elsewhere, and, most importantly, there was his inability to give the whole package of love, family, children, security. Jesus, she wasn't even gone yet and he felt as if his insides were being ripped out, as the battle between what he wanted to do and what he knew he should do raged inside him.

The days were getting longer. Miranda walked the beach and watched the sunlight stretch itself out across the calm water. *Eight o'clock at night and still light out.* She stood and studied the sea, looking for answers, for guidance. Something was wrong. He was pulling away already and she didn't know why. The audit was almost over. Could he really be finished with her? Could it really have been an in-the-moment thing for him? Everything she knew about him said he wasn't like that. He wasn't flippant, casual or light about anything, except maybe the weather. Intense, passionate, driven were more like it.

But ever since the weekend, ever since the night Roxanna's baby had been born, he'd been different. Later that night, they'd made love slowly, passionately. He'd ravaged every part of her body, but even then something had been different about him, something heavy and troubling in his loving, and he'd barely spoken a word. In the morning, when she'd woken, he'd been gone.

She knew he was busy, but these last couple of weeks since he'd returned from Portland, they'd spent every night together, even if they went the entire day without seeing each other.

Since that last time, it was as if he'd pulled a veil over himself and his emotions and she couldn't reach him. He'd hardly been around for her to even try. Was this his way of telling her it was over? Was he going to let her walk away? Maybe he didn't know she loved him?

"You idiot, you've been too afraid," she told herself. "You have to tell him. This might be the scariest thing you've ever done, but you can't leave here without telling him — you would always wonder, and that would be a worse pain to bear."

By late afternoon of the next day, she'd finished the audit. Early, nearly a week before the deadline. She should have been happy. Finishing audits always gave her a feeling of accomplishment, of success. One more puzzle figured out. She always felt relief when she was done. *Not this time.* They would get to keep the farm and their corporation, but the fines would be huge. It would be a financial blow, for sure. She'd never really hated anyone before, but she felt that emotion now, raw and angry inside her for a man she'd never met — T.D. Brockman, who, although he might be dead, was still able to harm these wonderful people of Brockman Farms. And she got to be the one who delivered his final beating. There would be no relief, no sense of accomplishment this time, only sickness and disgust. Afterwards? She had no idea what would happen after.

She wanted to avoid the moment when she had to tell them, but she needed to get it over with. And she was pretty certain Cruz, Jake and Adam were still in Cruz's office, going over their weekly meeting about the estate.

*Here goes, into the fire.*

They were laughing about something when she stepped to the doorway. Adam spotted her first. "Miranda. Come in," he said as he stood up.

"Sorry to interrupt," she said. She tried to look anywhere but at Cruz, because she'd noticed as soon as she stepped into the room that he'd gotten that veiled look on his face again. Where was the light, the happiness, the desire for her that he'd never been able to hide before?

"Miranda, good to see you," Jake said. "Is that what I think it is?"

"I finished the audit. Or nearly finished. I have to write my final report."

"Is the farm still ours?" Adam asked.

"Yes. But it's not great news. The fines will most likely total over one point five million dollars, but you won't know for sure until the IRS Criminal Investigation and Department of Justice finish their part."

"One point five million?" Adam said. "I think I might be sick."

"I know. I'm so sorry, but I think you'll be able to pay most of it from the foreign accounts T.D. had. You might need to sell a bit of land or properties, or come up with additional ways to make some extra money. It will be tight for a while, but I think you'll be okay."

Would Cruz say something, anything? That look of stone on his face was worse than any angry words he could throw out right now, even if they were aimed at her. She'd give anything to be his target if he would talk to her.

"It will make settling the estate easier now," she offered.

Jake must have noticed the tension in the room as he looked from her to Cruz. Cruz was burning a hole through the audit with his eyes. "Adam, I'll give you a ride to the barns," Jake said. Adam nodded at her before he and Jake left the room.

She walked over to Cruz, wanting to be near him. *If I can touch him, I can make that haunted look of his go away.*

"I suppose you'll be leaving then," he said, when she put her arms around him. He wouldn't even look at her.

"Cruz, I…" She couldn't tell him now, surrounded by this negative information of the audit while he stayed so visibly disengaged. But what other chance might she have? Maybe the good would ease some of the horrible feelings of the mess T.D. had left for them. This was the most important decision she would ever have to make in her life.

"I want to stay." She put her hand on his face, that rugged face of his so full of emotions. "I want to stay here with you. I love you, Cruz."

"Miranda, no."

It was like a slap. *No* was the last thing in the world she expected him to say. A numbness spread through her. She dropped her hands. "No? No, I don't love you, or no, you don't want me to stay? Or no to both, Cruz?"

She looked at him as if he was a stranger. This couldn't be the same man she'd fallen in love with. The anger in his eyes at that moment might haunt her forever.

"No. Yes." He raked his fingers through his hair and turned away. "It doesn't matter what I want. Miranda, this can't work. I was worried, but now I know for sure."

"Worried that I was falling in love with you?" The numbness was wearing off, leaving a slicing pain anchored in her heart.

"Worried about what the audit would mean," he said.

"Cruz, I knew the audit would upset you. I'm sorry for that. I hoped you wouldn't blame me, though. I thought we were well past that, but I guess I misjudged." Even she could hear the tension in her voice.

"It's not that, Miranda. I could never blame anyone for T.D.'s greed and deceptiveness," he said. "But I can't ask you to stay here and make these kinds of financial sacrifices for me, after what you've been through in your life. You'll grow to hate me."

Indignation quickly wiped the shock away. "Do you really think I care about your money, or the state of your financial affairs?"

He pulled away. "I know how important the issue is to you, and I can't give you what you want, what you deserve."

"I want you. That's all. That's everything to me, not money."

"Miranda, that's not all."

"I just told you I loved you, Cruz. That is *everything*," she said.

"Miranda, listen to me. There's a part of me that will always be less. I can't change that. I'm not good enough for you. I have to let you go."

"Less? Why? What? That's the stupidest thing I've ever heard, Cruz. Why would you think you're not good enough?"

He turned to look out of the window. The silence pierced through her.

"My mother was pregnant before she married T.D. It was one of the workers passing through one summer. He was gone, moving on to the next farm job before she knew she was carrying me. Her father married her off to T.D. to avoid a scandal. I'm not T.D's real son. You asked me why he hated me. It's because I'm a bastard, because my mother was already pregnant when he married her."

She shook her head to clear the shock of his words. "Cruz, you never told me, I—"

"It's not something I brag about," he said, his words harsh.

"That's not what I meant. I thought we trusted each other enough. I don't care about your past, who your fathers were, Cruz."

"Jesus, Miranda! Don't you get it? Two fathers didn't want me."

She knew he carried a lot of heavy baggage, but right then she was more inclined to hit him over the head with his stupid — and worse — mean way of looking at things.

"I'm sorry to hurt you. I never meant —"

"You're being stupid and insulting. Let me get this straight. You think you're not good enough?"

"That's what I said, Miranda. Please don't make this worse than —"

"Which," she talked over him again, "is an indirect way of saying I'm not good enough. Of all the stupid things you've said to me yet, that's the top."

"I'm talking about me," he said through his teeth.

She could hear the impatience in his words, as if he were trying to explain something to an idiot. Temper lit up her insides, like a match set to ignite a forest in one fast whoosh. "If you think you're not good enough because one father didn't even know about you, and the one that did was a bully, then what you're also saying is neither am I. Me, who wasn't wanted by her own mother. Hell, by your logic, your brothers aren't worthy either, or your mother. Not to mention you're completely disregarding all the people in your life who do love you, despite your crazy, ridiculous, hurtful rationalization. For crying out loud, your mother was seventeen when she got pregnant."

"I'm not talking about any of them, Miranda. I know my words hurt, but now you can be free to love someone who deserves you, someone who's capable of giving you all the things you want."

"You're afraid, Cruz. I can see it all over your face. Don't you know I can read your emotions?"

"Stop," he snapped. "You're making this harder on yourself."

"I'm making this harder?! I shared everything with you, including telling you about my past, so you could stand there and tell me in an idiotic way that I'm not worth love and commitment and family." Her voice rose and fell. By the end it was like ice.

"Miranda, you're putting words in my mouth," Cruz said. His tone, of reprimand, as if trying to calm down a child throwing a fit, was the last straw.

"Don't use that tone with me, you idiot. You insult me by talking to me like I'm a child who doesn't know her own mind, and you insult me further by belittling my choice, which was you." She shoved his chest. "I chose you and you're too pigheaded and afraid to grab on to love even when I'm tossing it at your feet with no conditions. So you throw that disgusting excuse in my face."

"It's not an excuse," he yelled. "It's different. I don't know how to make something like this work, like us."

"It is an excuse. You don't get to use your stupid logic on yourself then say it doesn't apply to the rest of us. You decide what your worth is, Cruz. It's up to you. You get to choose."

"It's not a choice like a selection on a menu, Miranda."

She couldn't hide the hurt she was sure must have flashed across her face at his condescending tone and the words. And worse, the fact that he wasn't brave enough, that he didn't want her, he didn't love her. Oh, it hurt alright. She'd never felt such pain, but she wouldn't run crying from him.

"Miranda, I didn't mean that the way it sounded."

"Is that what do when people get too close? You flick them off like a bug? Sex was fine and dandy, acting like you wanted to know about my life, my past, my dreams, inviting me to get to know your friends and family was allowed, but really it was all a bit of casual fun for you until it was time to shove me out the door —"

"That's not how it was, Miranda." Now his words were angry. She couldn't tell if he was angry at her or at himself, but it was too late. He'd hurt her heart too much. She had to salvage what she could of her emotions, of her self-esteem, and get out.

The pain took over. She could barely see straight. She'd told him she loved him and he'd chosen fear over love. No amount of arguing could change his mind. "It is a choice, Cruz." What was left of her voice was barely a whisper. "For me it was an easy choice. I see now how wrong I was." And she turned and walked away.

"Miranda, wait," he called. And he stood, shattered and disgusted with himself as the best thing in his life left him.

He felt sliced open, devastated. When had he miscalculated? He'd only wanted to set her free, and Jesus, she'd been like a tempest whirling around, like a hurricane crashing onto land. He'd meant to be rational and honest and somehow everything he'd said had come out mean and condescending. Hurt had flashed over her face and he'd regretted instantly the words that had put it there. That look when he'd answered so brutally, 'No,' to her expression of love. She loved him and he'd all but slapped her emotions away.

Shock and fear took over and he sat down in one of the chairs as his muscles started to shake. He couldn't even remember what he'd been trying to say or why it had seemed so important. He thought he might throw up.

# Chapter Twenty-Nine

Where could she go to bury her pain where no one could find her? She couldn't think. All she knew was she had to get far away from him, from the farm. Her whole body was beginning to shake, but she made it to her car and started driving.

The sun was setting when Lily pulled up in her driveway and found Miranda sitting on her front steps.

"Hey," Lily said as she stepped out. Her smile disappeared when Miranda looked up.

"Miranda! What happened?" She wrapped Miranda in her arms and sat down next to her.

"He doesn't want me, Lily. I fell so hard and fast and I knew he was holding back, but I thought he'd change his mind. I thought I could make him love me, that if I told him, it would change things for him, but…I was wrong."

Lily rocked Miranda as the tears came in a wave all over again. "Here," Lily said. "Let's get you inside and you can tell me what happened." Lily walked Miranda into the living room and left her curled on one of the soft blue velvet couches. "We need tissues and a drink."

"I don't think I can handle any wine right now."

"Phh." Lily swatted her words away. "What you need is bourbon, honey, a good stiff drink to clear your head so you can tell me what happened and get mad along with hurt, 'cause the hurt's going to be there, but the mad will help you deal with it."

She settled Miranda down with a bourbon and Miranda tried to tell her what had happened, each word like shards of glass on her tongue. But Lily was right. Mad helped, a little. She sat with a thick, soft blanket tucked around her. Once the shakes had started, she couldn't seem to get warm. "He said because his fathers didn't want him, he could never be worthy of me."

"The man's so afraid of love he came up with the stupidest excuse I've ever heard. I can't believe he didn't choke on his stupidity. I knew he wasn't T.D.'s biological son, but I had no idea it was still such a source of shame for him. Did you kick his ass? Because if you didn't, I will."

Miranda choked out a half-laugh. It felt like bitter herbs on her tongue. "I was too angry to see straight. I told him that by his logic, I wasn't worthy of love and his brothers and Katie weren't either. I told him our past didn't define us and that it was a choice, what we did with our own lives. And he said, 'It's not a choice like a selection on a menu, Miranda.'"

"He didn't." Lily's eyes were like slits, "Then you kicked his ass?"

Miranda sank back into the couch. "Then I left. I told him I had chosen him and that I obviously made a mistake and I walked away. I wish I were you, Lily. Maybe if I had kicked his ass, it wouldn't hurt so much right now."

Lily put her arm around Miranda. "You don't want to be like me. I'm irrational and overly emotional. Besides, from the way it sounds, you did good. Yours was more of an ass-kicking by words, which probably stings a lot worse right now than if you had literally kicked him with those pretty heels of yours."

"You really think he's hurting?" Miranda said.

"Oh, honey, just because he's afraid to admit he's in love, doesn't mean he's not there. He's head over heels for you. It's written all over him. Hopefully he'll catch up with what the rest of us can see before he loses the best thing that's ever happened to him."

"I thought I knew what it felt like to hurt, Lily," Miranda said in a quiet voice. "I'm not sure which is stronger right now, the pain or the fatigue. I should go." Exhaustion slammed into her.

"You are not going anywhere. I have plenty of bedrooms, my friend, clothes to borrow, a huge soaker tub and more bourbon. I'll feed you, cry with you, plan his demise—whatever you need. You can stay as long as you want."

"Lily," Miranda tried to speak, but her tears got in the way. "You know what's even worse?"

"What, honey?"

"I didn't only fall in love with Cruz. I fell in love with all of you, with Graciella, with the farm, the water, even those overgrown neglected orchards. I felt like I was finally home, that I'd found real friends and family and love to last a lifetime."

Lily put her arms around her and held on tight as her own tears slipped down her cheeks.

\* \* \* \*

Cruz was in the barn when he heard Lily come in.

"Evening, Lily. What are you doing here?" Adam stepped out of the barn office as she strode toward him.

"Where is the jackass? I know he's in here somewhere."

"For Pete's sake, everyone's tearing around here angry as feral cats," Adam said.

She brushed past him and followed the light towards Cruz at the end of the barn.

"What in the hell is wrong with you?" she yelled when she stopped next to him. "I never took you for stupid, Cruz Brockman, but there's a first time for everything." He was brushing one of the mares, trying to battle the demons in his mind. "Hiding, huh? A coward and an idiot." She sounded pissed and disgusted. More like she was spitting fire.

"Go away, Lily," he practically spat back at her. Anger and pain laced his words.

"Not until I'm done kicking your ass. Jesus, Cruz! She was too nice to do it herself, or too hurt. She told you she loved you and you ripped her heart out," Lily yelled at him.

"It was for the best." His back was to her, his voice raw.

"For whose best?" She was incredulous. "Her heart's broken, shattered into a million pieces. You look pretty shitty yourself."

"Such a way with words, Lily."

"Stop it," she said and shoved him around to face her. "What are you doing here brushing horses when you should be chasing after her?"

"I can't ask her to stay," he said, letting out a ragged breath. "Christ, you don't get it. With all this debt hanging around us, we'll have to cut corners all over the place, sell a good piece of land to stay afloat, Lily. We'll do it because this is ours. We'll do anything to keep it going. She's spent her whole life digging herself and her mother out of debt, keeping them going."

"Yes, and she did that out of obligation, Cruz. Imagine what more she'd do for love!" Lily said.

"There's no doubt we'll all keep the farm going. But aside from that, you're being stupid." Adam stepped towards them.

"Would everyone stop calling me stupid!" Cruz's temper snapped.

"Well, you're either stupid or blind if you can't see she's fallen in love with this place as much as she's fallen in love with you. She walks the land in the mornings as if she's trying to learn it. She peppers Javier and me with questions about the animals when she comes to the barns. She's been learning about cooking and gardening from Mom. Miguel and Roxanna have practically adopted her. Hell, she's even dreamed up great ideas for the future of this place, ideas that may help us stay afloat. And we all know how hard she worked to finish the audit, which I can't imagine was any great source of fun for her," Adam said. "Knowing that with each step she got closer to finishing meant bad news for us."

"That was before she knew what it would take, what it's going to take to get us out of this debt T.D. left us in. It changes things," Cruz said.

"Wrong, Cruz. She knew coming here that the farm's accounts were under investigation for tax fraud. The only thing she didn't know was whether we'd be completely shut down and ruined, or given a chance to pay off the debt," Adam said. "We have a chance. Why are you so afraid to take yours?"

"I can't ask her to make such a sacrifice."

"Being poor as a child, not being wanted by her mother, pulling herself up out of that to where she is now, all by herself—that takes brains and guts and grit," Lily said. "Maybe money and security have been the most important things to her in the past, but if you can't see the longing all over her face for love and family, that those are the things she really wants, that everything she has to give she wants to give it to you? If you can't see all that, then maybe you don't deserve her."

"You're afraid," Adam said as if he'd just come to understand.

"Damn right I'm afraid," Cruz swore. And the words raced out of him. He leaned over and put his hands on his knees, taking deep gulping breaths. "I feel like I'm going to be sick. Every time I look at her, I think, what if I'm not good enough? What if I'm a drifter like my biological father? And T.D., even though his blood isn't in me, he raised me."

Cruz rose and pushed by Adam to get out of the stall. "Jesus, I still have nightmares, once in a while, of the abuse, the way he used his belt, the way he belittled us. The man didn't have a heart. That's the fear that pricks at my mind, that I'm like them, those two men. I've never felt this crazy about anyone in my life as I do over Miranda. Am I afraid that I'll screw up big time? You bet."

"You are nothing like those men, Cruz." Lily put her hand on his arm. "Despite both of them, you are kind and good and generous and you deserve to be happy." She took his face in her hands and took one last look. "But you have to believe that about yourself," she said before she left.

"It's not that simple," Cruz said, but his words sounded weak even to himself. *Could it be that simple?*

"Seems simple enough to me," Adam said. "You've never let fear guide you, Cruz. Now's not the time to start. Lily's right, you know. You deserve to be happy. You deserve her."

Who was Adam kidding? Fear had driven him away from Graciella all those years ago. Fear had kept him away. Fear had prevented him from ever having a meaningful relationship with a woman until Miranda. Fear had been more than his guide, it had become his noose.

\* \* \* \*

It was late when Cruz got home. He stood and looked at his property, the house he'd spent years secretly waiting to buy so that when he finally came back here, this favorite spot of his in Graciella would belong to him. This place of beauty, peace and comfort.

The giant fir trees, black against the clear night sky and the almost full moon. The acres of grass to the right that would make a great yard for kids and dogs someday. All the things he wanted to do to renovate the actual house— restoring the fireplaces, adding a bathroom, a finished basement with a movie and game room, a gourmet kitchen with an island and room enough for his whole family to cook in… And beyond the house, through the clearing that led towards the steep path down to the beach and the ocean—his ocean.

He felt no comfort now, no promises of things to come. He felt nothing but empty.

Walking in, he realized Miranda was everywhere, her image, her scent. He could see her standing in his kitchen in his robe while he poured coffee, in his shower while he washed her hair, on the back porch facing the coast in the chairs they had sat in together, the two of them watching the sunset with his arms wrapped around her.

He could still feel her warm body entangled with his. Her love filled up a place deep inside him that had been empty for years.

He'd been so certain of everything he'd done the past few years—his career, the assignments he'd taken, the photographs. He'd been through war zones, natural disasters, deserts and droughts to capture emotions with film. He'd always been confident and sure and good at what he did. But he'd also always been afraid, afraid to get too close. Never in his life had he made such a mess of something so important. And he realized, as he looked around at his house, that since he'd come home, the fear had been easing up a bit, that he'd been dreaming of family and permanence and a place to be here all along, that all his plans for renovations and improvements included someone to share it with. His dreams were her dreams, ones that included love and family.

He was still afraid, but as he stood here imagining his future, he was more afraid of a future without her. She was everything to him. None of this mattered without her. He hoped it wasn't too late to realize it.

# Chapter Thirty

The knock startled Miranda, but the last person she expected to see at the door was Lily, since they'd said goodbye last night.

"Lily?"

"I need you to come with me, and not ask any questions." Lily pulled Miranda through the cottage to the back door. "Take off those heels and put these boots on. They totally don't go with that gorgeous skirt you have on, but we'll have to toss fashion aside for the moment."

"What's going on? I'm leaving as soon as I finish packing."

Lilly waited until Miranda obeyed and they left the cottage. "Well," she said, linking arms with Miranda and walking them through the orchards to a path behind the cottages Miranda hadn't seen yet. The scent of blossoms perfumed the warm spring evening. "I'm betting on the luck of this gorgeous land that you'll be changing your mind about that."

"Look, Lily, you know how I feel about this place, but I can't stay here now."

Undeterred, Lily said, "I know you don't trust people easily. Trust me. Look." They'd stopped at the edge of the cliff where an old staircase had been built into the side. It led down to the beach. It led to Cruz.

She hadn't seen him since she'd walked out on him in the office two days ago, after he'd shattered her.

"Oh," Miranda said. The pain hadn't lessened and now seeing him made it even worse. It felt like a stab from a broken rib every time she breathed.

"Now it's time to be brave," Lily whispered. "That man loves you. Trust him and most of all trust yourself."

He was so beautiful, standing there, right where he belonged, with the wide beach that stretched to forever and the nearly still water waiting behind him. Everything was calm today, as if waiting for something. She didn't know what to do, walk away or see him one last time. Apparently she was a sucker for punishment. His gaze never left her as she walked down to him.

"Hi," he said when she stood a few feet away. He wasn't calm. His voice was ragged and sounded nearly broken. "Miranda, I'm sorry."

"It's okay. I don't need another apology. I get it." She didn't get it, she would never understand and, she realized suddenly, she couldn't do this, be so close to him and not be allowed to have him.

"Wait." He put his hand on her arm. "I was a complete ass."

"Please let me go," she whispered.

"No," he said and stepped closer. "I made that horrible mistake once. I'm asking you to give me one more chance. I don't know if you can ever forgive me for hurting you, but I'm asking you to try because I love you too."

Whatever was showing on her face must have been enough of an invitation for him to continue.

"I want you to have everything you deserve, everything you want."

"Cruz, I want you."

"Shh, let me finish. I need to finish. Or I need to begin. Here, sit." He led her to a large tartan blanket he'd set out on the beach. "I have something."

She waited in confusion while he sat next to her and opened a basket.

"All this time we've spent together, I've held back because of my fear that I couldn't be enough. You were right. I was afraid. But with you it's different. Before, I've always been able to breeze through relationships. No one was ever important enough, but you scare the hell out of me in a different way. You're smart and gorgeous and vulnerable and amazing. You turned my world upside down. No one's ever turned my world upside down before. I stupidly held on to my fear because I didn't realize that with you, I don't have to be afraid of my past anymore."

He reached into the basket, pulled out a photograph and placed it on her lap. It was of a pile of lumber in front of his house.

"I don't understand, Cruz." She looked at him with confusion and watched as the smile spread across his face. The sun was behind him and it set a riot of colors around them as it bounced off the calm, gently lapping water.

"It's fencing lumber. We're going to need to fence in part of our yard if we're going to have kids. Can't have kids and dogs running around without a fence."

"Fencing lumber? Kids?"

"Or kid, if you only want one." He smiled such a hopeful smile she nearly laughed. "I see us having more than one. I see lots of kids running around that house and I've always wanted a dog or two."

"Dog? Or two?" He couldn't mean what she thought he meant. *Our yard, kids, dogs.* She was speechless. He put another photo in her lap. She looked down and this one was a black and white of that night in the hospital when Roxanna had had her baby. All of them, including Miranda, were crowded around, smiling over the baby and proud parents. Love and happiness practically dripped off the paper.

Before she could ask, he said, "Everything that's most important to me in this world is in that picture, except for my idiot brother Turner, who I hope will show up one of these days. That is my family, Miranda, and I want you to be a part of my family. If you'll have me." He'd let go of his fears and it showed in his smile, in the dreams he was sharing with her.

She looked up at him and couldn't stop the tears.

"We are going to get out of this debt. We will make it work, this place, all of us, but we need you. I *need* you, Miranda. I thought I was good at never giving my heart to anyone, but it had nothing to do with that. It had to do with the fact that I hadn't met you yet. You are my heart. I choose you. I think I did that moment you walked into my office and blindsided me.

"This place is only my dream if you're here too. Stay with me. Let me bring you all the flowers you should have." He reached into the basket again. This time it wasn't a photograph he pulled out, but a small bouquet of old-fashioned roses and a velvet box. He opened the box and inside was an emerald surrounded by small diamonds in an oval setting.

"It was my grandmother's."

"*Cruz.*" She covered her face with her hands.

He took one hand back and kissed it, that special gesture she loved so much, and her heart filled again.

"You are my home, Miranda. Marry me. Let me love you. Have a family with me."

"Say it again," she said as she threw her arms around him.

"I love you, Miranda."

"I'll never forget what that sounds like. I love you so much."

He kissed her, wrapped his arms around her and pulled her into his lap. "Look at that," he said, and nodded toward the water. She followed his gaze. The gentle, lazy water lapping against the shore, a huge blue sky with a few white clouds and the sun setting over the horizon. It cast the sky into pinks and purples and bright oranges. The scent of water and sand and blossoms drifted through the air. A heady, perfect scent. "Graciella," he said. "Our home."

"Yes." She nodded then wrapped her arms around his neck and kissed him again. "And, Cruz," she said when they broke apart, "I've never had a dog, either. And I want kids."

His smile lit up his entire face. "As in plural?"

"In fact," she whispered, "I think we should get started right now in this so very perfect setting."

# Want to see more from this author?
# Here's a taster for you to enjoy!

# Rescue Me: Salvaging Love
## Sara Ohlin

### *Excerpt*

Ellie was a soggy, soapy mess of bubbles and puppy fur. By some miracle, a few strands of her hair had survived the battle to bathe Chewie, one of the litter of four she'd found at the front door of her clinic, dirty, scrawny and huddled together in a cardboard box.

It wasn't the first time since she'd opened her vet clinic four years ago that animals had been abandoned at the door. Once, she'd even found a lovebird waiting for her. One lovebird. Everyone knew lovebirds were a pair. Ellie couldn't stand to see animals abandoned or put down, not if there was the slimmest chance someone could love them and give them a home.

Fortunately, these four babies would be adopted soon. Puppies always were. They were part Lab and part a whole bunch of mutt. Chewie was chocolate brown, like his namesake, and his hair was velvety and curly, more retriever-like. His shimmery brown baby eyes filled with longing every time he gazed at her. *I might have to keep this one.* As she poured water over him, he launched himself into her arms trying to cling to the large rubber apron she wore. Before she could disentangle him and put his butt back in the water, the bell over the front door rang. *Damn!* She'd meant to lock it. She kept Chewie attached to her chest with one hand, grabbed a towel to wrap around him with her other and headed out front.

*Holy cow!* "Can I…ah, help you?" The man stood by the front window, silhouetted by the fading evening light. Huge and gorgeous with rugged tan skin, black hair curling over his collar and the coolest blue-green eyes she'd ever seen. Ellie almost sighed, but that flash of beauty disappeared in an instant. Anger radiated from him.

"What the hell is going on, Ken?" he said into his phone, but he pierced her with his gaze.

His anger vibrated over them. Chewie started shaking in her arms and buried his head in the towel. "I'm sorry, sir, but can I help you? This is my—"

"What do I mean?" he ignored her to yell into his phone. "I'm standing here on my property that still has tenants in it. Explain!"

*Sheesh.* She leaned back with the force of his words. "It's okay, baby," she cooed to the shivering puppy in her arms. "Sir," she called louder this time, "we're closed right now and you're scaring the animals. If you wouldn't mind taking your phone call outside, I—"

He sliced his hand up to silence her.

*Excuse me?* She was not about to let this foul-mouthed jerk boss her around, but before she could say anything else, he hung up. "If you were closed, why was your door unlocked?"

"What?" It wasn't merely his size or harsh tone that had her brain malfunctioning. She couldn't keep up with his line of questioning.

"Your door," he said, his tone singeing her. "Why would a woman like you leave her door unlocked while she's here by herself?"

*'A woman like you?'* Ellie flinched. She didn't even want to know what he meant by that comment. She'd spent

eighteen years of her life with people putting her down. No way in hell she was going to listen to more of it, not after she'd clawed her way out of that filth so long ago. She chose to focus on only part of what he said.

"I'm not alone." She scrubbed the soft puppy.

"Jesus." He closed his eyes.

She certainly didn't know what *that* meant. His swearing said a lot, but at the same time it didn't really say anything.

"Would you mind not swearing?"

"Excuse me?"

"I said, would you —"

"I heard you."

Okay, now she was getting angry. "Listen. I don't know who you are or what you're doing here, but, like I said, we're closed for the evening and I need to get home. You can make an appointment or come back in the morning when we open." God, she hoped he didn't come back.

"You should have been closed for good a week ago. Closed and vacated."

"What? What do you mean? This is my clinic. I signed a lease through the end of the year. That's seven months away."

"I know when the end of the year is."

The man had a degree in condescending behavior. His tone, his attitude, his entire demeanor said power and money, and the tailored gray suit, black dress shirt and shoes all bragged of wealth. The way he tried to silence her with his hand in the air. She couldn't stand people thinking they were better than everyone else. It got her hackles up. That and the way he studied her, assessing.

"I was stating the terms so you could realize your mistake and apologize for barging in here with your atrocious behavior and yelling at me."

He stared at her again. His features transformed from a pissed-off beast to a quiet, controlled predator. As if he carefully leashed his temper, and instead saw her as a problem to be solved. His eyes were calculating. It sent a nervous tingle up her spine.

"Well?" she prompted, trying to act braver than she felt. Chewie's heartbeat raced against hers. He wiggled to get loose from her tight hold.

"Terms have changed." He raised an eyebrow. Those eyes of his were a mysterious blue-green, like a deep pristine lake surrounded by mountains. And when he wasn't yelling, his voice soothed. He took a step toward her which jarred her out of her observations. She leaned back.

"What terms? Who are you?" She had to look up now. Jesus, he was well over six feet tall.

"Jackson Kincaid. I'm the new owner of this block. I'm tearing the entire thing down. Everyone was supposed to be vacated last week at the latest," he finished, delivering the blow to her gut just when the wriggling mass in her arms threw himself onto the floor and shook his sudsy, wet puppy body all over the man. Unable to find traction on the slippery floor, the pup flopped over on his back and clung to Jackson's pants with his tiny claws.

"Christ!" He reached down and plucked the pup up into the air, holding him away from his body.

"The new owner? Of the whole block? And you're tearing it all down?" She was surprised she could even find her voice at the shock. "You can't."

"I can," he said, glaring at her with that raised-eyebrow thing he did that made her feel ten instead of twenty-seven.

"Can't." She'd found her voice again, getting pissed.

"Can," he said, leaning in.

"You're a bully!" Anger heated her blood. "You don't even know me or the Heelys, or Carl and his daughter. I know your kind. And I won't let you come in here and intimidate me."

"You won't?" He looked at her questioningly. Or was he teasing her? She'd been so busy yelling, it almost sounded now as if he were fighting back laughter.

"No, I won't."

"And how do you plan to stop me?"

But she didn't get a chance to speak because Chewie let loose and peed all over Mr. Bully, drenching his perfect-fitting suit and his expensive leather dress shoes.

Ellie watched, frozen in place while he blinked. *Oh, shit!* "I…I am so sorry. He's just a, well—"

"Puppy. Got it," he clipped.

"Someone left a litter at the door and I had to get them clean. He's not trained."

"Yeah. I got that too."

"Here," she said quietly, trading him a towel for Chewie.

"Fuck! This day keeps getting better. Slime of the earth in my office earlier. Get over here to check out my buildings, find the tenants still here, an ignorant blonde and now I have puppy piss all over me." He wiped at his wet shirt and jacket with the towel.

She soothed Chewie and bristled at the *ignorant blonde* comment.

"Look, I'm sorry about what happened, but there's no need to be rude. You don't know me, which means you don't get to call me ignorant. What *I* know from *your* behavior is that you're an arrogant jerk who needs lessons in manners."

His eyes met hers, and the heat in them made her suck in her breath. Okay, maybe she'd gotten carried away and should *really* learn when to stay quiet. He acted like a jerk, but it wasn't like she had to point it out to him. Belatedly she realized it was kind of like teasing a hungry lion.

"Not ignorant?" His voice had turned low. Yup, definitely poking a lion. "You're here alone. It's dark. Every store along this street is closed. It's a sketchy neighborhood at best, and you leave your door unlocked?"

"Why do you care?" Ellie was confused by this entire conversation.

"Why?" He prowled closer. Okay, she should definitely be more careful about locking her door. "You. Here. Alone. Any cracked-up junkie could come right in and take what he wanted." He waved his hand up and down her body to indicate what that might mean.

"Now you're freaking me out *and* being rude." Her voice wasn't above a whisper, but he heard it.

"Good!"

"Good?"

"Yeah, maybe you'll be freaked out enough next time to lock your fucking door."

Okay, she was exhausted, and hurt by his words, although she didn't understand why, since he was nothing to her. She wasn't good in situations like this — no matter how many years and miles away she was from her childhood, nasty people still affected her ability to be strong. It was painful to realize she hadn't gotten better at handling it at all. "Right. I understand," she began without any of the anger or passion lacing her words. "And I, ah, appreciate your concern, even if it's delivered in a yelling, jerky way, but you don't need to worry about me."

He braced back as if she'd slapped him. "You're kidding me?"

"No. Anyway, my night vet tech should be here any minute. Plus, I have Buffy. She's a great judge of character."

"Buffy?"

Ellie pointed toward the corner where her ten-year-old, one-hundred-pound Rottweiler slept on her dog bed, snoring away.

"Right, I can see how Buffy, who hasn't moved a muscle except to snore since I got here, is a perfect guard dog."

Ellie brushed back the curls that had slipped out of her ponytail. "If we continue this conversation tonight, you're going to throw your stuck-up disbelief and insults in my face, and as pleasant as it seems to be for you, it's not for me.

"I've been here since six, on my feet all day, which normally I don't mind because I love my job, but I had a horrible surgery on a dog. My assistant left at noon. I still have to get this little guy and his siblings settled for the night, which means fed, taken out to pee, shots and crates. I haven't eaten since breakfast. Dinner is a peanut butter and jelly sandwich before I face-plant into bed. You come in and threaten my clinic, no correction, my *dream,* which I worked my butt off to open. Maybe you could come back tomorrow, or we could meet for coffee and you can tell me, if you really are the new owner, what I have to do to convince you not to tear this block of buildings down. Then we can both go our separate ways and never see each other again."

It almost hurt her to say those words, because even though he was a total jerk, he was beautiful to look at. But horrors could hide behind beautiful appearances, something she was all too aware of. After all, her mother was a gorgeous model, but underneath she was crazy mean, and Ellie was the one who had taken the brunt of it.

He studied her while she spoke, silent and assessing again. Then he reached by her to grab one of her business cards from the counter. "Dr. Ellie Blevins, you think you can convince me not to tear this bag of bones down and build up a new condo development that will make billions?"

Billions? Did every battle she fought in this life have to be so outrageously difficult? This block was special. It wasn't only her clinic. It was the bakery, the hardware store that Carl and his daughter ran, her friend Ruby's spa, Lachlan's pub. This neighborhood burst with potential. And the park at the end of the block right along the river was lovely. The bonds she'd formed here, the true friendships, would make her fight back, even if she didn't feel brave enough for herself.

"It's not a bag of bones. It's a block of old, historic buildings that need love and care," she began. But standing there, taking in his polished rich-man strength, it was futile to convince him of anything. "You know what? Deal me the death blow now. I'd like to review the lease I signed before I throw in the towel and start looking for a new space and a new home, because I can tell there's no way you and I will ever be on the same page."

"New home?"

"What?" she said.

"You said, 'a new space and a new home'?"

"I live in the apartment above the French Connection Bakery. Mr. and Mrs. Heely have owned it for twenty-five years." There she was, exhausted-sharing again. And there he stood intense-staring. She closed her eyes at the craziest, weirdest conversation she'd ever had, and realized Chewie was asleep on her chest with his tiny head nuzzled in her neck. *Oh, soft love,* she thought, *if only people were more like dogs, so trusting, kind, and loving.*

"One month," he said.

"One month to be out of —"

"I'll give you one month to try to convince me."

"I… What?"

"You spend time with me for the next month. We get to know each other, and you can state your case."

"Spend time with you?" *Is he insane?*

"You said you wanted to try to convince me to change my mind."

"Oh," she whispered, confused again.

"You open tomorrow?"

"Yes," she said quickly, thinking maybe they'd tested each other's patience enough for one evening.

"Right, then. Tomorrow. Lock your door." Then he was gone, leaving her more confused than ever.

"Lock your door!" he yelled from outside, startling her out of her spot.

She went to the door, locked it, drew the blinds down and blew out a breath. "What in the heck just happened? I feel like a tornado blew through here and tossed us sideways into outer space. And what does 'tomorrow' mean? Is he coming back? Am I supposed to appear before him like a magician?"

She looked at Chewie and spoke into the empty waiting area with Buffy chasing squirrels in her dreams. *Holy cow! Holy freaking cow! This place is everything to me, more than my hopes and dreams — it's my safe place.* One single month to convince an angry lion not to eat her up? She might be an awesome veterinarian, but there were absolutely no instructions for how to communicate with a beast like Jackson Kincaid.

Home of Erotic Romance

Sign up for our newsletter and find out about all our romance book releases, eBook sales and promotions, sneak peeks and FREE romance books!

# About the Author

Sara Ohlin has lived all over the United States, but her heart keeps getting pulled back to the Pacific Northwest where it belongs. For years she has been writing creative non-fiction and memoir and feels that writing helps her make sense of this crazy world. She devours books and can often be found shushing her two hilarious kids so that she can finish reading. When she isn't reading or writing, she'll most likely be in the kitchen cooking up something scrumptious, a French macaron, shrimp scampi, a fun date-night-in dinner with her sexy husband, or perhaps her next love story.

Sara loves to hear from readers. You can find her contact information, website details and author profile page at https://www.totallybound.com